WHEN RICH MEN DIE

Also by Harold Adams

When Rich Men Die

HAROLD ADAMS

DOUBLEDAY & COMPANY, INC.
GARDEN CITY, NEW YORK
1987

*All of the characters in this book are fictitious
and any resemblance to persons, living or dead,
is purely coincidental.*

Library of Congress Cataloging-in-Publication Data
Adams, Harold, 1923–
When rich men die.

I. Title.
PS3551.D36W44   1987   813'.54   86–24148
ISBN 0-385-24005-8

To Wendy—
The daughter who turned out to be
exactly what I ordered

WHEN RICH MEN DIE

I

The digital clock showed 2:41 A.M. as I rolled to lift the receiver before the second ring and said, "Yeah?"

"I hear you got fired," she said.

"It was more like squeezed out."

I punched the pillow I'd been hugging and shoved it under my head.

"That's what happens to underdog champions. This is Daphne."

"Yeah, I recognized the overdog tone."

"If I didn't know you so well I'd think you were snotty just because of the hour. You *were* awake, weren't you?"

"Isn't everybody?"

"You never sleep."

"I do too. Right after making love and always just before the alarm."

"So you're alone."

"Yup. Everything's going your way. I'm unemployed and alone. Now if you're through gloating I can hang up and think of what I'm going to do about it."

"Don't be paranoid. As a matter of fact I called because I've got a little job you could probably handle if you stayed sober. Did you hear about Oren?"

"No. What the hell would your husband ever do that'd get in the news?"

"He's disappeared. Vanished. I'm a widow, I think."

"Oh."

"Is that all you can say, for Christ's sake, 'Oh'?"

She burned for a few seconds, then said, "He was down in Mexico."

"Ah."

"What's *that* supposed to mean?"

"Ah? It's used to express regret, delight, relief or even contempt. You have to catch the tone to know which. If I got the tone right it could mean all of those things."

"You know, if you weren't such a sarcastic bastard, things could've been a lot different between us."

"Of course. But isn't it lucky for you I was."

"What's *that* mean?"

"You might not have become a rich widow."

"That's not why I married him."

"So it was true love. What do you want from me?"

She took a deep breath. "I thought maybe you needed a job."

"Don't tell me—you've inherited a TV network?"

"Just try to quit being a smart ass, will you? You're an investigative reporter, right? I want you to go find out what happened to Oren down there."

It was my turn to keep quiet a moment.

"You'd pay?"

"Cash."

"You want me to find the body, right?"

"I can't inherit until it's found."

That had always been Daphne's most endearing trait; sudden, naked honesty, startling as the first lightning from a summer storm.

I asked why she was so sure he was dead.

"Because he's been missing for six months and his suitcase and portfolio and precious maps are all sitting in a hotel room in some miserable town down there where he never checked out and he hasn't been in touch with his bank or his broker or his lawyer or his wife. And finally, because his goddamned sweetie called to ask where he is. All that makes me just a teensy suspicious that something's weird. Does that seem strange to you?"

I silenced that one out and waited for her to go on. After a moment she did. Oren had been in Mexico City and Guadalajara the last she heard. I suggested he'd gone to Europe. She said not without his portfolio and maps. The maps were a security blanket; he used them to find places he'd visited the day before. That struck me as a touching weakness. I propped a second pillow behind my head and wished I still smoked. It would be so comfortable to sit up and light one and watch the glow in the dark. I wondered how significant it was that I missed smokes more than I'd ever missed Daphne.

"You say his sweetie called you?"

"She called our lawyer. She wouldn't *dare* call me."

"Is she Mexican?"

"Of course not. It's his old flame from college days. She ragged her first husband to death and now she's hooked Oren."

That explained the bitterness. Oren had dropped his young wife for an older woman. What could be more galling?

"Okay, what kind of money are we talking about?"

"What've you been making?"

"What's that got to do with anything?"

"I want to be sure the incentive is enough to keep you from looking for another job on my time."

"Okay, let's just make it a percentage of your inheritance."

"Don't be ridiculous. I'll give you one hundred thousand if you find Oren."

I wasn't exactly stunned, but for several seconds nothing intelligent came to mind as I compared that amount with what I'd been offered to work as an investigative reporter with the local newspaper.

"Are you still there?" she demanded.

"Is he really worth that much, even though untrue?"

"There's no question about that."

"And I collect, dead or alive?"

"You can only collect if you're alive."

I didn't give that hint the consideration it deserved, being distracted as I was by her offer.

"What if I can't find him?"

"Look, don't plan on failure, okay? Besides, if you do flop all you'll be out is some time. I'll cover expenses and reasonable compensation. I have to prove I tried to find him and it'll be a tax write-off so I've nothing to lose."

I told her fine, put it in writing with guarantees and she said no problem, fly down to Houston, meet her lawyer and work out the details with him.

I hung up, cutting off the telephone's soft glow, and glanced at my clock's glowing red numbers. It was 3 A.M.

Oren P. Fletcher III, according to newspaper archives I'd checked when he was my rival for Daphne, came from a banking family with a great reputation for flashy philanthropy. The third Oren P. had been a slow starter, but once he threw himself into the family hog trough, he demonstrated a fine genius for earning money and absolutely no interest in giving it away. Shortly after his fiftieth birthday his wife died suddenly of polio and the next year he had a near fatal heart attack. During his rehab period the doctors told him to slow down or forget about a long life.

So Oren had a revelation: it'd be better to give than to receive. He created the Frances Fletcher Foundation in honor of his departed wife and began searching for worthy causes.

Daphne was one of his earliest supplicants. She was about thirty years his junior but more than made up for that in natural cunning and persistence.

I met her before she'd worked her way up; she was merely a sidekick for the chairwoman of the Children's Hospital at a time when that matron was visiting royalty in Europe, leaving Daphne to deal with the press which was dutifully covering the story of the benefit ball being sponsored by their ever so benevolent organization.

I'd been writing news items and arranging interviews for our TV station for several months, so I took it for granted that anyone promoting anything would do somersaults and backflips to get five seconds on camera. It came as a jolt to find Daphne aloof when I called and announced whom I represented. It took several minutes to persuade her to set a time and once she agreed she hung up abruptly, as if she'd just got rid of an obnoxious salesman.

I hoped she'd make an ass of herself.

But no, she was perfect. Expressive dark eyes, the complexion of a professional model and a lustful mouth. She dressed like a millionaire; all class, no flash. I don't remember a word she said and neither did anyone else, but no one forgot what she looked like.

After the taping, when she knew she'd been superb, she was suddenly all charm and warmth. She told me confidentially that when I first called she'd been confused, thinking my station was the least instead of the most important in town. She also told me I was the first reporter she'd met who wore a clean shirt and a decent tie.

I told her that's how it is with guys in the TV world, they all dreamed of getting on camera eventually. She assured me I'd make it. I decided she was wonderful.

We met several times right after that. I was surprised to discover she was genuinely interested in the hospital and the kids. While she'd never been a mother, and probably never would be, she enjoyed watching and being around small children who were not her direct responsibility yet wanted her sympathy and succor. I think being with them made her realize how lucky she was to be healthy, beautiful and rich.

It soon became obvious that I was in competition with Oren the Third, but being young and cocky, I assumed my superior energy in the sleeping, or I should say, pre-sleeping activities would give me an unbeatable edge.

Besides, Oren was often out of town.

He was also pretty casual—so much so that once he stood her up for a weekend date in Mexico City. That made her mad enough to send me tickets to join her. Luckily for me I was able to go, but after two days I had to return and when I did she scornfully told me I was a peasant. A real man, she told me, was in charge of his own time.

I told her this man goddamned well was in charge of his time and he knew what was important and what was just fun.

That did it for us.

She didn't invite me to the wedding. I heard it was a very big affair and thoughtfully sent her a dildo as a wedding gift. It was rather a good one, of tasteful size and color, equipped with two B batteries.

She never thanked me.

II

As my flight approached Houston Sunday evening, I leaned against the plastic window and stared at the sparkling city below. The landing field with its blue lights and pale runways didn't appear until seconds before the wheels touched down, the tires squealed and the retros roared. A moment later tractors were charging out to our luggage bays, trailing their dark carts. I watched while eager passengers scrambled in the aisle, reaching overhead for coats and bags. When the aisle finally cleared, I got up and walked out.

The squat cabbie lifted his head and said "Ah!" when I gave him Fletcher's address.

"What's that mean?" I asked as he jerked us into heavy traffic.

"Ah? That don't mean much of nothing."

His voice rasped as if it hurt him to talk.

"Is it a long ways?"

"Not so far as Hawaii."

"Classy neighborhood?"

"It sure ain't no slum."

I settled back, studying the driver's picture on the seat back before me. The face was dark with a broad nose and wide, thin-lipped mouth. He looked like a man who'd precede a Mafia chieftain out of an elevator.

The trip took forty-five minutes and ended at the top of an arched drive before a great gray mausoleum. While I hadn't expected a bridge over a moat, it did seem a millionaire should at least have an iron gate with a guard and telephone.

The porch light was on, illuminating a handsome white door and wide, spotless steps. I considered removing my shoes before going up. A bell chimed remotely when I poked the button to my

right as the cab pulled away. For several seconds I listened to
cicadas which apparently filled the front lawn trees.

Finally the door opened and a man whose neck was long
enough to be articulated gazed down with disapproving eyes
under straggling brows.

I introduced myself, he nodded, waved me in with controlled
enthusiasm and as I passed him, Daphne appeared down the hall.

She'd been twenty-five when we met and the five years between
hadn't touched anything that showed. She was still slender, erect,
bright-eyed, dark-haired and rich. She wore a discreetly patterned black and brown silk gown that probably didn't cost much
more than the Taj Mahal.

"We'll go to the library," she said to me, and to the man with
the neck, "Bring coffee."

The library was no larger than a barn and lined with shelves of
matched leather volumes undoubtedly chosen by a decorator and
never touched by a genuine reader. A vast desk stood in one
corner flanked by a leather upholstered couch and a matching
chair, all squatting on a deep red Persian carpet.

Daphne waved me toward the couch and settled gracefully into
the chair while looking me over from loafer shoes to sandy hair.
There was a barely perceptible green tint on her eyelids and her
smooth cheeks had the gloss of a classic car with a hand-rubbed
paint job. We exchanged cool smiles.

"Well," she said, "I see you still wear clean shirts."

"I remembered it was important to you."

"You do this job for me and you might be able to buy one in
style."

I smiled tolerantly at the put-down and she smiled more
warmly and asked how the weather was in Minneapolis.

I said it was raining when I left.

She asked how the Vikings were doing. I said so far they were
doing fine. I didn't mention that the season hadn't started yet.

The man with the neck carried in a tray with a silver pot, cream
pitcher and sugar bowl, placed it noiselessly on a glass-topped
coffee table and straightened up, facing his lady.

"That'll be all," she said. He bowed and left.

"When did you give up Scotch?" I asked as she leaned forward to pour.

"When I got married."

"So? And when Lady Daphne goes on the wagon, everybody rides it, huh?"

"In my house, yes. You still use sugar?"

I shook my head, accepted the cup and saucer and settled back.

"You know Spanish, don't you?" she asked.

"I can find the men's room and follow simple road signs—that's about it."

"Well, you can always hire an interpreter if one's needed."

"Why not? I'll need a picture of your husband—we never met, you know."

"Of course." She lifted an envelope from the table and handed it over.

I pulled out three snapshots and spread them on the glass. The first was a candid of him walking along a crowded city sidewalk. The second showed him sitting on a park bench in bright sunlight. The third was a formal portrait. I'd expected him to look like an English aristocrat, but what I found was more like an Irish pug. The nose looked battered, the eyes were wide-set in a broad face loaded with laugh wrinkles. His jaw had a pugnacious thrust and his wide mouth formed a natural smile revealing good square teeth. Dense graying hair flopped across his forehead and half concealed his small ears.

"He's about five-ten," said Daphne. "Weighs about one hundred and eighty. His eyes are blue. He has an appendectomy scar and a birthmark on his left calf, just under the back of the knee. The teeth are genuine, in case you're wondering."

I studied the pictures.

"I suppose you thought he'd look like John Forsythe?"

"More like Melvyn Douglas," I said. That didn't register with her—she didn't watch old late-night movies on TV as I did.

I asked her what contacts I might find in Mexico.

"Well, there's Juan García, his banker in Guadalajara. I've no

idea how close they were, but he should know something of
Oren's coming and going. And there's a nightclub owner, Luis
Morales, in the same town. I don't remember the name of his
place. I suppose you'd best talk with Ms. Amsdecker, Oren's
secretary. She always knew where to reach him before he disappeared."

"I'd probably ought to talk with the old flame, too."

"What good'll that do? She's already been asking us where to
find him."

"Yeah, but she might have a notion why he'd disappear."

"Well, don't ask *me* where to find her."

"You know her name?"

"Believe it or not, it's *Elvira.* Elvira Mumford."

"Where'd he run across her again?"

"Damned if I know—or care. They always exchanged Christmas cards—she sent ugly arty ones—until her husband killed
himself and she was free."

"Are you kidding?"

"About the suicide? No."

I asked when she'd seen Oren last and she said it was almost
exactly six months and a half. I asked what were the circumstances.

"You mean, did we part in a rage? No. He'd been home about a
week. We hadn't seen a lot of each other—I was involved with a
new arts group. We're sponsoring a festival this summer for new
and unrecognized painters and sculptors. Oren met with a lot of
people. He told me about his old flame when I let him know I'd
heard about her. He pretended it was nothing, that she was an old
friend who'd had some bad times. He was only being kind. I told
him, and I made it plain, that philanthropy should have some
limits. He pretended that was very funny."

I knew how mad that must have made her. I got up, strolled
over to the bookshelf and pretended to examine titles.

"What kind of a relationship would you say you and your
husband had?" I asked without turning.

"You sound like a goddamned cop."

I turned toward her. "You sound like a hostile witness."

She put down her cup with a sharp click and glared.

"All I'm asking is that you find my husband. I don't think it's any of your business what went on between him and me. I'm not a suspect, I am the injured party and I thought when I called you that you'd come as an old friend with a talent for investigation who'd be my ally—"

"If I'm going to do any damned good I've got to know something about this guy—what his relationships were, why he'd jump whichever way he jumped. Yeah, I'm curious too, but I'm asking legitimate questions and you're smart enough to know it, so let's be honest—okay?"

Her glare subsided to a frown. Then she lifted her chin, asked if I wanted more coffee, poured for both of us and settled back, holding her cup with both hands.

"All right. We had a permanent truce. He was too old for me. I don't know why he married me, probably because I was decorative and knew people interested in charities and could be helpful socially, and, let's be honest, as you say, I kept after him. Maybe I caught him just at that time in life when a man thinks this is his last chance for a young one and he was afraid to pass it up. I found out he had very superficial tastes and intellectual scope. What he wanted was a kind of worship. That's why he loved giving away money. It made him God and he loved it. He told a group once that the giving by his foundation ranged from the whimsical to the capricious, and while he smiled sweetly to let them know he was kidding, he wasn't. That's one thing about Oren—he was almost always sincere with his humor."

"Was he jealous?"

She looked at me sharply. "Why do you ask that?"

"Older husbands of young wives usually are. Sometimes with good reason."

"I gave him no reason. Even if I had, I don't think he'd have paid a lot of attention. But I never tested him."

Remembering her enthusiasm in the sack, I found that hard to swallow.

"I'd guess," I said, "that you were never worshipful enough to keep a god happy."

She laughed and pushed her cup and saucer away. "You'd know that, wouldn't you?"

I sure would.

"I know what you're thinking," she said as I sat down again. "You're thinking he's left me. Just ducked out. Forget it. He had enough money to do anything he pleased and enough self-confidence to keep him from running from anything. Nothing real could touch him. He wasn't one of your weaklings who couldn't face fights or making choices—"

Her sweet smile let me know I'd been stabbed without malice.

"I've no doubt he's dead. Your job's to find the body."

"And not worry about who did it or why?"

"Just find the corpse, that's all I need."

Chimes sounded in the distance and her sleek head lifted swiftly.

"That'll be Harlan," she said.

She rose gracefully when the servant ushered in a tall man with a black mustache, fluffy waved hair and sculptured lips over a dimpled chin. She took his hands and gave him a quick peck on the cheek. He smiled brilliantly as his brown eyes drank her in before he pulled back to acknowledge me. His grip was firm and dry.

He accepted coffee and settled down on the couch beside Daphne, assuming a sober expression for the serious occasion. As we talked, he examined me like a lover checking out a predecessor he's heard too much about.

He explained that he'd inherited Oren as a client who had used Harlan's firm for years. I asked if they'd been close and he said theirs was not quite a father-son relationship, but they saw a lot of each other and shared a mutual respect.

"You think he's dead?" I asked.

"Well," he shrugged, "I'm not in the habit of jumping to conclusions, but certainly this thing looks extremely serious. When we first realized he was missing, I assumed he'd been in some sort of accident in one of those remote areas he fancied down there. People do disappear in Mexico, as I'm sure you know. There's a lot of primitive territory—"

Daphne interrupted, saying she thought our arrangements should be formalized before we went further and in a very short time our general agreement was worked out. Harlan promised to send me a formal contract in the mail and that was fine with me.

Harlan drove me back to town in his Porsche 990. He drove like a stunt man in a Burt Reynolds movie while I sat bracing my feet against the floorboards and caressing my seat belt.

"What's your impression so far?" he asked as we rocketed up a freeway ramp and shot into heavy traffic.

"It seems very responsive."

He laughed and eased up so we were only doing about eighty-five.

"I didn't mean about the car—I meant the case."

"Bafflement."

He glanced my way, then back at the pavement which streaked under us.

"What in particular?"

"How come she let six months pass before starting an investigation? And why pick me? Why not professionals—a whole team of them?"

He laughed. "She didn't tell you? That's typical of Daffy. Her conversation's always personal; she never gets around to tell anyone what's really going on. A month after he disappeared and the Mexican police hadn't dug up a thing and we couldn't push the State Department people to pick up on it, we went to a private agency."

"You couldn't get our government to ask questions about a missing millionaire?"

"Oh, that was no problem. But the Mexicans are very independent, you know, and what they implied was one can never tell what a rich gringo will do if he takes a notion. So I hired Gavillan's to find him. That's a company we've used for special pretrial investigations and they sent a Spanish-speaking agent. Very intelligent, aggressive man. He was on the case two weeks—"

He shook his head irritably as we were temporarily trapped in a slow-moving lane, suddenly downshifted and sent the Porsche darting across two lanes through a space a ferret would balk at.

I closed my eyes and asked what happened to the agent.

"He died. Food poisoning, they told us, from a place near León. We never found any notes from his investigation. It was all very mysterious."

He glanced my way to see how I took it. I looked enigmatic.

He grinned. "Don't let it worry you, food poisoning's not that uncommon down there. It *could* have been an accident."

He returned his attention to the traffic, downshifted again, cut in front of a blue Cadillac and made a right turn into an exit lane. The Cadillac's horn blared indignantly.

"Listen," he said, "you could probably use a drink—I know I could—how about we stop at a little place and talk some. Get acquainted."

That was fine with me and a few moments later we were seated at a corner table meant for romantic couples. A black waitress with something close to a butch haircut brought us towering drinks and a golden bowl filled with classy mixed nuts.

"I understand you were co-anchor for a TV news show up north," he said.

I nodded and he wanted to know what had happened. I said quite a lot.

"The way I hear it, you got squeezed out by a sexy blonde."

"That was part of it. She happened to be prettier, smarter and a few other things. Like, she knew what she wanted."

"And you didn't?"

"I didn't want the job bad enough to have her rubbed out, which is about the only way I could've won."

"It must've been pretty good while it lasted. I mean, having everybody recognize you everywhere you went, girls falling all over you—right?"

I admitted it hadn't been all bad and he asked how I got into it in the beginning.

I explained that I'd been working for the Better Business Bureau, doing consumer fraud publicity pieces. They got picked up regularly and led to interviews on camera which went over even better and suddenly I was offered a job with the top station in town. I wrote special news items, started arranging and running interviews, won a regular night spot as an investigative reporter and then one day they offered me the anchor job.

"How long did it take to get that?"

"About four years. I lucked out, actually. Their ace was hired by an eastern station and he left with pretty short notice. Their second choice turned them down so they turned to me on a temporary basis and reaction was good. I was kept on."

"And then they hired this witch?"

"She wasn't all witch. We got along fine for nearly a year."

"Did you quit or were you fired?"

"I quit before they fired me."

He nodded wisely. "Yes, you make a fuss in a deal like that and you never get another job, right?"

I admitted there was something to that. He kept watching me and I wondered if he was going to suggest I hire him to sue the station to get my job back.

"You look like you're in good shape," he said. "I bet you're an athlete. You run?"

"Used to. In high school and college. Mile relay, low hurdles. I tried out for football and basketball but the football coach said I was too light and the basketball coach said I was too short."

"What'd the track coach say?"

"He said I wasn't any too fast."

He laughed. I got a feeling he enjoyed hearing about my frustrations and figured he resented the fact I'd probably slept with Daphne and wanted anything he could find that'd put me down. I wished I'd skipped the athletic history.

I asked where he'd gone to school and he said Harvard in a tone that suggested didn't everyone? I asked what kind of law he specialized in and he said corporate, again as if the answer were so obvious only a moron would ask the question. But all the while he watched me with his rich, friendly smile. He let me know he had never indulged in group sports. He played handball, squash and tennis.

I decided to quit pretending I gave a damn about getting any better acquainted and asked what happened after the investigator died of food poisoning.

He said a second man was sent down there but didn't do any better except he stayed alive. After a few weeks he started insisting that Oren had taken off for Europe.

"I had the feeling he was right, but of course that notion infuriated Daphne because if that were the case, it would make finding him that much more complicated and drawn out, so she fired the man and came up with the idea of using you when she heard you'd lost your job. She said you had political savvy and a certain stubborn persistence. A bulldog, I believe she said."

I wondered why all these noble attributes came out sounding vaguely obnoxious.

"I think the real reason," he said, smiling beautifully, "is that she likes the idea of hiring a TV personality as her own private eye. It might give her better coverage when she becomes a millionaire's heiress."

I considered asking how long he'd been taking put-down lessons from Daphne but decided it was probably in his genes.

He finally asked me, very casually, how well I'd known Daphne.

"Not awfully."

His smile warmed. "That's too bad. She's quite a woman."

"Yeah, I know her well enough to know that."

He didn't smile so warmly when he let me out at my hotel twenty minutes later. When he wished me good luck, he made it sound as though I'd need it.

III

The gold leaf sign on the cherrywood door said FLETCHER FOUN-
DATION very quietly. I walked in, blinked at the snow-white carpet
and looked over the gleaming black desk on its chrome legs to
take in the receptionist. Her great brown eyes were warmer than
an electric blanket set on high and her smile said welcome, you
must be the most important man in the world.

"May I help you?" she asked and I knew she honest to God
wanted to.

"I'd like to see Ms. Amsdecker."

"Of course—you're Mr. Kyle Champion, right?"

I admitted it and she nodded, tipped her head, poked buttons
and announced me. Another quick nod and she said Ms. Amsdecker would be right out—would I like coffee?

She ordered it while I sank into a chair with a seat so low my
bottom was even with my heels, and as I reached into my pocket
for de Wetering's latest mystery, the lady appeared.

I climbed out of the pit, acknowledged her greeting and followed her trim figure down a gold-carpeted hall to the first door
on the right. The floor-to-ceiling window behind her desk displayed blue sky and Houston, spread-eagled flat into the hazy
distance. Ms. Amsdecker settled into a chair a Supreme Court
judge would envy and asked what could she do for me in a
manner that suggested she could hardly wait.

"You've been told why I'm here?"

"Of course."

She smiled. It brought dimples and showed cultured teeth. Her
eyes were faultless blue, so nakedly honest I was immediately
suspicious and then felt guilty about it. She wore her hair short
and it had the sleek perfection of chinchilla fur.

I asked if by any chance she had a theory about Mr. Fletcher's disappearance, did she know of any enemies or motives that anyone might have for doing away with him? She did not. He was a wonderful man whom everyone admired, respected and loved.

I asked if she knew Mr. Fletcher's wife.

Not well.

Her expression remained friendly, accommodating and respectful, but the tone of voice hinted at a change in attitude.

"Who called to say I was coming in?"

"Mrs. Fletcher."

"What'd she tell you to expect?"

She smiled. "Almost anything."

"Like what?"

"Oh, like, did I think his wife had killed him, had I slept with him myself, would I have dinner with you—"

"So what are the answers?"

"I don't think she killed him or made arrangements to have it done. No, I never slept with him. I was quite fond of him, but he was a good bit too old for me and I don't believe in dating employers."

"How long have you worked for him?"

"Two and a half years."

"Did you know he was messing around with an old girlfriend from college days?"

"No. He was rather good friends with a new member of the board—they grew up together. But it was hardly a flaming affair."

"How'd you know that?"

"I work here. I'm not blind or deaf."

"Did they meet here often—other than for board meetings, I mean?"

"A few times. They shared lunch hours occasionally."

"Long lunch hours?"

"Just average."

"She call him often?"

"I only screen calls when the receptionist is uncertain."

I nodded. "You think Mrs. Fletcher is having an affair with their lawyer, Harlan?"

"Probably."

"Did Fletcher know it?"

"I wouldn't be surprised."

"You think it bothered him?"

"No. He wasn't terribly interested in his wife."

"You think he wanted to leave her?"

"He left her all the time. I doubt they spent more than two weeks together in the last two years."

"But wouldn't he get sore if he knew people thought she was messing around?"

"No. If anyone got upset, it'd be her. *She* was the one with the delicate ego."

"Or maybe she was just afraid of losing all his money."

She made no comment on that. Her hands rested on the chair arms and she didn't fiddle or twitch as I watched her.

"Did he ever confide in you?"

"No."

"That surprises me. You strike me as a woman guys would naturally confide in."

She tilted her neat head. "Do I strike you as motherly?"

"I think guys more often confide in pretty women than in their mothers. At least once they've reached their teens."

She didn't think that was worth comment and I decided she was right.

"Did he usually carry a lot of money?"

"Quite a bit," she said, nodding.

"Was he ever mugged?"

"No. He never looked like a victim, if you know what I mean. He looked strong and terribly alert."

"But he mostly traveled alone, didn't he?"

"Always," she said soberly, "except when he was with someone."

I returned her sober gaze and asked if she'd have lunch with me.

"Will this be part of the investigation?"

"Would that make a difference?"

"Yes. I don't mix business with pleasure."

"Well, we won't know if it'll be a pleasure till we get better acquainted, will we?"

She smiled. "Unfortunately I have a luncheon engagement. I'm free for dinner, though."

"What time?"

"I'll meet you out front at five-thirty."

She came through the revolving door as my cab pulled up and I got out to hand her in. She wore a beige suit with a skirt to the knees and a white blouse with ruffles under the chin. All in all she looked like a New York model, except her face was a little too real. I wasn't positive about the eyelashes but the rest was genuine.

"Where are we going?" she asked.

I told her the restaurant my driver had recommended and she nodded, either in recognition or acceptance, I couldn't tell which.

"What do you normally do after work?"

"Go home and fix dinner. Once in a while I go out with men who want something."

"What do they usually want?"

"They almost always *say* they want to know me better. What they're really after is how can they get money from the Foundation."

"I think you underestimate yourself."

"I rarely underestimate men." Her mouth still smiled, but the words were stated soberly.

"Well, you know I'm not after a grant."

"Not from the foundation."

"I don't think Mrs. Fletcher'd like you much."

Surprise removed her polite smile. "Why'd you say that?"

"She resents remarks with double meanings."

She laughed. "Do you share her prejudice?"

"I share your weakness. So what do you figure I am after with you?"

"Anything you can get." She glanced out the window, then back at me. "About Mr. Fletcher, I mean."

"Of course. But this seems a great way to work at what I'm supposed to be doing."

"Right. And you can write the dinner off as an expense, I get a free meal and there won't be any wrestling around later."

So much for romance.

Our restaurant catered to expense accounts and the people who drink too much to care about taste, only quantity and style. She said she'd like white wine, so I ordered a Graves and we got through that while eating overcooked red snapper buried in sauce that needed more garlic.

I was pleased to see that while the waiter was better-dressed and probably handsomer than I, he got none of my partner's attention. Doubtless she was too professional to indulge in the roving eye.

After the meal she asked for decaffeinated coffee and showed a flicker of disappointment when the handsome waiter delivered a white pot of hot water with a packet of Kaffee Hag.

"Next time," I said, "you pick the restaurant. Now tell me about Fletcher."

She said he was punctual, thoughtful and always polite. He knew Spanish well and was a little fanatical about Mexico. His office was filled with mementos of his trips there; metal masks, clay figurines, silver, carvings, pottery and papier-mâché.

"Is he sentimental?" I asked.

I wondered why we were both suddenly speaking of him in the present tense when before we'd presumed he was dead. I decided she was remembering him favorably and unconsciously rejected his demise.

"No, I don't think he was sentimental," she said, suddenly letting him die. Her mouth drooped a little as she fiddled with the Kaffee Hag packet and dumped it into her cup.

"How about you?"

She met my gaze. "I liked him. I am not sentimental about him. I'm not sentimental about any man."

"Uh-huh. I can tell you're a real tough cookie. Got any pets?"

"I live in an apartment. No pets allowed."

"Got any stuffed animals?"

She smiled and I decided the eyelashes were real.

"I have a very beat-up teddy bear my nephew gave me."

"Haven't you got a guy?"

"Not stuffed."

We grinned at each other and drank coffee. She turned down brandy and said she'd stick with the coffee or its unreasonable facsimile. I ordered ouzo and a glass of water.

"That's Greek, isn't it?" she asked as the waiter delivered the ouzo in a sherry glass and set a tumbler of iced water beside it.

I said yes and dumped the ice and part of the water into my empty coffee cup and poured the ouzo slowly into the tumbler's remaining cold water. It turned ghostly white.

"Smells like licorice."

"Tastes like that. I think I should know your first name."

"It's Marigold."

"So you're called Mary, right?"

"Usually."

"I see. But not by friends, huh?"

"You're very perceptive, Mr. Champion."

"Okay, I'll call you Marigold if you call me Kyle."

I began asking questions which she answered casually. She saw about one movie a week, read *The New Yorker*, *The Atlantic*, *Savvy* and occasional novels. She played the flute, but not often. I did not find out if she had ever been married, dated regularly or was interested in men in general. She didn't invite such questions and volunteered nothing.

She didn't ask if I were married. Probably because she wasn't in the habit of believing answers she got in that line.

"Did you ever travel with Oren?"

She shook her head. He wasn't a man who liked toadies or sycophants and was content with handling his own luggage and sometimes even made his own travel arrangements. I asked if he ever sent her on personal errands.

"Sometimes." She smiled. "He occasionally asked me to buy fresh cookies from the specialty shop down the block. His fix, he called it. He asked so nicely I never resented it and he was very generous at Christmas and always remembered my birthday. When I missed work with the flu, he sent flowers to the apartment."

I suggested we try another place for a drink, but she said no thank you; she should get home.

Her apartment had a doorman and she told me I needn't escort her inside. We shook hands on the sidewalk and she thanked me for a nice time.

"I enjoyed talking about Mr. Fletcher." She frowned thoughtfully. "I keep thinking about him by his first name, but don't use it because it might sound a little disrespectful—"

I said I hoped I'd see her again.

She looked up at me as if surprised to see I was still there, then smiled gently.

"Well, yes, I guess that'll be up to you, won't it?"

IV

I took a Mexican flight from Houston to Guadalajara. The cabin was bright with hot colors, the seats comfortably shabby. Black-haired, dark-eyed stewardesses watched their passengers with calm detachment and a dark, slim steward rolled a liquor bar up and down the aisle dispensing wine, beer and highballs. I took a bottle of Bohemia and sipped from the plastic glass while staring out the window. Texas was covered with cities clear down to the Rio Grande. In Mexico there were occasional villages and tiny roads like erratic etchings on a map and all the earth was brown instead of Texas green. We crossed over a series of abrupt hills, then flat country again. I was baffled by the intricate patterns and varied shades of brown, distinct as pieces in a jigsaw puzzle and seemingly as arbitrary. I learned later the separating lines were stone walls, the most striking and omnipresent sign of Mexican landscapes. Near Guadalajara we passed over a spectacularly deep gorge. The entire area was gouged and lacerated by knifing streams and dry creek beds that twisted all over the land.

We descended without a glimpse of the city and emerged from the plane into eighty-four-degree sunshine. I hiked rapidly down the long concourse under an arching brick roof, made a ninety-degree turn and entered the main reception area where I retrieved my garment bag and moved on through customs.

The scene was frantic. One agent handled two counters, picked through the luggage with vandalous hands and left the piled mess for travelers to repack in a panic. I moved through quickly behind a group of young girls with an incredible number of suitcases, great cardboard boxes wrapped with twine, and bulky backpacks. A blonde pushed a half-assembled bicycle along on one functioning wheel. They were cheerful and full of laughter which even the rude customs official couldn't stifle.

Except for the girls, who spoke American, I heard nothing but staccato Spanish.

At the Hertz station I picked up a blue, two-door Maverick reserved for me, did a quick map study and headed for town. Guadalajara has over a million people, and judging from the territory I drove through, ninety-nine percent of them live in squalor. It was the ugliest city I've seen with the possible exception of Iráklion in Crete. The traffic matched the worst I've seen on the Chicago skyline freeway; so frantic it hypnotizes drivers into a half-controlled panic. For over half a mile I was trapped beside a huge old truck with an exhaust pipe aimed directly into my window. It was so vile it made my skin tingle and my eyes water. Despite the heat I rolled the window up, but somehow the poison seeped through until I was able to squirt ahead and change lanes leaving the truck behind me.

It took a couple of wrong passes before I located my hotel, found the garage entry and squeezed the Maverick down the ramp.

The lobby was cool and dark, the clerk efficient. In a few moments I was up in a small, characterless room with white walls and jalousie windows that let in lots of air and traffic noise. A small refrigerator harbored tiny bottles of vodka, gin, rum, whiskey and Scotch. Unfortunately the small ice trays were empty and a sign inside the door warned me against using tap water for refills. I found a water bottle with a sealed cap on the adjacent bureau and filled the trays, picked out a Johnnie Walker Black Label Scotch, emptied it into a tumbler and measured out a bit of tepid water to spread it a little. Then, after a couple of swallows, I hit the shower. I was still toweling my hair when the telephone rang.

"Yeah?"

"Mr. Champion?"

"Right."

"Welcome to Mexico. Mrs. Fletcher asked I should call. My name is Lalo. I am good friend of Señor Fletcher."

"Business friend?"

"Some business, some social, you know?"

"What's your business, Lalo?"

"People, Mr. Champion. I am what you call, ambassador of good will. I bring people together for mutual benefits."

"Who've you brought Mr. Fletcher together with lately?"

"No one, Mr. Champion. He is gone and no one knows where."

"So what do you offer me?"

"Service, Mr. Champion. I know the city, the language, the people."

I swigged my Scotch and studied the carpet. It was brown and tired.

"What do you get paid for your services, Lalo?"

"It depends. If we use my car, which I recommend, you save time and expense in the long walk since I know the way and the traffic."

"Did you work for the other two investigators?"

"Others? Ah, no sir. I did not know others."

"You didn't know anyone else was looking for him?"

"I know about the police, sir. They talked with me three times."

"But no private investigators?"

"Not that I recall."

"Is your memory poor?"

"No, that was just a way of speaking, you know? I am no so comfortable on telephone. Perhaps we meet? There is a bar downstairs."

I decided what the hell and told him I'd be down in ten minutes.

His head was round and his smile was "Have a good day," simple. A large-checked black and white sport jacket stretched across his thick chest over his solid paunch and a red plaid tie with a fat Windsor knot was half buried under his Adam's apple.

He gave me a balloon hand, warm and moist. Mirror-bright shoes gleamed under the knife edge of his pants.

He asked polite questions about my trip as he steered me into the bar and we took a small table beneath a large brown blowup of a desert photo that'd make a drowning man thirsty.

Lalo carefully tugged up his slacks at the crease as he sat down. I suspected he didn't dare cross his legs, with that crease he might cause an amputation.

"So Mrs. Fletcher talked to you about me?"

"Only to say you were looking for Mr. Fletcher and would need assistance. I have been a guide for fourteen years, I know everwhere and everone. First-class, professional guide."

As if to confirm his claim, the waiter appeared and greeted him as Señor Lalo. He beamed, ordered a gin and tonic and I asked for the same.

He asked if I'd been to Mexico before and clucked when I said no. I must return, he said, when I was not on such a tragic mission. Yes, he knew Juan García, the banker, and Luis Morales, the tavern owner. I asked how he knew Fletcher.

"Since he first come to Mexico I was his guide. He had little Spanish then, you see, and did not know our city. I taught him much. We were, you could say, constant companions—"

"Day and night?"

"At first, days only. Later, when he knew the business people and places, he was able to do without me for business but evenings I became his guide once more. I introduced him to Señor Morales and others—"

"Did you introduce him to any women?"

He drew himself up solemnly. "I am no a pimp, Mr. Champion."

"Not all women are prostitutes—or don't you know that?"

"Well, no, of course not—" For the first time he looked dismayed as he tried to decide if he should be insulted or pretend I'd merely misunderstood him. His thick hand blundered over his pumpkin face, then wandered back to the table. He tested his drink and the smile returned as he lowered the glass.

"Was he interested in women?" I asked.

"*Sí.* I mean, he had a quick eye for the pretty girl, you know? But he never ask I should take him where girls are. He was a little shy, I think. I ask him a couple times, you want to see different kind of show? and he would smile at me, very kind, and say, 'No thank you, Lalo.' "

"You have any idea what he *was* looking for?"

"Eh?"

"What'd he want, music, people, food?"

"Oh well, yes, everthing. Friends, good time."

"What'd he drink?"

"Whatever. Tequila with salt and lime—"

"Did he drink a lot?"

"Sometimes," he nodded vigorously, "but always the gentleman. Never loud or clumsy, you know. Sometimes, late, he would talk with special care, so no to stumble."

I kept asking questions and got the vague sense that he did not really know the man at all. It might have been because Lalo was too self-centered to observe anything closely; it was also possible that Fletcher simply chose not to reveal himself. I gave up and we agreed to meet at nine-thirty in the morning and go visit the banker, García. Lalo said he'd make the appointment.

I didn't notice anything unusual in my room until I hung my suit coat in the closet and saw the shirts were hanging a little awry. That wasn't the way I'd left them. I looked around the room and saw my hairbrush, which I'd left on the bureau, lay with its handle to the left instead of the right.

For several moments after putting the chain lock on the door I laid on my back, listening to sounds of traffic and a rock band down the block. I thought of the investigator Harlan mentioned, who had died of food poisoning, and made up my mind that after my meeting with Lalo in the morning, I'd make an abrupt change in tactics and locale.

V

I woke a little after 2 A.M. The sounds of traffic had fallen off and the music was done. I could hear occasional distant sounds in the hotel, a late shower running, a flushed toilet.

In the past I would have sat up, lit a cigarette and let my mind run with whatever problem I had at the moment. Now I lay on my side with my arm around the extra pillow and remembered Daphne.

After about ten minutes I sat up and dialed the operator. It took a while and she sounded sleepy but she gave me an outside line and I called Daphne's number.

She answered on the sixth ring.

"It's Kyle," I said.

"You bastard, d'you know what time it is here?"

"Uh-huh. About the same as when you called me last."

"That's different, I sleep nights and you know it."

"I sure do."

She grunted and I guessed she was rolling over.

"Okay," she said at last, "are you calling just to be snotty or have you found something?"

"I'm not sure. How'd you happen to send this bird Lalo to see me?"

"Who?"

"Lalo, the round-faced, balloon-handed guide."

"I never heard of him."

"He claims he knew Oren well, taught him Spanish, showed him around the world of business and pleasure."

"How old is he?"

"Thirty to forty."

"Oren's guide was an old man . . . Jim, I think. I told you that."

"No you didn't."

"Well, that's the only guide he ever had that I heard of. A courtly old man with sad eyes."

"You met him?"

"Yes. When we were in some funny little old town where they'd turned the riverbed into an underground highway. Spooky damned place."

"Why the hell didn't you mention him before?"

"Well, for heaven's sake, he wasn't anyone important. Am I supposed to remember every shoeshine boy and bartender?"

"Hell yes, if they knew the man and talked with him."

"Well, I don't remember any others."

"I don't suppose you'd know if there was an autopsy on the investigator who died down here?"

"I don't know anything about any investigators—Harlan handled that. Why do you ask?"

"Somebody searched my room this evening when I was out."

"Why'd anybody do that?"

"Either they thought they'd learn something about me, or they wanted to leave me a message."

She thought a moment and said, "Are you scared?"

"I'm not exactly thrilled over the idea of dying with the heaves in Mexico."

"If you chicken out, don't expect me to pay the bills."

"You've already given me an advance."

"I thought you were a professional."

"Yeah, I am. But I'd kind of like to know what the hell I'm into here, okay?"

"You'll just have to be careful about what you eat and drink."

"Sure, I'll pack my lunch. Was your lawyer ever in Mexico?"

"You mean Harlan?"

"How many lawyers you got?"

"I don't have any. Harlan's Oren's attorney."

"So has he been in Mexico?"

"You mean while working for Oren?"

"Jesus Christ, yes! Or on vacation or any other damned thing."

"I don't know. He hasn't told me everything he's done."

"You don't socialize with the hired help, huh?"

"Now what's the hidden meaning there?"

"There's nothing hidden there, I'm telling you not to bullshit me about you and Harlan, not after I watched you light up like a Hollywood opening when he showed up at the house."

"Why, Kyle," she said with delight, "you're jealous!"

"What I am is—I'm suspicious that old buddy Harlan had reasons to wish his old buddy Oren would become a permanent resident in Mexico."

"That's ridiculous."

"Somebody told somebody I was coming to Mexico looking for the man. Who the hell else knew besides you and the counselor?"

"Anybody *you* told, or the people in Oren's Houston office, my butler, maybe the taxi driver you gabbed with here or there—"

"Oh sure, every cab driver in Mexico's been alerted to tip off killers when I show up. Well thanks a lot for all your help, and if you just happen to think of somebody else like this Jim guy, put down the name and address and any other details so they'll be handy when I call the next time."

"Where can I reach you?"

I told her she wouldn't be able to from now on, I'd call her. She didn't like that one bit and warned me it'd better not be in the middle of the night and concluded that I should damned well get moving because it was excruciatingly awkward not knowing whether one was a widow or not.

She made me feel so sorry for her I promptly fell asleep.

VI

I called Ms. Amsdecker at the Fletcher Foundation just after 8 A.M. and wasn't surprised to find her at work and alert. No, she had never heard of Lalo and, yes, she knew about the old guide, Jim. She thought he lived in Guanajuato, but at one time he'd been in business somewhere in the Midwest before he retired.

"Who besides you in your office knows what I'm doing here?" I asked.

"Well, the receptionist arranged the reservation—"

"How long's she been with you?"

"About a year."

"Who hired her?"

"We have a firm that hires clerical help when we need it. They sent her."

"Okay, would you mind checking her out with them? See where she worked before and whether references were called."

"They're not likely to admit it if they didn't."

"Yeah, but give it a try anyway. What about you, where'd you work before?"

"I taught English in a Berlitz school in Mexico City."

That stopped me for a moment.

"So you speak Spanish, right?"

She said yes as calmly as if that were a sensible question after her last statement.

"How long were you there?"

"Nine months. And yes, I met Mr. Fletcher there. I was introduced by one of the teachers and agreed to attend a party with him where I'd act as interpreter. He learned I'd taken business courses in Chicago and offered me a job."

"So you *did* date him once."

"It was a business arrangement. No romance, no fooling."

I thought about that while listening to the deep hum of the telephone and distant voices murmuring.

"All right, check out the receptionist, okay?"

"Who will you have check me out?"

"Damned if I know, but I'll think of something. If things go okay, I'd like to take you someplace when I get back. Someplace where we could dance. You like to dance?"

"Yes."

"Okay, I'll be in touch."

Lalo was seated in a dusty blue Chevy Monza in front of the hotel when I came out at nine-thirty. His moon face beamed and he waved his fat hand in greeting.

"We got an appointment with García?" I asked.

"Of course—only it couldn't be till after ten so we take a little tour—no extra charge—part of package, eh?"

"Where?"

"City square. Is very grand. And if we have time, the church. You never see anything like it, I promise—"

I'm not thrilled by churches but it all sounded safe, so I slipped in beside him and we took off.

We parked on a grubby side street, strolled south and came to a huge rectangle with two huge, spouting fountains and a gross green statue. The rectangle was surrounded by flat-topped trees which spread their foliage over masses of citizens and shoeshine boys. It seemed the principal occupation in Guadalajara was shoeshining. Old men ran elaborate stands where the shinees sat enthroned above the peasant crowd, reading newspapers while the ancient ones slaved over their leather. Young boys carried portable kits and doggedly begged every man who came within range to let them do their thing and many obliged, standing on one foot at a time while the boys worked feverishly and their customers watched with approving smiles or eyed the passing señoritas.

Lalo escorted me to the base of the statue, which he explained was of the Liberator. It had heroic proportions but a peasant build and the maniacal face of a fanatic; frightening, yet almost ludicrously melodramatic. We moved southward and found a sub-square dominated by an elaborate bandstand with a roof supported by sculptured maidens with bare breasts and draped hips. While we watched, a young model in a red gown went up the steps at the bandstand front and posed for a young man festooned with cameras. We moved on and Lalo pointed out gaily decorated horsecarts hitched to flowered horses along the east end of the great rectangle. The stench was stout.

We strolled west to the church overlooking the broad open space. As I stepped up on the curb, a tiny, ancient, bowlegged woman with a pillow body blocked my way, and grinning toothlessly, pinned a miniature medal made of black ribbon, lace and a minuscule picture of Jesus on my shirt. I've long been able to resist beggars, but the old lady was too much. I dug out four pesos and dropped them in her hand. She gave me a coy smile and shook her head, as if I shouldn't have bothered, but clutched the coins tightly.

"You no should encourage them," Lalo told me tolerantly. He urged me on toward the church doors which were so huge the giant knockers hung on the brown planks seven feet overhead.

"My God," I thought, "they must be expecting the Jolly Green Giant."

We entered a small door within the huge one and I looked down as I stepped over the cross brace below. When I looked up, it was into the dark interior and I could see nothing but another opening about fifteen feet away.

"Careful," said Lalo, gripping my arm firmly.

As I turned in annoyance and started to jerk free, there was a rustle behind me and then my head exploded.

VII

The headache dragged me toward consciousness. Its intensity kept me from realizing at first that I was in a moving car and sitting between two people. My right knee hurt and I moved it cautiously and felt my slacks sticking to dried blood. I didn't dare move my head, I was afraid it would fall off.

I grunted and felt both arms restrained by large hands.

"*Silencio,*" cautioned a voice to my right.

I stayed silent and kept my eyes closed. I can remember times in college, how painful it could be to open your eyes with a raging hangover. Somewhere, in the vagueness of my stupor, I thought perhaps I'd bumped my head into some projection in the church, but the restraints and the alien voice made me realize I'd been assaulted. I felt a great rage at the unfairness of being sapped in a church.

The car took a corner, pressing me into the body on my left. I thought it must be a very small car or these were very large men. Blackness took over.

The headache dominated my life. I was aware of being lifted out of the car and moved into another and thought of telling my captors I'd be happy to cooperate if they'd just let me lie down and sleep a little while, but my mouth was locked as in a nightmare and my eyes wouldn't open. It seemed that if I willed it hard enough, maybe they would, but the will was missing.

I blanked out, then heard an engine start, felt my hands on a steering wheel, heard a door slam and felt the car in motion. I dragged my eyes open and saw the cliff edge before the hood of a gray Volkswagen, felt the sickening lurch as I went over and passed out with the crash some seconds later.

The ceiling was white, as were the walls, drapes and bed cover. The man in the chair beside the bed was dark-skinned with black hair and a heavy black mustache. His dark eyes stared into mine when I looked his way.

"Mr. Champion," he said.

I managed to croak.

He got up, took a glass from the stand beside my bed and offered it to me. He had to insert the glass tube in my mouth, but once piped in I managed nicely. The water wasn't cold, it was just the greatest drink of my life.

"You are in the Santa María Hospital," he told me. "Last night you lost control of a Volkswagen you rented in the afternoon and drove over the side of a cliff some forty miles west of Mexico City. Your car, fortunately, landed on a steep slope of loose shale which cushioned the impact and allowed you to live."

I finished the water, the man went to the door and ordered more from a dark-haired nurse, then returned to my side.

"My name is Moreno. Lieutenant Moreno, Mexico police. I know you are, or were, with television in the United States. Right now that is all I know. Where have you been staying?"

I named my hotel. It seemed like a great accomplishment, first to remember, then to speak. He said he knew of no such hotel in Mexico City. I said it was in Guadalajara.

"Ah!" he said. "How long have you been in Mexico?"

"What day is it?"

"Thursday."

"Came yesterday." I wondered if my arms would work and decided to wait awhile before checking that out.

"For what reason do you visit Mexico?"

"Assignment."

"By whom?"

Somewhere in my aching head a suspicion took root. Was this really a cop? Was it Thursday? Was I alive?

"Mr. Champion, who are you working for?"

"Channel 7, Minneapolis, St. Paul."

"You used to work there. I found your card and checked with

the station. They say you resigned a month ago. Think very carefully, why are you here now?"

My headache was too bad for me to be clever or even very paranoiac.

"I was hired by a lady."

That came out fairly well and he nodded encouragingly. I thought there was maybe a smile coming.

"Mrs. Fletcher. Houston. Wanted to find her husband."

"Very good. You are going to be all right, Mr. Champion. You have a concussion, not terribly severe, and you have been drugged, which is probably causing a great deal of your pain just now. Please tell me all you remember of what has happened in the time since you came to our country."

I asked for another drink of water and when it arrived, unconsciously moved my hand to guide the tube. It was a great comfort to find it worked. I stirred my left arm, clenched my fists as they lay on the white bed cover and began feeling better.

I told him all I could remember. He was as indignant about the attack in church as I was and clucked sympathetically as I described the moment before going over the cliff. I decided he was a sterling fellow.

When he was satisfied that I'd told him all I knew, he stood up, shook my hand gently and left.

Dinner was brown and I had trouble getting interested, but the pretty nurse was insistent and charming, so I felt it would be churlish not to please her and got through most of it. She patted my arm, then got me up and we walked the corridor. I learned her name, which should have been Carmen but wasn't, so I didn't retain it. They released me the next afternoon and by dinnertime I was on a plane heading back to Houston.

VIII

Ms. Amsdecker met me as I entered the concourse, had a young man take my bag and asked if I were strong enough to walk. I assured her I might even run if Hertz would pay, but I wasn't up to hurdling anything.

"Mrs. Fletcher's been very worried about you—you're to call her at once."

I couldn't picture Daphne getting gray hairs over me, but entered the first handy phone booth and placed the call.

She was more annoyed than sympathetic about my adventures and took the unreasonable attitude that one should expect to get clobbered in church. She asked what the Mexican police thought and was very interested in Lieutenant Moreno. She suspected he knew about me before I was hospitalized. Obviously it didn't take a cracked head to make people paranoiac.

"Now what're you going to do?" she demanded.

"I'll tell you what I'm not going to do, and that's tell anybody what I'm going to do and where I'll do it from. I'll keep you posted on progress and that's it."

She said that obviously getting clubbed made me snotty, but she'd put up with that as long as I stayed as stubborn about the job as I'd always been about everything else. She finally agreed to send more money through the Fletcher Foundation and broke off after telling me I'd damned well better report regularly.

"What'd she say?" asked Ms. Amsdecker.

"Come back with your shield or on it. Where shall we eat?"

"Didn't they feed you on the plane?"

"They threatened to, but I fought them off. Come on, pick a place."

"Okay, but first I've got to make a phone call."

She entered the booth and closed the door. I tried to look

elsewhere, but saw her shake her head firmly several times, and when she hung up, she did it with enough care to make me guess she'd rather have slammed it. She came out looking moderately grim.

The restaurant she chose was on a back street and I wondered if she was trying to keep me out of sight. Then the maître d' greeted her by name and I felt better. It was a clean, well-lighted place with a neat, fairly brief menu. I ordered a margarita and she had white wine. When the waiter left, she frowned at me.

"Shouldn't you be sticking with mild stimulants?"

"One's mild enough."

She asked what I'd like to eat and I said something not too brown. Mexican food had run too strong in that direction.

She suggested scampi, which was seldom brown except around the edges. I said that'd be fine and she ordered it too, which was nice, considering the amount of garlic used in it.

The margarita went down very smoothly. I ordered another over her mild objections and asked her to pick the wine for the meal. She did. The shrimp arrived, fat, juicy and pink, floating in butter. I swished them around in the sauce, drank the wine and admired Marigold. She ate with deliberate grace and a fine appetite. She also kept up with me on the wine, which was a considerable feat, since the headache did something for my thirst that only a steady flow could ease.

"Well," she said, "aside from the fracture, how was Mexico?"

"Fine."

"Did you learn anything?"

"Yeah, a guy could get killed down there."

"Were you terribly frightened?"

"No, I was scared shitless."

The alert blue eyes watched me with mild disapproval and some concern. She thought I must be drunk. I thought so too.

I mopped up scampi juice with my last roll, finished it off and wiped my mouth.

"Tell me what you think of Fletcher's wife, Daphne," I said. "I mean, what you really think."

She didn't like the question. "I don't know her that well."

"Come on, you must have some impressions. Level with me."

"They're very mixed. I knew before I met her that she was a lot younger than Oren, and pretty. That she'd done a lot of volunteer work for charity. Somehow, when I actually met her, she was a lot more aggressive and self-centered than I'd expected."

She sipped her wine and smiled.

"The fact is, I rather expected her to be a daughterly type, leaning on and looking up to her husband. I guess you know that's not her style."

Boy, did I know.

"How'd she and the man get on?"

"They didn't seem married. I mean, there was nothing personal in their relationship. No contact. You know, most married people develop a sort of comradery, they connect even when they're not getting along. Daphne and Oren just never seemed married."

"No love, no hate, no friendship?" I suggested.

She nodded and said she'd rather talk about something else.

"Okay. Tell me about you. Everything. From the beginning."

"You'll be sorry," she said, and began.

She'd been born in a small North Dakota town by the Red River of the north. When she was eight years old, her parents were trapped in a blizzard while returning from a visit with a sick relative and froze to death in their car. Marigold was raised by her grandparents, who died shortly after she finished college.

I said she was going too fast and asked what happened in high school. She said she'd been the yearbook editor, salutatorian, member of the debate team and a flute player in the school band.

"Sounds like you didn't have much time for guys," I said.

"Not much."

She went to the University of Wisconsin because her debate coach went there and knew people who gave her a room and meals.

I was tempted to ask for more details about the debate coach, but hadn't drunk enough yet to get reckless, so I asked what extracurricular activities she took on in Madison.

"I worked part-time as a waitress and started dating a lot."

"Ah. And did you get more out of that than debating, fluting and such?"

"I got a baby."

"Oh."

Her eyes narrowed.

"Does that bother you?"

"Hell no," I said too strongly. "What happened?"

"I had a girl. April. She lives with me."

"Hey, that's great. I always thought I'd like to have a little girl—"

"And have you?"

"No. Never married—"

"Well," she said dryly, "you don't have to marry to have a baby."

"Yeah, but it doesn't happen too often with guys."

"Unfortunately."

She said that with such asperity it didn't seem wise to comment. I asked who cared for the kid while she was working.

"Her grandmother. She lives with us and even helps pay the rent. That's how come I can live where I do, in case you wondered."

Actually I'd thought I could guess, but I didn't admit that.

"I thought your parents died—"

"They did. The mother of the guy who got me pregnant heard what had happened, came to see me, we hit it off and it's all turned out very nicely."

"What about her son, doesn't she like him?"

"We never discuss him."

The waiter came by and I ordered coffee with a shot of brandy. Marigold took decaffeinated coffee which was served from an orange-topped pot.

The moodiness that came over her during talk of her past was soon shoved aside and she said it was my turn to tell the life story.

"I want to know what it takes to become a TV star and then turn to private investigations."

"A high degree of incompetence helps," I said.

She shook her head impatiently and told me to be serious.

"Okay. I was born in Wisconsin, grew up all over the Midwest (Daddy was a traveling man), was a sprinter and hurdler in high school track, competed in speech and acted in plays. At the U, I majored in English and composition."

"What about girls?"

"I flunked that. In high school and college too."

"I don't believe it. What happened?"

"Okay, I fell in love my junior year in high school and had this big thing going clear through graduation. Only then I let a friend talk me into going to L.A. where his brother was supposed to have a great job waiting for us, but when we got there the brother'd been fired and I spent the summer parking cars and busing dishes. Didn't even make waiter. My girl, who was sore about me taking off to begin with, really got disgusted when I came home broke and we busted up. Then I went to college and fell for this willowy woman with sapphire eyes and a philandering husband. She was the instructor in a history course I took—the only history course—and I couldn't keep my eyes off her. I ran into her at the library one night and pretty soon that became a regular routine until one night we wound up in the back seat of her car. Afterward she cried and confessed she'd just been using me to get back at her cheating husband. She was awfully ashamed and apologetic—so much so I tried hard to be indignant because I could see that's what she wanted, but the fact is I was too high from the lovemaking to be bothered. I even promised to be her friend."

I'd felt guilty about that, knowing damned well I'd try to make her every chance I got and tried to make it right in my mind by telling myself I'd take her away from that son-of-a-bitch who didn't appreciate her.

"Things went fine for quite a while. She was really smart and I was fired up by our talks and arguments over books, plays, movies and music. Every once in a while she'd try to break things off when we were getting too physical."

I suppose that's what made it so exciting. I could never take her for granted, she was always being courted. We made love just often enough to keep the tension on a perpetual high. I never had enough.

"Then, when I thought I had her talked into leaving her husband and living with me, the dumb bastard got himself shot by the husband of a woman he was sleeping with. The bullet severed his spine and of course the selfish jerk lived and became a paraplegic. That finished off my romance. I think maybe she was happy. At least I like to think so. She's finally got the guy she loved from the time she was a little girl neighbor and now she'll never have to worry about the competition."

Competition had always worried her, she got jealous if I greeted a girl I knew on campus or looked too long at one near us. At first I'd felt flattered, she made it seem I must be irresistible to all those girls out there.

Marigold excused herself and got up to head for the ladies' room. I looked around and saw that while all the places seemed taken, the restaurant still looked uncrowded. Each table had its own fresh rose, some gold, others white or red. Ours was peach. It all had an air of senior romance.

The waiter strolled by to ask if there was anything I wanted and I said yes, bring us a bottle of champagne. He bowed approvingly and asked what kind. I asked for a Korbel, the driest, and he said they didn't have that but he could offer an equivalent and I accepted.

Marigold returned before the bucket arrived and said okay, now let's get down to how I got the TV anchor job.

"Well, I stayed in Minneapolis after graduation and worked for a year in a plumbing and heating wholesale operation. Great background stuff—I mean the staff of civilization—warm air and indoor johns, right? Only things went bad, my boss was bright and hardworking, but he was new and the competition cut his throat. Like, they'd offer all our customers a flat ten percent under anything my guy quoted. So we wound up with people who couldn't get credit anywhere else and went broke. Then I heard of an opening at the Better Business Bureau and the man in charge was looking for someone to write his Bulletin, so I told him what a great writer I was and sort of stretched the one course I took in journalism until it sounded like I was a bona fide reporter type and he took me on."

The waiter showed up with the champagne and Marigold's eyes opened wide enough to spill blue.

"What're we celebrating?" she asked.

"Survival."

She laughed and said she'd sure drink to that.

The cork was popped, the bubbly spilled a bit and then did its stuff in the tall glasses and we toasted each other and grinned a lot.

I went on with my story. Within a year I was starting to get some media attention to the variety of consumer protection stories appearing in our newsletter. That led to a couple of interviews on TV which were well received. The top local station began calling on me whenever they needed something short and grabby. Finally I was invited over for a chat with the station manager and came out with a job writing a weekly consumer report show.

"From there I went to handling interviews, then I was making direct appearances. The big break was when the news anchorman got an offer from the East and left us. The first choice for his replacement waltzed the station around long enough to get a better offer from a competitor and all of a sudden I was handling the show on a temporary basis. It went okay, so I got a contract."

Marigold's eyes sparkled above the champagne glass.

"So suddenly you were rich and famous?"

"Pretty famous and heading for fat."

"Wasn't it terribly exciting?"

"The first days I was flying. But you know how often you've read about entertainers who hit it real big early and they said they spent their days waiting for the world to discover they weren't all that special? That's the way it is. You just know it's all going to vanish. And in my line there were special problems. Back when I was with the Bureau, I kept getting worked up about a new fraud or scam and I'd develop an exposé like a madman. No doubts, these were bastards and I'd nail them. But the minute the release was made, I was scared. What if I'd made a mistake? What if they sued or sent goons to bust me up? And sure enough, every time they'd scream and come up with defenses and attacks and I'd be scrambling to defend myself. They never caught me in a serious slip or made me retract anything, but I'd be running scared for a week, and all the time asking myself, why'd I get myself in this mess? Then two days later I'd be off on another hunt."

"Well, when you got on TV it was different, wasn't it?"

"Yeah. Worse. With the Bureau release I sometimes reached thousands of people. On TV it got over a million. So okay, I handled regular news as an anchorman, but my specialty was the scam and I just naturally found them or had them brought to me by all those watchers and every time I let fly, the shit hit the fan again. And everybody knew what I looked like. In an article you're less than a name, on TV you're the guy who's been in everybody's living room, bedroom, bar or hotel."

The waiter came by and refilled our glasses. Marigold lifted hers toward me and said, "Let's drink to your next TV job."

"I'd rather drink to you."

She lowered her glass. "What's the matter? Gun-shy?"

"No. I just don't want to be that eager every night on a job that's so damned unreal."

"You'd rather be a private detective?"

"Well," I grinned, "it ain't all bad. Look at me now."

She shook her head, put the champagne glass on the table and leaned forward.

"What we have here is a loss of confidence. You made it too sudden and too easy, and when things went bad, you folded up and quit. And I'll bet I know why it went bad. People in that business measure everything by the dollar. They got you cheap because you were new, and when ratings dropped, they decided they had to have somebody expensive. You should've hung on and made them fire you. Then the competition would try to cash in on the sympathy thing."

"What I need, obviously, is a manager like you."

She picked up her glass, took a sip and studied me with her blue eyes.

"You're good-looking enough. Probably need more hair down across your forehead. You've got very dramatic eyebrows and terribly honest eyes. It'd help if you were more tight-lipped."

"You do plastic surgery?"

"Not lately. Okay, let's go back a ways. You met Daphne before getting the anchor spot, right?"

"Yeah."

"And you lost out there too?"

"That was no loss, just a passing fancy. But how'd you know?"

She smiled gleefully.

"I didn't know—you just told me. You two had a fling. I thought, when she talked to me about you, that there was a lemon twist in her tone sharp enough to make me suspect she'd been scorned or at least crossed. It made me wonder why she'd decided to hire you."

I'd wondered too but decided that in my increasingly woozy state this was not the time for further confessions. Telling her about people she'd never met was one thing, discussing the woman who might soon be her boss didn't seem too shrewd, even sober.

I said she hired me because she knew I'd been a good investigative reporter and that I was not working at the moment. It depressed me that I felt the need to be careful with this beautiful woman and it was even worse to realize that maybe I should be very suspicious of her. Obviously money and power were important to her and she had worked her way into a job with a millionaire and had learned all about the perks in plush city.

My headache, which I thought I'd drunk away, came back, dull but muddling. I finished the champagne, waved down the waiter, paid our check and escorted Marigold toward the exit without hardly staggering at all.

It took a few blocks before I realized she was trying to sober me up. When I looked around, I discovered we were in an area filled with quaint houses that looked like a movie set from a period picture.

She explained that this was a park. I didn't get the name but thought it terribly original of the city fathers to create a park with houses. I always thought you did it with trees, lawns, ponds and flowers.

"Are you all right?" she asked.

I told her I was wunnerful.

"For a man with a broken head, you've had an awful lot to drink."

"So I'll pay in the mornin'."

She let me take her hand. I told her she was a wunnerful lady to talk to, I'd known she would be from the moment I saw her.

"Yes, I cultivate that."

I dropped her hand.

"This's still all business, huh?"

She didn't answer but tilted her head so appealingly I was more smitten than ever and at the same time angry.

"So what's your trouble?" I demanded. "You hate all guys 'cause one got you pregnant and wouldn't marry you?"

Her smile disappeared but her voice remained calm.

"I never wanted to marry him. It wasn't passion that made me let him, it was stupidity. I let things go on till I couldn't have stopped him without a club and at that time I thought more about being ladylike than being a lady. Okay?"

"Yeah. Xactly. Shy people think it's not nice to raise a stink, so they get screwed. Story of the world."

We moved on until a red light stopped us. I turned to her.

"I want to meet April."

"Not tonight."

"Course not—tomorrow."

"Maybe." She didn't mean it.

"You figure I'm tryin' to hustle you through the kid?"

"Of course."

"Okay, the hell with it. I'll find a hotel and sack out."

"I've reserved a room for you; it's just a block away."

"Thanks, but I can make my own goddamned arrangements."

"You're in no condition to be wandering around alone."

Most women I've known would have made that an accusation; she put it as a fact.

"I'm just tired—I'm not drunk or crazy."

"And maybe a little hurt?"

When I didn't answer, she took my arm.

"Come on, you can trust me, Kyle. Let's go get you settled. After you've had a good sleep, call me, okay?"

"What, no aspirin?"

She smiled. "Maybe a Bromo."

I agreed.

IX

I woke with a rolling stomach and a sharp headache, but neither bothered me as much as knowing I'd been a damned fool. It was 2:30 A.M. The hotel was dead. The bathroom floor chilled my bare feet and I shuddered on contact with the toilet seat. The relief offered little and I staggered back to bed and the unyielding pillow. I thought of cigarettes and Daphne, my high school sweetheart, Rosie, the girls I missed out on in college because of the married instructor, and finally, of the last great debate I held with the studio manager who wound up suggesting that I would have a greater future elsewhere. Up until then he had been trying to explain to me how TV news is show biz and people prefer watching cooing co-anchors to hearing about a lot of depressing world news. Neither of us mentioned the fact that the bathing beauty opposite me on camera had been back-stabbing me off camera for two months and had everyone convinced our sagging ratings were all my fault.

The real problem was basic; more people wanted to watch our competition than us. My personal problem was that I hated TV news and all its oversimplification and the horrendous selectivity forced by shortages of time. I was ham enough to enjoy being on camera every weeknight and having people recognize me and light up, but I also got sick of feeling like a total phony.

So onward and upward, working for Daphne.

I checked out at 7:30 A.M. after booking a flight to Minneapolis over the hotel phone in my room. Then I took a cab to the airport, caught a bus back to town and boarded a Greyhound for San Antonio.

There a heavyset woman with a long mouth and short hair listened to my needs in a tourist bureau office, nodded sagely and set up reservations for my flight to Mexico the following morning. I paid her in cash and told her my name was Philip Marlowe. She said that sounded familiar and I said that was what all the girls told me. She gave me a cool look and a frigid farewell.

I'd asked her for a modest hotel; what I got was painfully shy. The desk clerk greeted me with the cool disdain of an untipped maître d' and found no record of my reservation. Luckily there was a room available. I noticed he gave my luggage careful scrutiny and after I'd signed in, realized why. He wanted to know its weight because he doubled as a bellboy.

My room overlooked an empty lot filled with rubble. There was no telephone and of course no TV or radio. That was okay, I hadn't planned to loll around or make calls from the room. I peeked into the shower stall. The shower head, an enormous affair which dripped lazily from an immovable arm, stuck straight out into the center and kept the entire floor mossy. In the morning I discovered it didn't run when turned on, just leaked a little more. There was no problem in adjusting the temperature; no matter what I did with the levers the water remained tepid. With some effort I managed to keep my sensitive skull dry and got dressed with one time-out to run down a pony-sized cockroach which tried to bully me with a hostile stare but succumbed to my shoe after about three full-armed swings. I left his corpse for the cleaning crew.

In the lobby phone booth I spent some time making an operator understand my pidgin Spanish and eventually got through to García's bank. There I was given a man with English, explained my desire to talk with the boss and made an appointment for ten-thirty. That was disturbingly close to the hour I'd supposedly had before, but I decided it wasn't significant.

Señor García was a dead ringer for the Hispanic lieutenant in "Hill Street Blues" during the episode when he wore a wig. I told myself as we shook hands in the modest office that I'd have to be careful not to trust this man on that dubious resemblance. Besides, this one did not wear a wig, I could see skull through the part and dandruff.

His English was far better than my Spanish, so we communicated without an interpreter.

I explained my mission.

A look of surprise and concern took over his round face. I asked if he hadn't been aware that the man had disappeared.

He shook his head and explained that Mr. Fletcher was often gone for long periods of time.

"No one's been here asking about him?"

"No one."

"How about telephone calls?"

He hesitated half a second, then shrugged. "Not that I remember—"

I felt that my stare made him nervous, but he met my eyes and didn't blink.

"I'd think his lawyer might have called. Fletcher's wife thinks her husband may have been kidnapped, maybe murdered."

"Fantástico! Tell me about it—"

I did. He kept shaking his head, then called in a young woman and talked in Spanish too rapidly for me to follow. She returned after a brief absence and they exchanged more incomprehensible talk before stopping to stare at me in unison.

"His account has been withdrawn," he said. "Six months ago— one week after we talked right here. He said nothing about taking his money out. Not a word."

"Was it a large amount?"

"Substantial, yes. We had handled his account for five years."

The young woman left and García slumped in his chair.

"What can you tell me about him?" I asked.

He slowly sat forward, resting his thick forearms on the clean desk, and frowned.

"A gentleman. Thoughtful, interested. Very nice."

"Did he ask a lot of questions?"

"I never thought of it that way. It was just that he did not talk much of himself. He listened much. No hurry. Patient. What do you call it? Laid out?"

"Laid back," I said.

His smile stretched his black mustache and he shook his head. "There's a big difference, no?"

"Do you remember if Mr. Fletcher had a guide with him the first time he called on you?"

"No. With me he needed no interpreter."

"You ever heard of a guide named Lalo?"

He shook his head.

"How big was Fletcher's account?"

He sat up straight and regarded me reproachfully. "I can't tell you that sort of information."

"Did you ever socialize with him?"

His dark eyebrows went up.

"I mean, did you ever dine out with him, have lunch or dinner together?"

"Ah, social. No. We talked when he came to the bank, which was not often. He would simply drop in, you know. How are you? How's the family? Is business good? That sort of thing. No gossip or jokes."

I thanked him and got up. He stood politely.

"One thing puzzles me. Mrs. Fletcher hired two other investigators before me. You say no one came to ask about the disappearance? I can't understand that."

He gave a massive shrug. "Perhaps they were aware that we were not that close, or maybe they were not as thorough as you."

"You know a nightclub owner named Morales?"

He frowned and shook his head. "I do not go to nightclubs."

"Ever hear him mention a man named Jim?"

He shook his head again.

"That might have been an Americanization—this fellow was an older man who worked in the States and returned to his home when he retired—"

It meant nothing to him. We shook hands and I left.

I went through a telephone directory in the bank lobby and tried three Luis Morales listed, but all I learned was that the people who answered couldn't understand my Spanish.

Back at the hotel I asked the clerk if he could recommend a

guide with good English. He was delighted to help; said he could call just the man at once. I told him I'd be in the café down the street and he said he'd send the man along.

I strolled down the narrow walk under the bright sky and felt the burning sun through my summer jacket. Mexican sunlight has a scent all its own, a spicy, almost perfumed garbage smell, rich and old.

An ancient man in wrinkled white pants and shirt served me coffee in the small café and meandered off.

I stared through the open front door at passing Mexicans and thought about the banker, García. It was hard to imagine why he would lie about being called on by previous investigators, but I couldn't believe Daphne hadn't sent them to him or that they had neglected to make the call. How many leads had she offered? I was beginning to think I should have done more preliminary checking in Houston. Perhaps I could call Marigold, the proper secretary, and recruit her for some snooping on my behalf. At the very least, it would be an excuse to talk with her again.

A young man appeared in the café entrance and looked about eagerly. He wore splendidly chromed sunglasses that masked the upper half of his face, and a white jacket with a fur collar and fleece lining which showed at the cuffs. His cotton slacks were gleaming white as were the loafers on his small feet.

"Señor Champion?" he said. "I am Carlos Mayor, official guide and interpreter, at your service."

I stood up to accept his hand and he beamed at me. I asked if he'd care for coffee; he nodded enthusiastically, called the waiter and settled down as if he expected to spend the day there.

"Would you mind removing the glasses?" I asked after the waiter delivered coffee for Carlos.

The radiant smile suffered an eclipse.

"It makes me feel like I'm talking to a masked man," I explained.

He nodded, unconvinced, but removed the glasses slowly.

His irises were black, surrounded by bloodshot yellow. Black brows and eyelashes, long as an actress's, gave him the look of a badly done mask.

"I was up late," he apologized. "Very big party."

"You should've slept later."

"My wife, she is no *simpática*—kind, I should say. She was angry I stay out late. She is pregnant." He shrugged, indicating that explained everything.

"So, you're going to be a father. Congratulations."

He laughed. "Fourth time," he said, holding up four slender fingers.

A good Catholic, I thought, and smiled back at him. He put the glasses back on, muttering something about "you don't mind," and I didn't. There was an infinite sadness in the exposed eyes that the fine-toothed smile couldn't obscure.

"How many of the children live?" I asked.

"Two," he said, and crossed himself. "Well, what you like to see? I know all of Guadalajara—"

"I want to talk with a guy named Luis Morales. He owns a nightclub."

"Ah, you are no a tourist?"

"No."

"You have been to Mexico before?"

"Yeah, I've already seen the square and the cathedral. I just want to see some people. Mr. Morales and a man named Jim."

He nodded wisely and asked if I had a car. I shook my head. He smiled.

"We will need a car, señor."

"We'll take a cab."

The smile flickered and I was glad I couldn't see his eyes. No doubt a kickback had just died.

"Of course."

He drank his coffee with loving sips and tried to make conversation, asked if I wouldn't like another cup and sadly gave in when I shook my head and looked impatient. He finally rose and we went to a public telephone where he called the numbers I'd tried earlier. In no time he had the address of Mr. Morales's nightclub and we flagged a cab.

"This place," he said as the cab careened through narrow streets, "is called La Reata, which is from lariat or what you call the lasso." He grinned. "It is for to rope in the customers, you know?"

The cab pulled up in front of a white Cadillac which looked freshly polished. It was the kind that has a computer in the dash and nags you about seat belts, locking doors and low oil.

We approached fort-like doors set in a blank-faced building which reflected heat on us and Carlos grasped the giant pull handle and hauled the door open for me. It moved smoothly and we entered a vestibule warm and dark as a womb. Then we went through double doors into the cool interior.

"*Buenas tardes,*" said a young man in a black suit and white shirt as we approached the reservations station.

Carlos pulled his chromed glasses down for a quick peek at the scene, beamed his happy guide smile, returned the greeting and introduced me as a gentleman from the north who wished to meet Señor Morales. He added, with an attempt at mysteriousness, that it was a personal visit.

The man in black examined me. I felt measured, weighed and grilled by the dark eyes, but they gave no hint of how he added up the appraisal.

He turned his sleek head and a man approached from the shadows. This one had a thick body, like a jaguar, and moved with the same animal grace. I expected him to frisk me, but he simply nodded, tipped his head and moved off. I followed with Carlos at my heels.

Mr. Morales held court in a booth near the kitchen entrance. It was a large booth with high backs and padded benches. The table held two stacks of paper, one to his right, the other to his left and one sheet was in the middle. A white lamp illuminated the stacks, his face was in shadows.

"Señor Champion," announced the jaguar in a furry voice. He added a word I didn't recognize.

I saw the gleam of a smile in the shadowed face. Luis Morales waved me into the seat across from him. He was all in white; shirt, tie and suit. His large hands were dark with black hair down to the knuckles. His nails were manicured.

I moved toward the wall on the bench, making room for Carlos who took his place at my side gingerly.

Morales spoke in rapid Spanish. I looked at Carlos.

"He wishes to know, Señor Champion, for which periodical do you write?"

The question startled me and I said without thinking that I was not with a newspaper but with TV news in Minneapolis. That obviously confused Morales. I assumed he didn't know where my town was and had Carlos explain, but Morales cut him off. He wanted to know why a northern TV man, without a camera, was asking about his club.

I explained through Carlos that I was not here asking about his club but was seeking information about a man named Oren Fletcher who I'd been told had been his friend.

That brought on a long cold silence. Soon more Spanish was exchanged at top speed before it slowly came out that Morales had been expecting a writer from a travel magazine who was doing stories on the finer eating places in Mexico.

Mr. Morales's one-track mind took several seconds to absorb the fact I was not interested in his food. I figured the interview was a total bust but Carlos, despite obviously believing we had lost face, hung on stubbornly and after a while our host admitted he had known Fletcher.

"Muy simpático," he said several times.

"Ask him," I told Carlos, "if they were close friends."

That brought a shrug which I guessed indicated modest agreement.

"Where is he now?"

There was another brief silence after the question and then some rapid Spanish from Morales.

"He says he hasn't seen him for six months," Carlos said. "He wants to know why you're asking."

"Tell him Fletcher's disappeared and his wife and friends are worried."

That brought a cluck of sympathy and a repetition of his statement that he hadn't seen Fletcher in over six months.

I asked if that didn't surprise him.

The answer was no, he often disappeared for long periods. He traveled much.

I asked if Fletcher had ever talked about his contributions. Carlos's translation of Morales's response was severely abridged. It was clear that Morales was not interested in charity.

I said I understood they had been close friends; what did they talk about?

"Mexico," was the answer.

"Did he have a mistress here?"

Carlos didn't know what a mistress was until I explained. Looking somewhat apprehensive, he posed the question.

Morales's smile was tolerant. He spoke easily, leaning a little more into the light but still not far enough to show his eyes. His nose was broad with a firm, straight bridge.

"He says, 'Of course, a man many miles from home needs a woman wherever he is.' "

I asked if he'd met her.

He had met one, yes.

"How old?"

The answer was quick and Carlos grinned.

"He says he does not ask ladies their ages."

"Was she about his age?"

"Women are never a man's age," translated Carlos, smiling broadly.

"What color was her hair?"

"Negro."

"Natural?"

"Who ever knows?"

"What was her name?"

"He called her Little Rabbit."

Mr. Morales was enjoying all this and Carlos shared his good spirits. I stopped asking questions for several seconds and stared into the shadows above Mr. Morales's nose. The whites of his eyes were barely discernible.

"Ask him," I said, "if he has any favorite charity of his own that Mr. Fletcher gave to."

Morales pulled back, leaving only his shoulders and chest in the light.

"He says he does not beg anything *from* anyone *for* anyone."

I had touched a sensitive spot but couldn't understand what it meant. His withdrawal was complete, he wanted to end the interview. I hurried to ask what impressions he had of Mr. Fletcher's feelings about Mexico.

He leaned forward but again stopped before his eyes came into the light. His voice took an edge. Fletcher's view of Mexico was sentimental, he was attracted by the poverty and hopelessness, he liked to think the people were simple and childish, in need of the great benefactor. He had asked Morales why the people were so poor and Morales told him it was because they were good Catholics and in a Catholic country, only the church could be rich.

I asked if he were Catholic. He suddenly grinned.

"*Sí,*" translated Carlos. "A poor one. Poor ones sometimes get rich."

"You think he wanted to make his home in Mexico?" I asked.

"He said he would be buried here."

Carlos frowned as he translated that and crossed himself. He had removed his sunglasses and his naked eyes revealed a painful sadness. Or was it fright? I guessed he was strongly Catholic and deeply guilty. Did he think his dead sons were punishment for his sins?

I looked back at Morales who sat in his shadows, immobile and sober once more.

"Where'd Fletcher spend his time in Mexico?" I asked.

He said he wasn't sure, but he probably spent as much time in Guanajuato as anywhere. That was a town of many tourists which kept the spirit of Mexico. It was small, very old and had lots of poor people and many places where the rich could stay and dine.

"What was his favorite?"

"El Castillo de Santa Cecilia."

"A castle?"

It was a hotel that had once been a mine which was remodeled. That seemed a highly unlikely transition to me, but I didn't question him. I asked if he'd ever heard of an elderly companion to Fletcher, a man named Jim.

No, but there had been a Hymie. He was old and once lived in the United States. I questioned Carlos on the name and learned it was spelled Jaime.

Bingo.

"Where'd he stay?"

"El Castillo."

Bingo *dos.*

I thanked Mr. Morales who shook hands without rising and a few moments later Carlos and I were standing in front of the nightclub, blinking in the hot sun. Carlos signaled for a cab and asked me where next?

I said my hotel.

He was disappointed but cheered slightly as I paid him in cash the amount we had agreed on. When we said good-bye in front of the hotel, he asked what time I wished him to return.

I told him he'd taken care of all I needed.

He looked shocked. "There is no more?"

"Nada más. Thanks, you did a good job. If I need you some other time, I'll let you know."

His crestfallen face made me feel guilty enough to give him a token bonus, but when he asked what I was going to do next, I lied and said I didn't know but he should not worry. He sighed, looked at his day's earnings, cheered up, smiled and waved good-bye.

X

I checked out, cashed some traveler's checks and visited a tourist bureau where I learned Guanajuato had no airline connections. So I rented a car, bought a map and set off.

The countryside was mostly bright red dust and its stone walls made big and little squares, corridors, triangles and rectangles all across the wrinkled, arid land. I thought of all the churches and guessed there had to be a religious motivation for the walls, something Christian to account for the prodigious labors. Perhaps they were built for penance, to gain absolution, something more tangible than recited Hail Marys. But my God, what a sinful people they must think themselves to be.

The entire country smelled of tortillas, urine, manure and blossoms.

The road took me through Tepititlán, where streets were narrow and directional signs appeared erratically on building corners and fences. The sign painter must have been a very shy man; why else would he place his work in such obscure places? Soon I missed a turn and was in the city square where the traffic was ox-cart slow through the narrow ways. After circling the square twice I eased my subcompact Ford into a freshly vacated space and set off in search of directions. A half a block's walk brought me to a uniformed cop standing before a big church, talking with a black-shawled young woman. They both stared apprehensively at me. The man was stocky, bronzed and very neat in his khaki uniform and billed cap.

"You speak English?" I asked.

A look of dismay crossed the brown face and he turned toward the young lady who raised both hands and fled.

"*Lo siento,*" I said, hoping it meant "sorry," and then, very slowly, told him I was lost and needed help. The Spanish was just accurate enough to make him beam happily and at once he launched into an explanation so rapid and complete I felt sure he not only provided directions out of town but all of the way back to Houston and maybe even on to Minneapolis.

I raised my hands and, not being able to think of the word for slow, begged him to speak less fast. That tickled him and I think he honestly tried, but there was no governor on his speech delivery. Still, after about three rounds and considerable gesticulating, he gave me enough information to make a try and I escaped the town.

The map failed me again about twenty minutes later and I got lost in an even smaller town called San Juan de Lago where a bus driver set me straight once more.

It was afternoon when I reached León and I decided to stop for lunch. As I got out of the car, a herd of goats shepherded by a raggedy man shuffled by and I gazed until they moved far down the dusty road.

The front entrance of the café looked as if it had been damaged by an earthquake. When I got inside and saw the crowd of young toughs, it seemed quite possible they had done the damage. They were in a fiesta mood as they crowded around large tables in the dim light, drinking *cervezas* from cans and eating lustily. I made my way through the gloom to a brighter porch area on the north side and sat down in the cool shade. After a while a pockmarked young man approached carrying a gray cloth which he spread over the scarred table before me. The tablecloth was wrinkled and dirty, matching the menu he handed over.

I ordered a *cerveza, muy fría,* and tried to read the menu. When the waiter returned with a frosty glass, I thanked him and asked if they had anything like a cheese sandwich. His sober face strained for understanding. I said, "Queso sanweech?"

He brightened, nodded and hurried away. I got up, found the toilet and went in. It reeked and the toilet wouldn't flush—I doubted if it had for years. After adding to the mess I hurried out, breathing through my mouth, which left a very bad taste. In my absence the waiter had delivered two oblong ceramic bowls of sauce. One looked like unstrained tomato juice, the other like a very unsuccessful vegetable soup. Both bowls had metal spoons, one of them crusty with debris from past meals.

I sniffed but didn't have nerve enough to use the crusty spoon or even the relatively clean one. While I was trying to decide, the young man returned carrying a double plate gingerly with a folded towel and set it down. I stared at the shallow bowl filled with sizzling, bubbling cheese. The waiter then delivered a basket of hot tortillas and stepped back, beaming at me. I lifted the beer glass in salute, he nodded and left.

I rolled a tortilla, dipped it into the steaming cheese and tasted it cautiously. It was delicious. In the next few moments I mopped the bowl clean and wiped out the tortillas but never did have enough nerve to try the sauces.

The road from León to Guanajuato was uncomplicated, and when at last I drove down the hill road into the city, I was greeted by a mob of young men who shouted greetings and urged me to stop. I felt like a long-awaited rock star as I looked into the white-toothed, smiling faces and carefully drove through as they gesticulated and bent down to peer into the car. Finally I understood they were guides, offering their services. I was so busy avoiding them I didn't realize quite where I was going and all at once I was in a tunnel. It was dimly lighted, one way and winding. I slowed down even more only to have a truck move up so close the hood seemed to hang over my trunk. I pressured the gas pedal until I found a wide spot where I pulled over. The truck driver leaned on his horn and roared around me, followed by an ancient Volkswagen and a mufflerless pickup. The truck driver's horn echoed off the walls long after he was out of sight. I searched for turnoffs and began to feel more and more claustrophobic, but the tunnel ran on and on and now a cab began tailgating me. At last I spotted an exit, swung into it and felt my chest expand as I burst into the sunlight once more. All the streets were up and I stuck the Ford in second and followed the flow, thinking I might reach a point where I could get an overview of the town's terrain. Up and up I went. A towering, pilastered brown stone wall came in view. I drove toward it, passed along its southern edge, and glancing to the right, saw a vast gray swamp, dammed on the valley side. I realized it was filled with silver mine tailings. The great wall protected a silver mine. I parked by the road and wandered over to a strange little amphitheater which had a Greek look and eventually figured out it must have been a stone-walled water tank. I gazed around at walls all about the surrounding hills, some crumbling and fragmented, others high and in good repair. I stared back at the jumbled city below and knew at once that nothing seen from here would help me down there. I got back in the car and started down.

Soon I was on a narrow, twisting street that became narrower every block, and after inching around my third parked car, it dawned on me they were all facing uphill. I was on a one-way street going the wrong way.

I inched on. Old ladies observed me from open doorways, children smiled from narrow sidewalks. No one embarrassed me by commenting on my error, but then, they also might have been hoping to see the excitement when I met a native driving up. Maybe that was why they looked so happy.

Finally I escaped the trap and moved into normal, wild traffic. Soon I saw the young guides again and realized I was back where I'd started. Trying to avoid the young men, I made a sudden turn and promptly found myself in a cul-de-sac. I made an aborted U-turn, backed and advanced twice, faced the main street once more and stared into the sunglassed face of a young man wearing a white sport coat over a red T-shirt with "Welcome to Guanajuato!" across the front.

I braked to a halt and sighed.

"Good afternoon, sore," he said with the voice of a guardian angel. "May I offer my sorvices? Manuel my name, guiding my game. Show you all the best sights, scenes and settings. I am licensed, trained and experienced. Make you feel like home."

"Be my guest," I said, waving at the seat beside me. He bowed, opened the door, slipped in, leaned back and sighed serenely. I suspected it was the first time he'd sat down in hours.

"How do I get to the Castillo de Santa Cecilia?"

"No problem. Torn left at the corner here."

I turned left. Rival guides hooted at Manuel who waved lan-guidly.

"How you like tonnel?" he asked turning to me.

"Not much. How'd you know I was in it?"

"Saw you drive in. Everybody without guide do that. Never happy. Was river once, you know. Thass why he wind so. In 1905 our people grow tired of spring floods, torn river to go another place, then they build fine road through center of city where river ran. Like subway, you know? Very clever."

"You mean they knew back then that tourists would come and be scared to hell and hire guides to save them from doing it again?"

"*Sí!* Smart people." He laughed with childish delight.

"And clairvoyant."

"Sure thing," he said without understanding. "You got reser-vation at Castillo?"

"No. Will that be a problem?"

"Not with Manuel to help. You see."

We passed a walled area with a barred entrance and a number of men in green uniforms standing about.

"Cheapest hotel in town," said Manuel.

"Looks like a military post."

"Is jail."

It didn't look like a place I'd care to stay in at any price.

Eventually we drove through a towering, arched gate into a broad drive between walls festooned with flowering vines and came to the hotel which was sprawling, towered, arched, crenel-lated, balconied, landscaped and covered with brilliant blossoms. I parked beside the front entrance and we walked inside a dark lobby furnished with bulky easy chairs and a great round table. Manuel spoke with a slender, swarthy man at the desk who nod-ded and offered me a ballpoint pen and a registration card. I thought briefly of using a false name, but that seemed foolish when I was carrying a pocketful of traveler's checks, charge cards and general identification I'd undoubtedly use soon.

Before heading for my room, I made a deal with Manuel to return the following morning at 9:30 A.M. He promised me the greatest day of my life and took off jauntily.

A red-jacketed, stocky bellboy led me up a wide flight of steps with a narrow, red-patterned carpet, through archways, down a high, windowed hall with graduated steps every dozen or so paces which followed the slope the building had been set on. It looked at least a city block long. We turned off into another hall, through another archway and he halted at a tall, heavy wooden door with an arched top which he carefully unlocked.

I walked inside. The ceiling was beamed and bricks the size of paving blocks formed shallow arches between the beams. Wall lamps of wrought iron, with naked bulbs, jutted into the room from stucco walls. The double beds looked solid as marble with heavy, almost black head and footboards and deep maroon woolen spreads. A window with an arched top opened on a vast view of the hotel courtyard and entrance.

"Okay?" asked the bellhop with a proud grin.

"*Bueno, magnífico.*"

He saluted when I gave him a tip and bowed out.

The bathroom was wide, poorly lighted and had a crooked mirror that reflected my chest when I stood before the sink. There was no insect life visible in the shower stall which was big enough for four people and had a faint odor of mold.

"Don't bitch," I told myself. "You've never been in a neater place."

It took about thirty seconds to get settled in and then I set off to explore. I still couldn't imagine the place had ever been a mine, or if so, why it had been built like a Disney version of a Moroccan castle. Whatever the reasons, the builder had been as liberal as a Hollywood scene designer and I was determined to enjoy his work.

I found the bar appropriately set in the highest end of the hotel just off the small swimming pool. It offered a splendid view of the town below and the hills to the east which at dusk took on a wild, castle appearance, purely fairy-story stuff. I took a stool at the dark bar and ordered a margarita which was delivered in a vast glass with a generously salted brim.

I tasted it and said, "Good!" The ample bartender nodded solemnly.

"Is Jaime around?" I asked.

He smiled. "Jim?" The "j" was so soft it was almost an "h." I nodded.

He tilted his head toward the corner to my right. I turned and met the mild gaze of a slender gray man, so settled into the scene he seemed painted there.

"It can't be him," I thought as I picked up my drink and moved over.

"Do you speak English?" I asked.

"I do. Please sit down."

"You're very kind." I sank into the dark chair across from him.

"Not at all. I enjoy speaking English now and then. Where are you from?"

I told him.

"A very cold country."

"In the winter."

"But the winter is ten months long, isn't it?"

"Sometimes eleven. You must've been there."

"I've been close, just ninety miles east. But I met a lady from there not long ago."

"Would her name have been Daphne?"

His eyebrows lifted. It didn't take much effort, they were very light.

"Yes. Daphne Fletcher. Is the world really so small?"

"At the moment. I knew her a few years back, before she was married."

"Remarkable. Did you know her well?"

"Fairly. When'd you see her last?"

"Oh, I only saw her once. I knew her husband much better."

"Good. Where's he now?"

"Oren?" He smiled. "Who knows, maybe Spain, possibly Tibet. You never know."

"Does he travel on business?"

His smile was as serene as a priest who's been in the sacramental wine. "Oren travels as he pleases. What business are you in?"

"I used to be in TV news, but that went sour. Right now I'm a tourist."

"And how do you like Guanajuato?"

"Well, except for the tunnel, it seems like a nice town."

He laughed softly. "Even that's all right when you get used to it. Much better than a raging river every spring. Have you eaten here yet?"

I shook my head. He assured me I'd enjoy the food and would love the breakfasts.

"When did you see Oren last?" I asked.

He examined my face solemnly. "The habits of a newsman die hard, eh? Are you sure you're not still in the business?"

He spoke with an undertone of amusement. I had the feeling we were playing chess on a board only he could see.

"The fact is, I heard from Mrs. Fletcher not long ago. She called because her husband has been missing for over six months. She asked me to look into it. That's why I'm here."

He nodded, glanced toward the bar and lifted his empty glass. *"Como se llama?"* he asked me.

"Champion. Kyle Champion."

"You know some Spanish."

"Un poco."

The waiter delivered a frosty glass, set it down gently and moved off. Jim took a drink and placed the glass on the table.

"Doesn't it bother you that Fletcher's disappeared?" I asked.

"I think he has only disappeared from his wife."

"Oh? Then you've seen him in the last six months?"

He shook his head. "But that means nothing. I often do not see him for months."

"His office in Houston believes he's disappeared. His banker in

Guadalajara says he withdrew his account there about six months ago, without an explanation or a farewell."

"Was this banker so close that he had reason to expect explanations and farewells?"

"He seemed to think they were due."

"Well, you know how sentimental bankers are about money. They don't understand love and hate too well. The difference between women and money is that men never hate money."

"Mr. Fletcher left his luggage in Guadalajara and didn't check out of his room or pay his bill there."

Jim tilted his head and squinted slightly.

"What about his briefcase?"

"Left in the room. And two investigators hired by Mrs. Fletcher came up with nothing. No, that's not quite right, one of them came up with food poisoning and died."

"Ah!" he said, and shrank a little.

"Why'd you say you thought he'd only disappeared from his wife?"

He looked at me blankly for a moment, sat a little straighter, took a good swallow from the frosty glass and shook his head.

"Theirs is not a happy marriage."

"What makes you think that?"

He shrugged. "They were seldom together."

"I hear he had a woman. An old sweetheart from college days."

"Elvira? She was very close to him, yes. But only in the past couple years. The marriage was not a success for any of its five years."

"A bar owner in Guadalajara told me he met a woman he thought was Fletcher's mistress."

"It is seldom wise to believe bartenders."

"This was a bar *owner.*"

"Es igual."

"Equal? You mean the same?"

He smiled and nodded.

"What does Elvira look like?"

"A lady. Rather solid. Handsome face, very intelligent, you see it in the eyes."

"White hair?"

"No, rather light brown, with red highlights. A little bit of gray mixed in."

"You know her pretty well?"

"No. We met in Mexico City one time and Oren carried a picture of her. I think he idealizes her in his way. He's a romantic man."

"Sentimental?"

"Oh yes, like all we old men."

He glanced past my shoulder, smiled gently and lifted his chin. I looked around and saw a slender young woman approaching with quick, assured steps. Jim rose, I followed suit and she stopped by the table and acknowledged me with a polite nod and a brief glance from magnificent brown eyes. Shining black hair framed her oval face and its dark, flawless skin. A white, sleeveless dress showed off her tanned arms. She wore a single silver bracelet with a large turquoise inset.

Jim told me, with obvious pride, th..t she was his daughter, Juanita. He gave her my name and asked her to sit down. She did so, I felt with reluctance, and when he spoke to her softly in Spanish, she responded with swift words. All I caught was *"solo"* and from her tone and attitude I guessed she was disappointed to find he was not alone. My first reaction was that she was not his daughter at all, then I decided that was a foolish notion.

I stood up, bowed toward Juanita and told Jim it had been nice talking with him.

"Maybe we can meet another time to talk about Mr. Fletcher."

Juanita's head jerked up. "What? You know him?"

"No, but I'd like to."

She glanced at her father, then back at me.

"Why?"

"His wife has asked me to try and locate him."

"You are a detective?"

"Not really. More like a reporter between assignments."

I felt a little foolish about the euphemism but hoped Jim wouldn't put me down. He smiled tolerantly.

"Please stay," said Juanita.

"We should not impose on Mr. Champion," said Jim. His voice was gentle, but his eyes were stern. She avoided his look and watched me.

"It's no imposition—I just didn't want to intrude—"

"You understand Spanish?" she asked.

"A little—"

"I'm sorry I was rude," she said.

I assured her there was no offense and apologized for upsetting her and we both talked stumblingly until Jim laughed and suggested we stop babbling and have a quiet drink.

Conversation lagged as orders were placed and stayed feeble until we had fresh drinks and tried them. Juanita had something orange and sipped it cautiously, glancing my way when she thought I was looking at her father and otherwise gazing around the room with a bemused expression on her lovely face. Her high cheeks, soft mouth and not quite snubbed nose fascinated me. Her perfection was something one sees in porcelain works pictured in *The New Yorker.*

Conversation still failed to take life and finally I began explaining why I was in Mexico and what I'd been told. I didn't mention the attempt on my life, I think because I was afraid of dramatizing myself and feared she would guess as much and think less of me for it.

I wanted to tell her she made me wish I were an artist or a sculptor. The impulse to praise her would have overpowered me but for Jim, sitting quietly with his drink and his sad eyes.

When I ran down, we sat in silence for a few moments. Then Juanita leaned a little forward.

"Mrs. Fletcher, is she terribly upset?"

"I wouldn't say she's prostrate."

"You think she is more worried about money problems than what has happened to her husband?"

"That's my impression." I knew I should feel guilty about

disloyalty to my employer, but somehow, looking into Juanita's eyes, that didn't concern me much.

She looked down at her drink, lifted the glass and finished the small remnant.

A disturbing question came to mind as I stared at her dark hair. I didn't want to ask it but couldn't hold back.

"Have you ever been to a nightclub in Guadalajara, called La Reata?"

Jim stirred and Juanita's dark brown eyes met my stare directly and did not blink.

"No."

"The owner there described a dark-haired companion of Mr. Fletcher's who sounded like your twin."

The lie had no apparent impact. I caught another slight movement by Jim out of the corner of my eye, but he did not speak as his daughter continued to meet my eyes. I smiled and said, "Well, I suppose all men describe an ideal when they recall a lovely lady."

She did not seem to understand the intended compliment and slumped back in her chair, breaking eye contact.

"When did this bar owner say he saw Oren with a young lady?" asked Jim.

"He didn't give a date and I didn't think to ask at the time."

Jim nodded, as if that were significant. The sternness had left his eyes, leaving only sorrow. I asked if he had ever been to La Reata with Fletcher and he shook his head.

I returned my attention to Juanita who looked away, giving me a moment to admire her profile as she gazed soulfully across the barroom through the open door at the hills beyond which were fading into the twilight.

"Were you fond of Mr. Fletcher?" I asked.

"Yes. He was very kind and pleasant. He told stories of people who needed help and about the other people who tried to serve them."

I glanced at Jim to see if he reflected any awareness that Juanita spoke of Fletcher in the past, but he only gazed at his drink.

I asked Juanita to give me an example of Fletcher's conversation.

"Well, he was very concerned about old people who've outlived their friends and families and live alone and helpless. He said there was this organization called the Little Brothers which believed in the philosophy of flowers before bread. That meant they thought old people needed attention and reminders of beauty in life just as much as they needed food. He said there were people who resented this, that a rich woman told him at a dinner party that these young people working for Little Brothers took one of her tenants out for dinner and a concert and brought her home wearing a corsage. She couldn't believe they did it for any reason except to get money away from her. And besides, she said, old people had no business gadding about, they should stay home where they belonged. Oren was very sad about that."

"Did he let the woman know?"

"Oh no, he would never have done that. Oren didn't like to embarrass anyone, not even those who deserved it."

I thought he sounded like a sweet wimp.

"Did he give the Little Brothers any money?"

"I've no idea. He never said anything about where he gave away money. I guess he thought it would sound like bragging."

When Jim said it was time to go for dinner, Juanita invited me to join them. I began a polite refusal, but Jim insisted and I was happy to agree.

We walked through the open arch from the bar and passed along the deserted pool where stars sparkled on the dark surface, then descended gently curving stairs to the drive. I glanced up at the small towers and the crenellated walls, half expecting to see dark figures with spears or arrows guarding the parapets, but they were deserted.

A moment later we entered the bright dining hall with its linens, shining silver, tinkling glasses, bustling waiters and bright-faced diners. The maître d' welcomed Jim with special warmth, beamed at Juanita and even let some of his enthusiasm spill over me as he escorted us to a table by the north wall and handed out menus.

I considered ordering another margarita, but when Juanita asked for wine, I changed my mind. It didn't seem likely she'd be as tolerant of a drunk as Marigold had been.

I asked if either of them could think of anyone who might have hated Mr. Fletcher and they shook their heads.

"Look, I don't want to be offensive, but I've really got to ask some nasty questions—you understand that, don't you?"

Juanita looked doubtful, but Jim nodded thoughtfully.

"Is it just possible that any people around here figured there was something between Fletcher and Juanita?"

Jim lifted his narrow shoulders, Juanita frowned.

"You're wondering if Juanita had a jealous young man?" asked Jim.

"I'm trying to think of everything. So far nobody's given me a thing to go on except Mrs. Fletcher and the fact is, she's the only person who seems to have a logical reason to want him gone. Everybody else seems to think he was a saint or close to it."

"Saintliness is no protection against madmen," said Jim. "Look at Gandhi and Lincoln."

"They were both politicians. That's a whole different can of worms."

"I have no jealous man friends," said Juanita.

"But you do have admirers, you must know that."

She shrugged them off.

"Look around," I said. "You see them anywhere you go where there are men."

She dismissed the oglers with another shrug.

I gave up on Fletcher and questioned Jim about his working life in the States. He brushed it off as a dull story, but I pressed him until he related quite a bit of it. He confessed, sheepishly, that he'd wanted to be a composer and conductor and went to an Eastern college to study music. While there, he met a businessman with a closet dream of being an opera singer. They had quickly become good friends. When Jim ran out of tuition money, the businessman offered him a temporary job in Milwaukee and two years later he was a supervisor.

"Eventually he sent me to Eau Claire where I took charge of his plant."

He married there and Juanita was born. The mother died of childbirth, he said.

"And you raised her all by yourself?"

"Yes," he said with sudden, radiant pride, and smiled.

Juanita smiled too, reached over to pat his hand and said, "Poor Papa."

XI

I rose at seven and shaved while bending nearly in half before the crooked mirror over the sink under a dim bulb. The shower water was warm and I had a minor struggle remembering to keep my mouth shut so no water would enter and give me the trots. Normally I rinse my head while breathing through my mouth.

By seven-thirty I emerged from my room in fresh clothes and felt the morning air cool on the still moist hair on my neck.

Brilliant sunshine streamed through the east windows of the dining room on the white tablecloths and a ten-foot-long table loaded with fresh-cut melons, papaya, pineapple and great glass pitchers of fruit juice.

I loaded my plate with fruit, took a glass of orange juice and picked a table under the windows. A white-clad waiter brought a basket of biscuits, rolls and sugared corn muffins. After a brief conference, I ordered *huevos rancheros,* bacon and coffee. When I'd finished my fruit, the eggs arrived with whites as pure as fresh snow and yolks an orange-red, like the rising sun seen through thin fog. A watery-looking sauce crouched around its edges, looking harmless.

The first sample was a shock. The eggs tasted as though they'd been poached in Tabasco sauce. I ate all my rolls and drank three cups of coffee trying to keep the fire under control and probably did more damage to my mouth and throat with the hot coffee than the eggs but never realized it at the moment.

"You like the *rancheros?*" asked the waiter innocently as he filled my cup the third time.

"Like?" I said, wiping my mouth. "I respect them, but no, like is not the word."

"Wake you up, no?"

"*Sí, mucho.*"

On the way out I paused beside the maître d' near the door and congratulated him on his splendid dining room, excellent service and food. He nodded, looking modestly pleased, and then I asked if he had known an American named Oren Fletcher who had stayed at this hotel.

"*Sí.*" He smiled more directly. "*Un caballero.* Gentleman."

"When did you see him last?"

He frowned in thought, shook his head slowly and said it had been quite some time, several months—

"About six?"

"*Más o menos.*"

"Was he here long at that time?"

He looked at me and the smile did not return.

"There is a problem?" he said formally.

"He seems to have disappeared," I said, and explained that I had been asked to try and locate him.

A group of four entered and he excused himself to speak with them and escort them to a table. When he came back he was still smiling, but sobered as he joined me.

"I would say Mr. Fletcher stayed with us three, maybe four times in the last two years. About a week each time."

"Was he alone?"

"No. Usually he dined with Jim."

"And his daughter, Juanita?"

"Sometimes. And occasionally with other friends of Jim."

"Did Mr. Fletcher have a lady of his own?"

He gave me a knowing smile. "No."

I smiled back. "Would you tell me if he did?"

"But of course."

I wasn't supposed to believe him. I said thanks, offered my hand which he took along with the generous tip in my palm.

It was nine-forty when Manuel walked slowly up the drive. He stepped carefully, like a man with a hangover who suspects he will suffer catastrophic damage if he steps in a hole that would jar his swollen head.

I called good morning through the open window and he winced, raised his head cautiously and upon recognizing me, smiled and lifted his hand. I told him to wait, I'd be right down.

Since I had no clear idea of what to do or see, it seemed reasonable to accept whatever tour the guide suggested and gain at least a little familiarity with the city and places that might have been known to Fletcher. Manuel said things would go much more easily if I let him drive and assured me he was licensed, insured and highly skillful.

Our first destination was a cemetery at the top of a hill.

"All funerals pass this way," he said as we drove up. "Even I, who live on the hill, will come down and return on this street when I die."

It was a grand avenue for parades; wide with broad sidewalks atypical of Guanajuato. The pavement was pitted and spindly trees lined the way.

At the hillcrest a fat cop directed us into a parking space directly before the Hall of Mummies and opened my car door with a flourish. I expected him to linger for a tip, but he moved off, radiating hospitality and the joy of life. I found his spirit reflected all over the hill. It was like a carnival. There were dozens of souvenir stands and boys surrounded each new arrival, offering shoeshines or great, shining machetes for sale while people wandered back and forth, peering into stands, stopping in clumps to gossip, laughing and gesticulating.

I paid three pesos to enter a great long corridor and found glass-covered cabinets lining both sides, filled with small brown mummies, five to a case, men and women wired erect, mostly nude except for a few who still wore decaying shoes which hid their feet.

All had apparently died in agony. Every face was a permanent scream. To my consternation, Manuel launched into a memorized lecture, describing how each one had died. This one of cancer, the next in childbirth (the baby was in evidence), the next had been buried alive during an epileptic fit. As we passed before the epilepsy victim, I nearly stumbled over a boy busy at work shining the shoes of a tourist who was gazing at the mummy.

At the end of the hall the cabinets displayed baby mummies exclusively.

We moved outside into the welcome sunlight and Manuel explained, as we approached the crypts, how people were interred there. The families paid for five-year periods in advance. If they could not afford to renew this rent, the body was moved to the catacombs. I gathered that those which had mummified in a satisfactorily horrifying state made their way into the display cases for the edification of those who needed a jolt toward the true religion.

I tried deciphering some of the crypt inscriptions but had little luck. My favorite, translated eagerly by Manuel, stated the departed's name and life span, and ended: "Born innocent, Died ignorant."

Manuel asked if I'd care to buy a candy mummy for my family or lady, saying if so, he could get them for me cheaper downtown where his mother ran a shop. I thanked him politely and explained that I was short on family and ladyless at the moment.

"Is fine candy," he assured me. "Very nicely made. You find nothing like it anywhere else in worl'."

I didn't tell him how grateful I was to hear that.

We drove on to a crafts shop where they had intriguingly detailed wood carvings, far too delicate to survive baggage handlers, and after admiring them excessively, I suggested we move on. He was obviously disappointed in me. I wanted to think he was let down by my lack of appreciation for things Mexican, but suspected he got a cut if his client bought anything in the shop.

We drove downtown and visited an astonishing baroque theater where a troupe of young people energetically rehearsed a musical show. Manuel couldn't tell me the name of it, but seemed a little mollified when he saw how impressed I was.

Manuel hurried me from there back to the car and we first-geared up a steep hill to see a monument built to a miner who had set fire to a warehouse fortified by seven hundred Spaniards besieged by three thousand Mexicans. Of course the brave miner had died in the battle and had been rewarded with an ugly, monstrous statue of pinkish tan which overlooked, with baleful eyes, a magnificent view of the city below and the surrounding hills.

Manuel was dismayed when he realized I had no camera and concluded, silently, that I was a very strange tourist.

Next he drove us to a church called San Cayetano which was near an old mine on a hill northeast of the city. It was grotesquely baroque, inside and out, with a huge wrought-iron gate and a front covered with gingerbread facing on pink block walls. A great clock with a Roman-numeraled face stuck out of the left bell tower, looking anachronistic. We went inside and stared at the three gold-plated altars, obscenely ornate, a vast, incredible salute to garish bad taste. It was so ugly it was awesome. All it needed was a waterfall and colored spotlights.

We moved on to the nearby mine which was decorated with towering stone points designed to give a distant impression of a giant crown, symbolizing Spanish domination. Manuel told me that the mine, which operates night and day, has been in continuous operation since 1594.

Flowering vines covered the stark walls and I commented how strange it was that anything so beautiful would grow wild in such a place. Manuel smiled tolerantly and told me they were planted and nourished.

"We like flowers," he said.

Since it was well past noon, I suggested we call it quits and return to the hotel. He was disappointed, probably hoping for a free lunch, but I was afraid he'd take me to another church or something like the other depressing places we'd already visited and decided I was wasting time. I didn't think these were places where Fletcher would have wandered.

Which will give you an idea of how wrong a truly amateur detective can be.

As I walked into the dining room, I met Jim and Juanita coming out. He gave me his sad smile and asked if I'd had a pleasant morning.

"Edifying, I think."

"You make that sound painful."

"It was. I visited the mummery, a gross church and a cruel mine."

He laughed. "That's very interesting; your route must have been the same Oren took on his first visit. He was particularly horrified by the mummies and the crypts."

"Don't tell me he was afraid there wouldn't be enough money to prevent him from staying put?"

"I don't think so. But it truly weighed on him—he had a morbid fear of the ignominious—well, why don't you plan to go out to dinner with us this evening? We'll try to show you the more cheerful face of Mexico."

I said that sounded fine and we agreed to meet in the bar at eight.

After lunch I slipped into the dark lobby telephone booth. The light didn't come on when I closed the door, which was fine for privacy but didn't help me read my little black book. Finally I managed and got through to Milwaukee.

The city desk woman at the paper told me to wait and I sat listening to my money hum away for about five minutes before Al Lutz finally growled, "Yeah?"

"I need help, Al. Got a minute?"

"We got no openings for TV guys."

"I want information. I can even pay for it."

"I'd figure the Walter Cronkite of the prairie could pay for a story—what do you want?"

"Anything you can find on a guy named Jaime Durado. Probably called himself James, or Jim when he lived in your town. He worked for Goldstein, Inc., a tool manufacturing and specialty mail-order house. Durado's Mexican. Went to Milwaukee in the fifties, then to Eau Claire, Wisconsin, in the sixties. Had a wife who died giving birth to their daughter, Juanita. I want anything you can give me on all three of these people."

"He ever kill anybody?"

"Not that I know of—yet. Mostly minded his own business and probably made some nice change. I'd guess Goldstein was loaded pretty good."

"If it's the Goldstein I remember, he was. A nut, too. So what's the big scoop here, fraud, embezzlement?"

"It's pretty complicated. If you can get me what I need, I'll fill you in with an exclusive."

"Okay. Gimme your number."

"I'll call you. Right now I'm in Mexico."

"Mexico? What the hell, you been canned?"

"Why'd you think that?"

"I heard a few things down the line. So the gal got you bounced."

"I resigned."

"Uh-huh. Well, old buddy, I think I'm gonna need a retainer on this one. Can you handle that?"

"You don't trust me?"

"Not even God. Cash. In advance."

"I'll wire two-fifty. You do the job, even if you have to hire help, and I'll cover expenses."

"If you didn't talk so fast, I'd think you'd been swimming in the old tequila. You sure you're sober?"

"Sober as Burger. Get on it, huh?"

"Sure, if you send the dough."

"Done. But don't let anyone know why you're doing this or who asked you to, okay?"

"I won't have any trouble with the second part, for Christ's sake, but why *am* I doing it?"

"For money. I'll call tomorrow."

XII

The Durados were having a drink in the bar when I arrived just before eight. His blue-and-white-striped suit hung limply over his slender, stooped frame. Juanita glowed in a red and white dress that left her shoulders bare and showed off her small waist and supple hips.

Jim suggested we walk to the place he had in mind and we set off down a curving street between ancient walls where there was little traffic. It was getting dark. The warm, still air was filled with the usual scents of manure and sweet blossoms. Despite her high heels, Juanita walked along the rough street with grace, lightly holding her father's arm.

It should have been cozy and romantic, but I felt very uneasy. I wished I were Archie Goodwin with a gun in my shoulder holster, ice in my veins and the self-confidence of Zeus. My only weapon was a penknife with scissors, toothpick and tweezers.

"Where are we going?" I asked.

"To a nightclub owned by an old friend," said Jim.

"Did he know Fletcher?"

"We have eaten there together, yes."

A car approached from behind us and I moved instinctively closer to the wall and looked around. It was a very large car. It passed us slowly. The rear lights seemed unnaturally large and bright as it passed and disappeared around the corner.

"How much further?" I asked.

"Not far."

"You are nervous?" asked Juanita without audible scorn.

I shook my head. The high walls on each side of us had no windows before the second floor and there were no breaks between buildings. The doorways looked stout and secured.

We turned the corner and sighted a building on the left with a canopied entrance and cars parked in front. I wasn't sure but thought I recognized the car that had passed us, now dark and immobile at the curb.

As we passed it, I peeked inside and saw empty seats.

The nightclub was dark-paneled, had wrought-iron sconces, a dark-tiled floor and polite people. The gray-haired maître d' smiled, bowed and led us through a low-ceilinged room to a table beside a railing over a deep, indoor pool. Blue light in its depths silhouetted large goldfish moving casually through the clear water. A candle in the center of our table flickered gently. I held Juanita's chair and glanced around. The patrons were well dressed, mature and mostly self-centered. No one paid any attention to us.

We ordered drinks from a prompt waiter.

"It seems a very pleasant place," I told Jim.

The soft lights, low talk and the unusually wide spaces between tables gave an impression of privacy that should have been reassuring, so I wondered why I still felt threatened. My hand wandered to the shirt pocket where there were no cigarettes, drifted over my coat lapel and touched the nylon tie which I knew needed no straightening. I rested my forearms on the table edge and leaned toward Juanita.

"Your dress is very becoming."

She looked momentarily startled, then glanced down as if to be certain what she was wearing and nodded.

"Yes. Thank you."

"Juanita gives much thought to her clothes," said Jim. "She gives much thought to her appearance in every way. And yet she doesn't seem much interested in the attention she draws. You will notice, if you are observant, that she does not gaze into mirrors as most young people will."

I couldn't make out whether the objective-sounding comments were meant to be critical, but his tone and expression reflected only fondness.

I asked what sort of a child she had been.

At first, he said, she was in poor health, slept badly, ate very little and was often ill with childhood diseases. This went on until she was six and she had aged her father almost fatally. But after this initial testing, God had taken pity and suddenly she became a healthy, loving child. When she was a junior in high school, he had brought her to Mexico for a visit and she had loved the land immediately.

"I had great difficulty in persuading her to attend college anywhere but in Mexico City. Eventually she gave in and went to Eau Claire Normal, a teachers college, then went to Milwaukee to teach and finally returned to me when I came down with pneumonia and nursed me back to health. Then I retired and we moved here."

"That was her idea?"

"It was a mutual decision."

"Do you teach anymore?" I asked her.

She shook her head.

"She looks after her father. It is almost a full-time job, or so she says. She does some painting and drawing and a little needlework. I think she is marvelously talented. She tells me I am a ninny, a doting father."

She was not amused by his teasing and frowned.

I asked if Fletcher had always carried large amounts of money and he said yes, that was his custom. Did he make it obvious? Not directly. That is, he did not flash a big roll, but on the other hand he tipped lavishly, never allowed anyone else to pay at his table and bought expensive wines.

"He dressed beautifully," said Juanita.

"Nothing showy," said Jim, "but always rich. Clothing that good waiters and smart shoeshine boys immediately identify with money."

"Was he generous with his wife?"

"I've no way of knowing. In view of his generous nature, I would find it hard to believe he could be penurious with anyone. Why? Do you think she might have had something to do with his disappearance?"

"Well, obviously she had the most to gain. But if it was something she arranged, why hire me to find him?"

"Ah," he said, nodding, "perhaps she is devious. She wishes to give the appearance of being the loving wife."

"And hired an amateur to do the job?"

He smiled. "Wise women know that men do not expect them to act wisely."

When I looked skeptical, he leaned forward, folded his hands on the tablecloth and said, "Consider: what if the lady did manage it. Only the persons she hired disposed of the man in a way to avoid early discovery, allowing themselves time to establish alibis or distance. And say they were so successful at postponing discovery that time stretched out, making matters awkward for the widow. Then she would have to find the body to establish her inheritance, at the same time avoiding any revelations that would incriminate her?"

It was a cute scenario, but I'd talked enough with old police-beat reporters to know that murder is ninety-nine percent immediate, sordid and stupidly emotional. Worse, if Jim were right, my chances of solving this case were less than remote.

I glanced at Juanita who was staring at her father with her lovely mouth set in disapproval.

"What do you think?" I asked her.

"I think it is very bad form to talk about our friend as if he were part of an unimportant little riddle that amuses you to puzzle over."

I started to apologize, but Jim raised his slender hand to interrupt me.

"This is not as casual as it may sound, my dear. Kyle is on a serious assignment. I have only been trying to offer a little help in my own way—"

"You were making conversation. What you should do is really help. He is looking for our friend. You've told me we are responsible for our friends."

For a moment they stared at each other. Finally he nodded.

"Very well," he said, turning to me, "I offer my full assistance, for whatever it's worth. I admit, I've had trouble taking this all seriously—it seems too farfetched. Yet I know what can happen. Are you absolutely convinced Oren's dead?"

"Just about. Otherwise why'd two professional investigators fail to find him? Why did one die and the other turn cautious? And why was I attacked in a church in Guadalajara and driven over a cliff outside Mexico City?"

Juanita looked shocked and Jim frowned.

"You didn't tell us any of this before—"

I told them all I had. Juanita listened with fascination and stood up to examine my skull. This drew attention from the nearest patrons, embarrassing me roundly, but also gave me a certain satisfaction, since it was the most personal attention she'd ever given me.

Jim asked about my movements from the time Daphne called me until the night I appeared in the Castillo. When I was all through, he settled back, took a good drink and shook his head.

"This is truly awful," he said. He looked down at his plate, still nearly filled with *pollo mole* which he'd dabbed at while I talked.

I apologized for ruining his appetite and he said no, no, I had simply answered his foolish questions. He drank some wine, fidgeted in his chair, ordered coffee and after only a couple of swallows pushed it away and placed his hands on the table edge.

"It is late, I have much to think about. We will talk of these things tomorrow—"

Juanita started to push her chair back.

"Please," I said, leaning toward her, "if you are not too tired, I'd like to talk with you a little—" I looked at Jim. "Is that all right?"

"I will stay," she said.

He looked at her with something between surprise and concern in his long face, then nodded, wished me good evening and walked off. I watched him go, vaguely disturbed by his melancholy, then looked at his lovely daughter and smiled.

"It's very kind of you to stay with me."

"I'm not sleepy."

She was not a flatterer, but I noticed that for the first time since we'd met she looked at me as if she were interested.

"Were you terribly frightened," she asked, "when you went over the cliff?"

"Yeah, but it would've been worse if I hadn't been so damned bewildered. I kept thinking, 'This is all a mistake.' I guess that's the standard cliché for victims. Every time I read about people getting picked up by state police or being attacked in the street, they always say there's been a mistake—as if no one would do anything like that to *them.* Not deliberately. It's pretty stupid."

"I think it's very natural. We all think of ourselves as rather special and, you know, nice. We can't believe anything awful can happen to us and it's usually true, right?"

"Not in the world I cover, no. What I'm saying is, *I* shouldn't have reacted that way."

"Well, you had an excuse. You'd been hit on the head."

I looked at her closely, trying to decide if she was a deadpan comic, but if she was, she was too good at it for me to tell.

"You like to dance?" I asked.

"Oh yes." Her lovely face lost its serious cast and she actually smiled. For me it lighted our area like the candles on a centenarian's birthday cake.

"Is there a place near here?"

"Of course." She began to rise. I rose with her. The waiter appeared at my shoulder and I sat down again to fish out my credit card and cover the check.

We were out in the street again before I remembered my earlier paranoia, but by this time I had trouble taking it seriously. Juanita continued to glow as we hiked briskly along dark avenues, and when I asked if it were far, she said no, nothing was far in Guanajuato. No large or small cars passed us and we met only one couple who were too absorbed in each other to notice us. Juanita held my arm and each time I asked, "How far?" she said, "Not far."

Soon we entered a small dark bar filled with bright young people who were mostly drunk and the music was romantic and exuberant by turns. I didn't know all the steps in use but faked my way along and felt I was doing very well with the slow pieces. To my surprise, Juanita was a clinger. It excited me so much I was afraid she'd be offended, but if she was aware, she didn't let on. I wondered if she were so virginal she simply didn't know.

A squarely built, gray-haired man approached our table between numbers, greeted Juanita with great solemnity and asked about her father. She assured him he was fine and introduced us. He turned cold eyes on me and nodded.

I ignored their chill and complimented him on his fine club and the musicians. The dancing had intoxicated me more than any of the drinks and I wanted approval from outside to match what I felt within.

Juanita translated my comments, the square man nodded stiffly and she translated his response which in effect said that the music was loud, which is what the young want.

Through my good spirits came the message that I was an alien.

They exchanged a few more words, he bowed to Juanita, lifted a shoulder my way and moved off.

"I don't think he approves of me," I said when we were seated once more.

"He does not like Americans with Mexican girls."

"But you're American."

"Not to him. He knows only my father, never saw my mother and pretends she was Mexican."

"Did he know Fletcher?"

She shrugged. The gesture was a little too casual. My excitement began to wilt and my paranoia returned. I looked around and saw a young man a table away, watching Juanita. He caught my glance and gave me a hard, challenging stare. The girl at his side touched his arm, but he ignored her. There was another man across from him also looking our way.

I turned to Juanita who sat with her chin high, bobbing gently to the rhythm of the band.

"Is there hostility here toward Americans?" I asked.

"Among some," she said indifferently.

The fast number ended and they began playing something slow. I asked her to dance and she rose at once and met me. The floor became crowded and people bumped us gently and there was little chance to move except against each other.

"You are a very lovely dancer," I said into her ear. She smiled. I could feel the smile against my cheek and her hair tickled my temple.

"I'm awfully glad you aren't hostile," I said.

"I'm American."

"But you didn't want to live there."

"I wouldn't have minded."

"Really? I thought your father said it was a mutual decision."

"He's a little embarrassed to admit to Americans that after all his years in the north, he wanted to come back home when he grew old. He thinks they are offended—you know? That he has, in this way, rejected them."

We finished the dance in silence and returned to our table. The young men watched us. I looked around and decided we had not attracted the attention of any other patrons except for occasional admiring glances cast by men who noticed Juanita. So why were these two guys so intent? They both had women of their own who looked attractive enough. Of course they weren't in a class with Juanita; no one I'd seen yet was. I looked at their women. They were talking to each other with great animation but suddenly stopped in unison and looked our way.

"You sleepy yet?" I asked.

"No."

I glanced back toward the nearby table. The first young man was on his feet. He walked our way. So which is it, I thought, a foolish young man with a hatred for Americans, or someone hired to play the role and get rid of an investigator?

He stopped by the table and said, "Juanita."

She glanced up. Her expression told me nothing—at the moment I couldn't tell whether she even recognized him, then suddenly she looked bored and tilted her head toward me.

"Mr. Champion, this is Mr. Rodríguez." She looked back toward the young man and said something like *"amigo de mi padre."*

"Otro?"

She shrugged. The man looked at me. I guessed he was not my height but probably had a weight advantage of fifteen pounds or more. He did not look fat. His fists were clenched and large, his forehead wrinkled in a scowl. He spoke a few words in rapid Spanish, and while I caught none of the sense, the tone was clear.

"What's his problem?" I asked.

"He wants to be insulting. Don't get up, it will only cause trouble."

I saw two waiters approaching with exaggeratedly casual haste. They flanked the young man, not touching him, and the taller of the two spoke softly. He ignored them and called me a Yankee something that sounded porcine. I looked to Juanita for a translation. The waiters crowded the young man away and he moved without resistance while still scowling at me.

"What'd he call me?" I asked Juanita.

"Nothing. He is childish. Let's go."

"Is he an old boyfriend?"

"No, he only wants to be. He is stupid."

She was very angry and I felt, as I paid the bill, that much of the anger was directed at me.

The hush of night was a relief at first, but as we walked down the dark street, it became oppressive. Before we had gone half a dozen yards, I heard voices from behind and glanced back to see two men exiting from the club.

They had left their women behind them.

I halted. It made no sense to try and run and I preferred a confrontation near the club to one in a more remote street. Juanita apparently shared my view; at any rate she halted with me and faced the approaching men.

"Will I have to fight them both at once?" I asked.

"There'll be no fight. Be sensible and keep still."

I noticed that Rodríguez walked stiffly and wondered if he might be drunk. That could help. His partner didn't share his huskiness, but he wore a smile that was not reassuring. I'd seen it on bullyboys in gangs when I was a boy. It belongs to the jackals who jump on the fallen.

Juanita addressed Rodríguez in a tone that would mentholate Mexican hot peppers. He halted a yard away with his head thrust forward and stared at her. Then he looked at me.

"Vaya con Dios, Yankee."

I'd never heard that expression used except as a blessing and for a second had no notion of how to take it.

"Go ahead," said Juanita. "I'll be perfectly all right."

"The hell with that."

"Don't be childish—go!"

"I can't, and you know it. What the hell *is* this?"

Rodríguez stepped forward and tried to shove me with a hard straight-arm, open-handed to my left shoulder. It was another reminder of schoolyard days, when boys went through preliminaries leading to full battle or simple retreat. But I had been expecting a punch, not a shove, and retaliated with a right cross that caught him flush on the jaw. He wheeled away, staggered, tripped over his own feet and sat down. For a second he stayed there, his mouth sagging in astonishment while the three of us stared down. Then he gave a bellow, lunged to his feet and charged.

Things got very busy.

From the beginning my major fear was that the second man would jump me from behind and I kept maneuvering to keep Rodríguez between us, but he kept charging like a wounded bull and I had all I could do to keep him from swarming over me. Twice I caught him moving in and hammered right crosses toward his chin, but each time he swung his arms enough to deflect my fist. Very soon I became sure he was too drunk to catch me alone. I also realized he was strong enough to be dangerous if we clinched.

Juanita kept shouting, "Stop it!" and "No!" while we fought in grim silence.

His last rush almost cornered me against the wall, but I ducked under his right-hand swing and buried my fist in his gut. As he neatly folded, I brought both hands down on the back of his neck. He dropped to his knees, lowered his hands and rolled to the ground in a fetal position.

I looked around for his friend and found his fist with my cheek. It wasn't a really good punch, but I was already tired and off balance, so it dropped me. I rolled to all fours and came up in time to catch another blow, only this time it was a kick and that was much more effective than his fist.

Once more I found myself coming to with a raging headache.

"Are you all right?" asked Juanita.

"Lovely," I said. *"Mucho bueno. Grandísimo."*

I opened my eyes and saw light and shadows and people. And a cop. He was bending over quite formally with a notebook in his hand.

He spoke in soft Spanish, rather slowly. I understood *"llama"* and told him my name, but Juanita said no, she had already told him that, he was asking who had attacked me.

"Didn't you tell him?"

"I told him I didn't know."

I squinted at her. Her lovely face was composed and very thoughtful. She looked at me steadily.

"Then certainly I don't," I said.

She spoke to the cop.

He solemnly put away his notebook and offered me his hand. I accepted it, got to my feet and let him lead me to his squad car.

"Am I being arrested?" I asked Juanita.

"He is going to give us a ride back to the hotel."

I looked at him. He was very young and a little too good-looking with black wavy hair and brown eyes. He smiled encouragement, showing marvelous teeth. I smiled back, hoping mine weren't bloody.

Juanita entered the back seat and I followed her. The door closed firmly behind us, sending a stab of pain through my aching head, and then we were off. He spoke to Juanita and she responded briefly. She called him José. They talked more and more rapidly, or at least he did. I decided he was very fond of his voice. He played it like a clarinet. It trilled and swooped, lilting and mellow. A virtuoso performance. I sat dumb. When a man is with a beautiful woman, all the world is in competition for her attention. An intelligent man, I told myself, would choose plain women. I remembered Sinatra's old hit "Paper Doll."

"Are you asleep?" Juanita asked.

"Wouldn't dream of it. Might miss this guy's chatter."

José turned to look back.

Juanita spoke to him and he beamed at me.

"What'd you tell him?" I asked.

"That you admired his Spanish."

Maybe I was wrong. Perhaps she did have a sense of humor. She just wasn't fond of smiling. I smiled back at José and he grinned back in the mirror. There's nothing like a happy cop all full of Spanish.

He drove us through the Castillo arch and opened the door for Juanita who accepted his hand as she climbed out. I managed on my own but shook hands when he offered and we smiled at each other with, at least on my part, naked hypocrisy.

Juanita said I should go to my room and get some rest, but I told her I was too keyed up to relax without a nightcap so we made our way to the bar. Jim, who I'd assumed had been in bed for hours, was at his usual table and rose to greet us. He showed great concern over my battle scars and it took some effort to persuade him I didn't need medical attention. He insisted we go to the men's room and there he washed the cut on my cheek and clucked over me before agreeing to return to Juanita. They exchanged a lot of Spanish before I got my tall gin and tonic.

Anticipating my questions, Jim told me he had intended to sleep but couldn't when he tried.

"All of this thing about Oren, it kept tumbling through my head and then I began worrying about you and Juanita."

"Did you send the cop to check on us?"

He looked embarrassed and waved his slender hand.

"I made a suggestion. José is a nice fellow, he was happy to help out."

"How'd he know where we went?"

"Oh, I know the places Juanita likes."

His face was so sad and tired it was hard to be suspicious and yet I felt uneasy about the entire evening and kept thinking of Rodríguez. He had said something about *"el otro,"* the other. Had Juanita danced with Fletcher in that same club? It seemed unlikely but—

"Who is this Rodríguez guy?" I asked.

"An acquaintance, nothing more," said Jim. "A headstrong young man with romantic ambitions."

I looked at Juanita.

"Why didn't you give his name to José?"

"I didn't want to get him in trouble."

"What's his friend's name?"

She said she didn't know.

"Anyway, it was all nothing, really. Just drunken young men, one of them jealous."

"Has he attacked your partners before?"

"No."

"He has made threats," said Jim in mild reproof. "Juanita is not good at discouraging unacceptable suitors. It makes men like Rodríguez presumptuous."

I decided I was too tired and sore to ask more questions, let alone evaluate answers, and said I guessed I'd turn in.

Jim agreed that would be wise and promised to be available in the morning. "I know some people with the police—it might be helpful."

I hoped so and departed.

My room looked unshakably secure with its heavy wooden headboard, the bulky blankets, the sturdy wooden chairs with leather seats and the fine, arched ceiling with its massive blocks and great beams. All very reassuring.

I told myself that this castle was my home for now, undressed slowly, strolled to the bathroom, brushed my teeth with bottled water and examined my face. It was puffy on the left and scuffed on the right, but I'd avoided blows to the nose and would not suffer the embarrassment of a black eye.

Back in the bedroom I jerked back the heavy blanket and started at the sight of a green figure resting between the white pillows. It took half a second to recognize it was one of the candy mummies I'd seen in the stalls at the cemetery that morning. I leaned close and stared into the tiny face with its stretched mouth frozen in a perpetual silent scream.

After a while I put the figure in the top bureau drawer, climbed into bed and stared at the dark ceiling. Sleep wouldn't come. Even trying to get lost in sexual fantasies didn't work because each face I imagined eventually wore the mask of the mummy.

XIII

I had finished my breakfast and was drinking coffee while reading P. D. James's *An Unsuitable Job for a Woman* when Jim appeared beside my table and asked if he might join me. I said of course, asked where Juanita was and learned she had stayed in bed.

"Like most young people, she's not hungry in the morning."

He ordered coffee and rolls and we exchanged innocuous talk until finally I asked, "Does Juanita often inspire scenes?"

He put his roll to his mouth, took a small bite and chewed thoughtfully.

"No," he said, after swallowing. "I hope that nothing I said last night gave you such an impression."

"No. What impressed me was how cool she stayed during the hassle. Most women I've known would've screamed or run for help or even got in the way."

"Well, she's only half Latin."

Most of the women I've known weren't Latin at all.

I asked if he'd go with me to police headquarters and introduce me to the top policeman he knew so I could ask questions about the investigation of Fletcher's disappearance. He said of course, he'd be delighted.

We agreed to meet an hour later in the lobby, and after a quick visit to my room, I went down and telephoned Al Lutz in Milwaukee. There was an expensive delay before he finally growled, "Yeah?"

"What've you got?"

"Arthritis, among other things. I told you it'd take a little time."

"So what've you done?"

"Called Goldstein. He's not answering his phone these days. Been dead three years."

"Old age?"

"Car accident. Truck broadsided him."

I thought about that a moment and then asked what had he learned about Jim.

"There's no obit on record for his wife."

"You're sure?"

"You doubt our computer?"

"I suppose I don't dare. Can you find out if she died in Eau Claire?"

"It'll cost."

"I'll pay."

"Done."

"See if you can find out what kind of a deal Jim had with Goldstein—did he have stock, was he on a salary, what the retirement setup was, what kind of money he made—all that stuff."

"You're really fishing, huh?"

"Yeah, and so far all I've got is an empty lake. I'll call you tomorrow."

"If you're smart, you'll make it afternoon. This kind of stuff takes time."

"Money's no object, Al, just get those fish for me."

"Sure."

The outside walls of the police station were a bilious green, inside they were baby-shit yellow. Lieutenant Juárez's office was about the size of a cell and furnished with a stark wooden desk, a straight-backed chair and a bench. We sat on the bench.

I suspected the room was seldom used for anything but interrogations.

The lieutenant's face was brown and wrinkled, his dark eyes wary and strangely moist. All the time we were in his office I expected them to leak tears but they never did. His grizzled hair was neatly brushed and his slightly wrinkled uniform looked clean.

As Jim asked questions, the wary brown eyes fastened on him.

When I spoke and when he answered, he gave me his full attention.

He explained very precisely, as though he were speaking to retarded children, that Mr. Fletcher had not disappeared from sight in Guanajuato, he was last seen in Guadalajara. It was his understanding that the Guadalajara police had investigated the matter most carefully and had concluded that the gentleman had left their city on an impulse, probably bound for a rendezvous. He had not taken an airplane, at least not under his true name. He was a man of ample means to go where he pleased when he pleased and there was no reason known to the authorities to suspect any form of foul play.

Jim translated all of this with an apologetic air.

The lieutenant concluded with a short lecture about the foolishness of drunken brawling outside of nightclubs.

I have a fairly low tolerance for condescension and none at all for uninvited advice, but the setting was intimidating, so I managed to keep my temper and asked Jim to describe to him the attempt on my life in Guadalajara and ask him if that did not suggest that something strange was going on?

Lieutenant Juárez smiled and an "I'm glad you asked that question" smile creased his broad face. He spoke to Jim while watching me.

Jim took a moment before translating, but he needn't have bothered. In essence, the lieutenant said that men who drink too much are notoriously accident-prone.

I asked if he had talked with the officer who investigated the incident. He responded, Jim said, that he had seen the written report on the entire affair.

As we walked under the bright sun along the dusty street, I talked to Jim.

"Lieutenant Moreno, the Guadalajara cop who talked with me at the hospital, never questioned the authenticity of my story. I don't believe he wrote a report saying I'd driven myself over that cliff because I was drunk."

"Perhaps someone else wrote the report from that officer's notes."

"Nuts. This bastard just doesn't want complications."

"Well, the unfortunate brawl last night was not helpful."

I stopped dead and glared at him.

"You think that was *my* fault?"

He smiled gently. "You think it was Juanita's?"

"I think it was Rodríguez's."

"You asked if Juanita were often involved in such scenes."

"That doesn't mean I was blaming her—I was just surprised she didn't seem upset by any of it."

"Of course," he said, and began to walk on. "She was very impressed by your performance. She says you are a brave and *'muy formidable'* fellow."

"I didn't feel formidable after the kick in the head."

He shook his head sympathetically and went back to talking of Lieutenant Juárez.

"He was, you could say, predisposed toward skepticism. He may believe your concern for Mr. Fletcher comes from a convoluted desire to save face. Unfortunately I mentioned your background; like most policemen, he is suspicious of the media, even as the media is often suspicious of policemen."

"Well, I guess we've both got our reasons for that."

He laughed, patted my shoulder and said, "We will not be discouraged, not while you keep your sense of humor."

"I don't know, I think I could be."

Back at the hotel the room clerk told me I'd had a call from Houston and handed me a slip of paper with a telephone number.

I recognized it as Daphne's.

I was halfway to the booth before it dawned on me she wasn't supposed to know where I was. For several seconds I fumbled with my charge card, trying to figure that out, but finally got the telephone call placed.

Harlan, her young lawyer, answered.

I asked for the lady of the house and he wanted to know who was calling.

"Philip Marlowe."

"Well," she said sweetly, "I hear you're having a lovely time."

"There's some good news and some bad news," I said, matching her treacle.

"I assume you have a perfectly rational explanation for your little brawl last night?"

"How about we quit the cat-and-mouse shit and you tell me how you knew where to reach me?"

"It was a matter of deduction, Mr. Marlowe. I got a telephone call from the Mexican police. They wondered if I were aware of your manner of investigating the disappearance of my husband."

"What'd you say?"

"Why, I told them you had your own unique methods, what else could I say? I'd already admitted to another policeman that you worked for me. You must be running up quite an expense account for those people down there. Were you too drunk to remember what happened last night? I'm awfully curious about it all. I understand there was a beautiful, very young señorita involved—"

"I wasn't drunk, and yes, there was a girl—she's Jim's daughter. Jim's the guide who knew your husband—the one you forgot to tell me about. I located him and he's agreed to help me, so at least there's that much more progress made by me than by your other investigators. I was with him last night, him and his daughter. He pulled out early and I had a couple drinks with the young lady, who, incidentally, may have known Oren pretty well."

"I see. So you were interrogating her, right?"

"I even danced with her. She's something of a stunner. Did Oren go for the young ones?"

"Don't you all?"

"I could go for this one," I admitted.

"Well, do it on your own goddamned time. You aren't really getting anywhere at all, are you?"

"I didn't think so until I got back to the hotel last night and found somebody'd left me a warning in the room. There's got to be some reason people keep giving me a hard time—which brings me back to how you knew where to reach me. When did you get the call from the police?"

"About an hour ago."

"Exactly what did they tell you—who called?"

"How do I know? It was a man. He said you'd been involved in a drunken brawl outside a nightclub last night. He wanted to know if you still worked for me. I said I'd let him know after I talked with you."

I might have been grateful for that if I hadn't known that she was simply too stubborn to admit she might have made a mistake to any stranger.

"So, am I fired?"

"You're on probation. What'll you do next?"

"Go back to Guadalajara."

"Well, get on with it then. Harlan's managed to free some money for me, but I'm sick of fighting for what's mine and I want it settled."

"Yes, ma'am."

She hung up. It seemed to me she could at least suggest I take care of myself. After all, I still had quite a bundle of her money.

Jim was perfectly willing to join me on my trip to Guadalajara. I wanted to suggest that Juanita come too but didn't quite have the gall. I was pleasantly surprised when, after I'd rented a car and come around to pick him up, she appeared in a white, sleeveless dress with spaghetti straps delicate as spider webbing over her brown, smooth shoulders. She was carrying a Gurkha overnight bag.

She sat in front with me, Jim got in back and leaned forward to guide me through the exit from the city, which is a reverse maze that has no way out for the uninitiated.

Once we were out of the valley and on the highway, Jim settled back, stretched his legs across the width of the seat and leaned against the car side opposite me. Juanita sat primly, with folded hands, watching the road. The air conditioner didn't work, so we

drove with the windows wide open. After about twenty-five miles
Jim's eyes closed and a few moments later his mouth opened.

"I'm curious about your friend, Rodríguez," I said, leaning
slightly toward Juanita. The rushing wind through the open windows made it hard to hear.

"He is nothing."

"If he's nothing, why didn't you tell his name?"

She made a petulant mouth and turned my way.

"Did you want him thrown in jail?"

"It might've been good for him. He had no call to jump me."

"He thought so. You were with me."

"So what's his beef? He had a girl of his own."

"He is in love with me."

She said that with a finality that cut off discussion. Men fell in
love with her; it couldn't be helped and she couldn't condemn
them for it, because it was natural.

I drove for a while, digesting that, and every now and then
glanced her way. She stared ahead, her chin raised to give her fine
profile its full advantage. I thought about the fractions of inches
that made the difference between beauty and ugliness. Her face
had been designed in perfectly proportioned curves, the deli-
cately rounded chin, the lips just ripe enough to entice without
being gross, the nose of perfect length and artistic shape.

"Well shit," I thought, and then spoke aloud. "Do you think
I'm in love with you?"

She glanced at me archly. "Aren't you?"

"I hardly know you."

"You were willing to fight two men over me."

"I stayed and fought to keep from being run down."

"No," she said, shaking her head gently, "you were more afraid
of being ashamed than of being killed. I know."

"I'd have done the same thing with any other woman standing
by."

She smiled.

I looked in the rearview mirror and caught Jim's face. His eyes
were slitted and his mouth was set in a gentle smile. I slowly

became aware of being trapped. What the hell was I going to do in Guadalajara with this old man and his spell-casting daughter? Would we troop into the bank and the nightclubs like a vaudeville act, youth, age and postadolescent? It could be disarming, I supposed, but hardly effective in the long run. And would I be expected to provide three hotel rooms? What would happen if Daphne found out? A stupid question. Probation ended, that's what. She might even hire hit men. Or sue to recover her advance. She slept with a lawyer now; suit would be her new obsession.

I drove on, squinting into the hot sun at the dusty country-side and roller-coaster road being swallowed by the hood of my rented Ford while I inhaled the sweet and sour air full of dust and heavy with heat.

XIV

As we entered the outskirts of Guadalajara, Jim leaned forward and put his hands on the seat back between Juanita and me.

"I suggest you move into the right lane now," he said. "We should take the turnoff about a mile from here."

"You've got a hotel in mind?"

"Oh yes."

I looked at him in the mirror and he smiled. His face had nothing sinister in it and I looked away, feeling foolish about my earlier sense of entrapment, and guilty because a certain suspicion lingered. I would prefer to find a place unfamiliar to the three of us, but that didn't seem particularly vital, since there would be nothing at all to prevent one or the other of them from passing on our location to associates if that's what they wanted to do.

"I'm going to introduce you to an old and trusted friend. More important to you, he knew Oren well and is a man with many connections."

"What does he do?"

"Camillo is retired. He consorts with priests, in preparation for the day he dies. After a long life of making much money by exploiting people, he must hurry to recover the grace of God for the sake of his soul, so he does good deeds and demonstrates his basic piety."

I made the turn as directed and followed other directions until eventually we pulled up before what appeared to be a small hotel. A shabby green awning extended across the walk to the curb where I parked, and a shabby gray man, with a sharp jaw and wild white hair, stepped from a glass-fronted foyer and greeted Jim with liquid Spanish spoken softly as a whisper.

"He will park the car," Jim said, and led us into the lobby.

Another old man in an ancient suit with wide lapels and a large, patterned tie with a vast Windsor knot which lifted his collar like limp wings nodded at us graciously and smiled, revealing yellowed false teeth with pale gums.

"This," Jim told me, "is Paco. He is Camillo's right-hand man."

I was introduced as a friend and expected to sign in, but instead was immediately ushered to the elevators with Jim and Juanita. The operator looked so old I wondered if he were resurrected each morning for his duties in this hotel for the ancient. Jim thanked him when he opened the creaking doors and he nodded while giving me an enigmatic, hooded stare.

As we walked down a narrow, dim hall on a threadbare carpet, Jim explained that this was a residence home for the indigent, aged men which Camillo had established with his own money and maintained with the help of wealthy friends.

"As you can see, he offers those who are interested jobs in running the place as much like a hc .el as possible. There is a dining room and a coffee shop, a barber, a tailor and a tobacco shop. Men unable to work steadily can get by very nicely without ever leaving the building if they wish. There is a television room in the basement and a piano. Sometimes an old lady comes in and plays old tunes they like and they sing a little."

Paco opened the door to a room at the extreme end of the hall and waved us in. I entered the short hall flanked by a closet on the right and a bathroom to the left and moved on into a spacious living room with a large, crystal chandelier. The furnishings were grossly overstuffed and had claw feet clutching glass balls that sank halfway out of sight in the lush gold carpet. The room was oblong with three doors spaced along the right-hand wall.

"This will do very nicely, Paco," said Jim. "Is Camillo in his suite?"

"He is. He asked that you get settled and comfortable, and then come down for drinks and dinner."

"You're quite a manager," I told Jim when Paco had left. "What if I'd objected to coming here?"

"I didn't think you would—but if so, no problem. What do you think of this hotel?"

"Are all the rooms this plush?"

"Few are as large," he smiled. "This is an executive suite. Camillo uses it for private parties and people like Oren have stayed in it."

"Potential donors?"

"That's right."

I looked around. "It doesn't suggest philanthropy. It looks more like a room for romancing and intrigue."

"Camillo says that is what philanthropy is today."

The three bedrooms were painted blue, yellow and pink.

"Don't you think Juanita should have the pink?" asked Jim.

"Very appropriate."

"And for you, the blue."

"Are you fond of yellow?"

"Not at all. But it is the middle room and there are adjoining doors."

A knock on the door interrupted Juanita's "Oh, Daddy!" and Jim, grinning broadly, went to open it. The old man who'd parked our car was in the hallway with our bags.

We met Camillo at seven-thirty that evening in his private alcove in the dining room. The walls were gold, the floor blue-tiled and a crystal chandelier, twice the size of the one in our living room, hung over a table covered by a deep blue cloth and set with bone-white China and glistening silverware.

Evidently Camillo was not convinced that the way to salvation lay through austerity.

He entered the room from the waiter's entrance as we came through the guest door. Jim greeted him and he approached us with a vague smile. Curly hair, half dark, half gray, framed his aged cupid's face and he carried his chubby hands thrust forward from the elbows. A light gray cotton suit draped over his stocky figure and white shoes gleamed under his pants cuffs. The dark eyes were bright but strangely unfocused—they never quite met mine as we were introduced—yet they didn't strike me as evasive, only preoccupied. We took seats around the table with me on his left, Juanita on his right and Jim directly across. A waiter of about sixty, who seemed young compared with the retainers we'd met before, appeared with a towel on his arm and an expression of deep concentration, like a cat in a sandbox, and bent over his employer's left shoulder.

"Bring the Mumm's," said Camillo.

"Jim tells me you're on a mission to locate Oren Fletcher," he said when the waiter left. "Is that wise?"

"I'm beginning to wonder," I admitted, "but what makes you ask?"

"Well," he said, touching his chubby fingertips together, "when a man like Oren disappears, his friends suspect it was by his own choice. Why bother him?"

"Because it's a lot of bother for his wife."

"Why? Because she's financially embarrassed or wants to marry another man?"

"I don't think marriage to somebody else is important to Mrs. Fletcher."

"But the money is, eh?"

"Well, she has to maintain his home and she gets pretty concerned when his business associates come to her for help and she can't do anything—"

"He raises and gives away money. What can be so urgent about handling that?"

"I'd think that as a man who runs a charitable organization himself, you'd know people involved usually consider their needs pretty urgent."

"I don't run a charitable organization, Mr. Champion. I administer a home for the elderly. They don't even have to be indigent. I take in people I like. It just happens that these days I seem to like more poor people than I used to, but I don't discriminate against those who aren't starving. I think that's a rather snobbish attitude in its own way."

"You mean that those who can afford to pay their own way?"

"People, poor or otherwise, pay here in service if they're able."

The waiter carried in a magnum of champagne nestled in a silver bucket of ice and went through the opening ritual. The cork popped discreetly, trapped in the draped towel, and the waiter struggled a little, pouring from the great bottle. He spilled some and his master ignored the waste.

We all sipped and I glanced at Juanita whose dark eyes watched Camillo with calm interest. He spoke to her in Spanish, she smiled and sipped more champagne while watching over the glass. He spoke again and she responded languidly.

"Is she not lovely?" Camillo said to me.

"Beautiful."

"Later I will have a look. I am not totally blind, it is just that my glasses are so thick they give me a headache when I wear them for long and mostly I can do all right without them. All things in the room, for me, are like a distant vista and I need powerful binoculars to see what is out there. A long time ago, a comedian from your country, Caesar, did a TV sketch where he was a musician with glasses like mine. He kept gazing into the audience saying, 'It's *dangerous* out there!' It was quite funny then, I could see and I laughed. Now when I think of it, it is not very funny anymore. Do you wear glasses, Mr. Champion?"

"No sir, not yet."

"They are a very large nuisance. I envy those who can wear contact lenses."

We had downed several glasses of champagne by the time our salad arrived, and when Camillo ate, there was no conversation. The salad was removed and more champagne was poured.

"Oren," he told me, "is a fascinating man. You would think, from his face, that he'd be a man of action, a boxer or hockey player, but nothing more violent than an electric razor has ever touched his cheeks. He greets people with warmth, like a politician, as if he needed their favor, yet he has never *needed* anyone. So what is it he wants? Why is he so eager to be loved, why is he so *interested* in us all? Always watching and asking questions—I asked him, I am a very straightforward man, what do you want?

"You know what he said? Love. When he was in college, he became friends with a young man whose father was an evangelist. During the summer Oren joined his friend and they traveled with this evangelist in the Midwest and Oren watched the crowds who listened to this man and gathered around after his sermons and flocked to his side wherever he moved. Oren told me there was a warmth there, a happiness and joy more beautiful than anything he'd ever known. Only Oren was not himself a believer. He could not accept Christ or the Holy Father. So you know what? He wanted to be Jesus himself. He couldn't preach about eternal salvation, but he could do miracles because he had money. He wanted love and learned he could buy it if he were clever. Love is leverage, you know. He convinced people they could be rewarded if they were worthy. *He* was the way and the light, God Almighty. Now, a man like that does not disappear involuntarily or in a moment of despair. God never despairs. Escapists flee from boredom, responsibility, problems, disgrace— Oren has gone into seclusion, that's all. It does not matter to him that he was entrapped by an ambitious young woman who came on him during his foolish period—which we all go through after forty— sooner or later—you'll see. That time when you see, all around you, thousands of beautiful girls, so desirable you're driven to a frenzy, knowing you're growing too old for them. You *have* to have one or a dozen for yourself before it's too late."

I couldn't remember when I hadn't felt that way but nodded wisely and drank champagne.

"We're having lamb," said our host. "It's been butterflied and marinated in olive oil, lemon, garlic, ground pepper and one other spice—a Greek recipe I particularly favor."

The waiter delivered a steaming platter of meat redolent of garlic, glistening with juice, and placed it reverently before Camillo who picked up a silver-handled carving knife, a matching two-pronged fork, and began carving long, thick slices which he placed on plates stacked before him which the servant passed on.

As my dad would say, the meat was so tender it almost wept.

"Have you asked Fletcher to help fund this hotel?" I asked.

"Of course."

"And?"

"He refused. Very politely, of course. He said he did not give money for hobbies. We both laughed. It was an irony, you see. Giving money is a hobby with him. I always told him that and he never denied it. Of course he worked hard at it—some men will always work harder at hobbies than at making a living."

"He ever say what you'd have to do to get his money?"

"*Sí.* Take in the hopeless. Men who can't walk or hold their wastes. I tried to make him understand I was helping make life bearable for men who still had self-awareness, men capable of something beyond the vegetable wait for death. Have you ever visited a nursing home, Mr. Champion?"

I had not.

"Well, I wasn't born to wealth. My father was poor and my grandparents were poorer. My grandmother died in a nursing home. It was not light and clean and regulated like those in your country—it was a dump heap for the dying. If I told you details, I know you wouldn't eat for a week. The fires of Milton's hell are not worse than living with the dying who are mad, helpless, hopeless and filthy, watched over by indifferent, retarded and lazy, if not vicious, dogs who couldn't get employment anywhere else. It is all a nightmare. So I prepared this place for those who still have their wits and some interest in living, to give them a few final, tranquil years."

"What happens when they deteriorate?"

"They know when they come that when they must have constant care, they leave. I make exceptions for those whose minds remain reasonably keen."

"You just send them away when they're helpless?"

"It is more complicated than that, unfortunately, but in essence, you guess right. If I had my way, we would run a room in the basement where those who were ready could go and find final escape, quietly and with dignity. I do not have my way, so we must thrust them back into the cruel world."

"Not having good eyesight must, at such times, be quite convenient."

He smiled tolerantly. "It doesn't really help that much. My imagination is formidable, my hearing excellent. I know what happens. And I concentrate on taking in another old man to give a period of comfort and contentment."

I looked at Jim who watched me with his gentle eyes, and at Juanita who daintily feasted on the tender lamb.

I thought of telling him about the attempt on my life, but Camillo's style did not encourage volunteered information. It seemed unlikely he'd listen, let alone believe such a story. He was like many self-made men I've interviewed or questioned over the years, totally immersed in his own ideas and interests, a man who listens only to what reinforces or supports his own theses; not stupid, sometimes not even insensitive, but so taken up in achieving results for his own projects and dreams that he was incapable of assimilating anything irrelevant to the direct pursuit of his goals. I believed he was sincere in what he was doing in his hotel, and that he'd have been insulted if I were to point out that it provided him with unlimited retainers and worshippers.

When I asked how many men lived in the hotel, he waved his plump hand vaguely and said it varied from forty to fifty—occasionally a few more.

I refused the after-dinner cigars, which he said were Cuban, but accepted the brandy. After the table had been cleared, Camillo asked his man to bring the camera and his glasses. He hadn't exaggerated; his lenses were easily the thickest I've ever seen. He placed the heavy frame gingerly on his thick nose before leaning forward to gaze at Juanita who sat radiantly at ease under the soft glow from the muted chandelier.

"More beautiful each day," he said, and lifted the camera, the latest from Polaroid, and snapped four flash shots of her. After careful examination, he picked his favorite, pocketed it and offered us the others as souvenirs.

He then pushed his chair back, told us it had been a lovely evening and he looked forward to seeing us tomorrow.

Back in our room we found a bouquet of two dozen long-stemmed peach-colored roses and a bottle of Kahlúa beside three small silver goblets set on a round table between the windows.

"Well," I said, "Camillo is a unique kind of host."

"I'm afraid you don't approve of him," said Jim.

"I didn't mean to make it obvious. The trouble is, when a guy's that thick-skinned, I can't quite resist trying to reach him."

Jim poured the dark chocolate liquid slowly into the silver goblets, filling them almost to the brim, then handed one to Juanita, another to me and lifted his own.

"To youth," he said, looking at me.

"To beauty," I said, looking at Juanita.

"To experience," she said, looking into her goblet.

We sat down and I asked if Camillo was all he pretended or did he dramatize?

"He does not dramatize. He was born poor, became rich, lived hard and hopes to die in grace. And he is genuinely, perhaps fanatically dedicated to giving these old men some rich years before they die."

"Then how can he throw them out when their need becomes greatest?"

"For the benefit of those who remain. If the hopeless and mad remained, before long this would be just another house of despair, like the nursing homes that haunt him."

I wanted to argue about that, but could see that Juanita was becoming bored and gave it up.

In a little while we finished our drinks and stood up to go to our rooms.

Jim paused before turning to his door.

"Try not to offend Camillo again," he said gently. "He is far more sensitive than you realize, and quite vindictive when he feels insulted."

I looked around my room, half expecting to find another warning of some sort, but could find nothing out of order. Even so, I found myself thinking of Jim's warning. I thought about it a very long time and it gained significance until I finally slept.

XV

In the morning I heard Jim rise early and dozed as he passed some time in the bathroom. At eight I woke fully, got up, checked the living room and found it empty. Jim's door was open, so I took a peek. He'd drawn the covers up, leaving the bed looking almost unused. The bureau top was clear and all of his clothing put away.

Juanita's door was still closed.

I took a shower, dressed, and after thinking about it awhile, went to the telephone and asked if I could make a long-distance call. The switchboard octogenarian didn't speak English well and after a while someone else came on the line and told me yes, they'd give me an outside line and would bill me for the call with a fifteen percent surcharge.

A few moments later Al Lutz was on the line.

"I'm not too sure about this line," I told Al, "so let's not mention names or anything too specific—okay? That is, if you've got anything."

"I'm not sure what I got. First, there's no obituary because as far as anybody knows, the lady's alive. She took off with a young man when the daughter was four."

I thought about that a couple of seconds and asked if he'd picked up anything interesting on the father.

"Considering what the lady did—who knows the husband was the father?"

"It was like that?"

"Let's say it could've been. Anyway, the man with the horns did okay in the bread department. Besides the business he went there to run, he got into real estate, and I don't mean he was selling outhouses. Downtown properties, some heavy stuff. Lots of connections, one of those backroom politicians, you know? The guys that run for nothing and manage to run everything. Maybe not that big, but enough so he was always selling the right property at the right time for the very all right price, you know? This boy made a roll."

"Anything on the daughter?"

"Oh yeah. Very popular, very big on campus. Story goes that the boys swooned. One nut killed himself over her. And not a student, a teacher."

"How old was he?"

"He was old enough to teach."

"Are you passing rumors or is there something to this?"

"It's solid. I hired a reporter there, son of an old friend, a real nosy son-of-a-bitch. He read yearbooks from the school, talked with the old principal, gossiped with lodge brothers—"

"Have him find out how old the teacher was."

"You care what the guy taught?"

"I'd like all you can get on him."

"You got a line on something?"

"I'm not even sure I've got one in the water, but follow up on this, okay?"

"It's your bread, which reminds me, I'll need another fifty."

I heard stirrings in Juanita's room.

"I'll send it. Thanks."

Juanita emerged from her room in an emerald-green robe that flowed over her body. She had brushed her hair and the sun coming through the east window brought out highlights of red in the blackness that fell to her shoulders. Her eyes were somber, her mouth looked swollen and a little sullen.

I said good morning.

She nodded and went into the bathroom. After a few moments I heard the shower turned on. I imagined her removing the green robe and later turning her body under the water and thought it might be wise if I simply went down to breakfast but made no move to do it.

When she came from the bathroom, she smiled at me and stopped in the center of the room, combing her long dark hair.

"I'm not civil when I wake," she said, "and I don't wake till I've had my shower."

I grinned a little oafishly, reassured by her sudden friendliness while feeling a bit ridiculous that a smile could lift me so.

"What do you think of Camillo?" I asked.

"He's a charming old show-off. A flirt."

"You like that?"

"Of course. I'll get dressed and we'll have breakfast, all right?"

She left the bedroom door open about a foot and I fought the impulse to rise and stroll about the living room to see if I could get a glimpse of her dressing. I settled for walking over to the door but to the side that gave me no view.

"How long have you known him?" I asked.

"About three years."

"Is he married?"

"Three times. He says that's enough, now he just has girl-friends."

"Young ones?"

"I've never met any of them, I wouldn't know."

She didn't seem much interested in that subject and my own thoughts were too much involved with picturing her brushing her hair before the mirror. I kept imagining that she was doing it after having dropped the robe on the bed.

Then Jim unlocked the hall door and came in. By the time he could see me, I was standing beside the nearest window, looking out at the sunlit street below.

Jim smiled at me with a look that said he knew perfectly well just what I was thinking about his daughter.

"Well," he said, "I suppose you've been wondering what happened to your chaperon?"

"Yeah," I lied and wondered how I could have become so besotted by Juanita that I'd forgotten him entirely for several moments. All I could think of, besides her body, was the man who'd killed himself over her.

Jim told me he had been unable to sleep and developed back problems if he lay in bed too long, so he'd gone downstairs and talked with some of the elders who'd convinced him he should eat breakfast.

He told me the *huevos rancheros* were not so strong here as at the Castillo.

Juanita and I went down to the coffee shop, which was in the lower level. I much prefer breakfast in a room where I can see the sun is shining and was not charmed by the bright colors of the plastic chairs and oilcloth table covers. This was the only section of the hotel that I'd seen which looked institutional. The fruit was good, I took two slices of watermelon, and the semisweet rolls went well with the rich black coffee.

"Where'd your father meet your mother?" I asked Juanita.

She was buttering a roll and stopped momentarily to look at me with her wide, dark eyes.

"In Eau Claire."

"How'd it happen?"

"Does that make a difference?"

"I'm curious about how people meet who later get married."

She smiled. "You're a strange fellow. Well, Father was at a little nightclub between Chippewa Falls and Eau Claire. They had dancing there. Mother was with a fellow from Chippewa Falls and Father saw her and was very excited and he went over and asked her to dance while she was alone—her man had gone to talk with some friends. So they danced and Mother was afraid her fellow would be mad and he was, but when Father talked to him, he got over it and they talked and laughed and Mother was rather annoyed because they didn't seem to think she was important enough to fight over, but the next morning Father called her— he'd got her name straight right away and called all the people with her last name listed in the telephone book until he got her. He wanted to see her that afternoon and they went on a picnic at the park in Chippewa Falls and later got married."

"Did she tell you about all this?"

"No—she died delivering me, don't you remember? Father told me all about how it was."

"Do you take after her?"

"No. She was very fair, and more delicate."

"What else did Jim tell you about her?"

She ate slowly and talked without looking at me very often.

"She was gentle and good."

"Was she Catholic?"

"Of course."

"Was she a lot younger than Jim?"

"Yes, I think so."

"You have any pictures of her?"

"Not anymore. They got lost during one of our moves. We moved a lot. Are you going to have more coffee?"

I said yes, and when we had our cups full, asked if she remembered any signs of prejudice in Wisconsin.

"You mean, because Father was Mexican?"

I nodded.

"No. I don't remember anything like that. And the school people were always nice to me."

"You mean the students, or the teachers?"

"Both."

"I bet you were a good student."

"Oh yes. And I was always pretty. That helps very much, you know. And my clothes were nice. They also knew I had no mother, so they felt they had to be kind."

"So what made you want to leave when Jim retired?"

"I hated winters. So did he."

"Then you didn't mind leaving Wisconsin at all?"

"Not much, no. One should move on sometime, you know."

"No matter who's left behind?"

She gave me a quick, guarded glance.

"There was no one that important to me."

I suspected she had never known real acceptance. People had been nice because, as she said, she was pretty and not poor and had no mother, but she was an alien who never belonged. Her father was tolerated, perhaps even admired for his enterprise, but he would not have belonged to private clubs or been invited into homes for intimate parties and dinners.

"Ever wanted to go back?" I asked.

"Sometimes I think it'd be nice to live awhile in one of the bigger cities, where all the kids I knew planned to go, in California, Chicago, or even New York."

"What'd you most like to do?"

She cradled her cup in both hands and gazed into space.

"I'd like to marry a very nice man who had a lot of money."

"A man like Oren Fletcher?"

She met my eyes. "Yes."

"You're more comfortable with older men, aren't you?"

She gave me a kindly smile. "Well, I've lived with one all my life, maybe that has something to do with it."

"Did a young man disappoint you?"

"All young men disappointed me," she said, and looked away.

We found Jim reading a Mexican newspaper in the living room while two old men worked silently in the bedrooms changing sheets and making beds.

Jim saw me staring at them and smiled.

"This is probably the only hotel in the world without maids," he said.

I suggested we visit the police. He agreed and we left Juanita in the room, painting her fingernails.

"Won't she be bored?" I asked as we stepped into the already hot street.

"She's seldom bored," he assured me. "Juanita is an uncomplicated girl; she has no ambition and little curiosity. Her mind is mostly at ease. It makes her an ideal daughter."

The tragedy, I thought, was that she had no expectations.

The police were polite and rigidly formal. We talked with several people, or rather, Jim did. No one we met admitted to having any English. I suspected that the captain who spent the most time with us was perfectly able to understand my comments to Jim, but he never let on and all we learned was that while they had been very concerned about Fletcher's abrupt disappearance, their investigation had turned up nothing to suggest he met with foul play. The room was orderly where he spent his last accounted-for hours and there were no notes left.

I asked if any mail had been delivered to the hotel since Fletcher's disappearance. Yes, it had all been forwarded to Mrs. Fletcher in Houston.

Did they have any theories about Fletcher's abrupt disappearance which left personal effects in the room, including a briefcase the man habitually carried everywhere he went?

The squat captain answered with an elaborate shrug. He said the switchboard woman had said she thought there had been a call for Mr. Fletcher not long before he left, but she was not positive, there had been many calls around that time.

Was the call from a man or a woman, I asked.

The operator thought it was from a woman. No one reported seeing Mr. Fletcher leave the hotel.

"Did you know that Fletcher made a substantial withdrawal from his bank that morning?" I asked.

"*Sí,*" he said when Jim made the translation.

"Do you know the amount?"

"He says it was exactly $375,250," Jim told me.

The captain looked very proud, I suppose because it was the first time I'd asked a question he could answer with precision.

I asked if Fletcher had had any visitors.

The captain frowned and shook his head as he answered. There were none who asked to be announced, but there had been a lot of people coming and going in the lobby, so people who knew their way could have gone up without being noticed.

"It seems to me," I said, "that since Fletcher took a third of a million dollars from his bank and promptly disappeared, it would be pretty damned obvious there was foul play."

Jim glanced nervously at the captain and back to me.

"You want me to pose that as a question?"

"Yeah. Politely, of course."

"I don't think it wise to offend the man."

"Jim, you're the most inoffensive man I've met, put it to him pretty, okay?"

After a few seconds of thought Jim released a flow of soft Spanish. The captain responded calmly.

Jim looked a little relieved and turned to me once more.

"He says yes, they were very suspicious, but they simply have not been able to find anyone who saw visitors approach the man, or who saw him leave the hotel. They find it hard to believe that anyone could have kidnapped him without someone seeing something suspicious."

I stared at the captain for a moment and thought, "Well shit, back to nowhere." He stared back, not hostile or even indifferent, perhaps just a little amused. Then he pushed his chair back and rose.

"Muchas gracias," I said and managed not to sound sarcastic.

"De nada," he responded.

"Yeah," I thought, "of nothing or for nothing."

"You know what I think?" I said to Jim as we walked back toward the hotel.

"I'm afraid not."

"I think they positively *do* believe he was snatched but haven't got a notion how to find out, so they're playing games, trying to make us think everything's okay and Fletcher's just in the sack with some woman."

"Yes, that's quite possible."

"Somehow he was coerced into taking that money out. Somebody had something on him, that's got to be it."

"I don't know—he wasn't a very vulnerable man."

"As long as he was married to Daphne, he was vulnerable. She's that kind of woman. Finding vulnerability is her number-one specialty."

I telephoned Marigold from the hotel lobby booth. She almost sounded glad to hear from me and asked if I'd sustained any new damage.

"Aside from paralyzing frustration, I'm in great shape. Can you tell me exactly when you last heard from Fletcher?"

"The second Friday in March."

"What time?"

"Four-thirty P.M."

The precision stopped me for a moment.

"Are you impressed or disbelieving?" she asked.

"Some of both—when did you look it up?"

"The morning after you took me to dinner. It seemed likely you'd ask. Only I thought it'd be lots sooner."

"Yeah, well, when I make an ass of myself, I get shy."

"You weren't that bad. Considering what you'd been through, you were almost noble. Have you checked me out yet?"

"I'm working on it."

The wire hummed during our mutual silence and then she asked if I were making any progress.

"Apparently not—nobody's tried to kill me lately, but a young guy did try to punch me around. I don't think it had anything to do with Fletcher. When you checked up on the date and time, did you note what he called about?"

"Sure. He asked if I'd received a grant request from a man named Camillo, in Guadalajara."

"Had you?"

"Yes. He'd asked for one hundred and fifty thousand dollars for a rather special home for the elderly. It was called the Casa de la Hora."

"What made it special?"

"Well, it wasn't like a nursing home, it was sort of a rest stop between a working life and being a vegetable, you know what I mean?"

"Yeah. Was it a detailed proposal?"

"Hardly. Terse would be more like it. Two pages. No financials. It was more like a memo than a grant proposal. It was the sort of thing Oren asked for from people with projects he particularly liked."

"So what'd Fletcher say about it?"

"He asked me to read it to him and I did. He laughed when I finished and asked what I thought of it. I said it seemed worth considering if we could get more details. Then he told me he'd spent a couple of nights in the place and had told the man who ran it to make an application.

"I said, 'So you plan to give him a grant?' and to my surprise, he said no, he wasn't about to fund people's hobbies, but it might be a worthwhile venture to support somewhere in Texas or maybe Montana."

"So why'd he ask the guy to make a request?"

"Well, he wanted to go through the motions and I suspect he knew the man wouldn't really make a proper application. I thought it was cruel to give the man false hopes and Oren could tell how I felt right away and told me not to worry, this fellow would find all the money he needed, probably in his own bank account if it came to that."

"You think it's possible he wanted to take this guy Camillo down a peg?"

"Well," she said slowly, "it's not out of the question. Oren was inclined to do that with people who irritated him."

"He didn't like competing gods," I suggested.

She laughed. It was a short outburst and stopped almost immediately.

"That's awful," she said, and began laughing again. The sound faded as she lowered the telephone or covered it temporarily.

"I don't know what's come over me," she said after a moment, "it's really not that funny."

"But you think it's true."

"I'm afraid so. Oren never mingled much with people of his own class, and when he did, they seemed to make him irritable. His wife remarked on it once and he told her there was just so much room on Parnassus."

"You heard him say that to her?"

"No, he told me about it."

That seemed like a strange thing for a man to tell his secretary, but I decided not to comment on it.

I asked if she'd checked out the girl in her office, Danielle.

"Yes. The people at the hiring service didn't have much—she's very young you know. She did well in school—went to business college—"

"Is she married or involved?"

"She's not married. I don't know about the other. The service doesn't go into that sort of thing."

"What about the old sweetheart revived, Elvira? You got her address or number?"

"Of course."

I wrote them both down and asked if she had access to Fletcher's address book.

"Yes, why?"

"Do me a favor and get it."

She was back in a moment and I asked her to see if she found a Juanita Durado listed.

"Not under 'D'; wait—yes, here's a Juanita—"

"In Guanajuato?"

"That's right, you want the number?"

Well, well.

"Ah, no thanks, I know where to find her. Listen, I'm going to be back in Houston for a day or two, could we get together? I'll stay sober."

"When do you have in mind?"

"How about Saturday?"

"Okay, but don't make it too early. I try to spend most of the weekend with April."

"No problem, we'll take her to a movie."

"Like what?"

"Oh, *Annie,* or something. You pick it; I'll like it. I really want to see you and meet April."

She remained skeptical but eventually agreed to give it a try if April were willing. I hung up and began to worry because I was feeling too optimistic.

XVI

Camillo had other commitments that evening, so Jim, Juanita and I dined as a threesome amid the old-timers in a large, softly illuminated room at the hotel. Jim told Juanita of our frustrating afternoon and she listened with barely polite interest.

My problem was how to raise the question of Juanita's number in Oren Fletcher's little black book. It seemed wise to ask her when we were not with Jim.

"You know any of the men living here?" I asked Jim when we were having coffee after our pleasant meal.

"Not really. I've talked with one or two—"

"What do they think of Camillo?"

"That's interesting," he smiled, "because it's a thing I've wanted to know and somehow, they haven't been willing to say. They aren't exactly evasive, it's more as if the subject makes them shy. I don't know whether they're embarrassed by their gratitude, or offended by it."

"Did you ask them directly?"

"Oh no, never. All very indirect. Mostly I listen to them talk. They call him 'The señor' or 'Patrón.' When he talks, those close listen. Or most of them do. I suspect only sycophants seek to sit close, but then, I rather suspect that most of these people are of that order, since who comes and who stays depends entirely on Camillo's private whims."

"Is it really that simple?"

"He says as much. I don't know why he'd lie, although he might exaggerate to make himself seem more impressive."

I looked around at the men and tried to imagine how I'd react in their position. I couldn't quite picture it.

"Let's visit a bar near here," I suggested. Jim seemed unsurprised by the idea, and as usual, Juanita agreed by action without comment.

We found a place just a block away which was filled with scents of old beer and burned corn. Its patrons were mostly men of my age or younger and they gave close attention to Juanita who ignored them. She had a way of withdrawing that was so complete I couldn't believe she either saw or heard anyone more than three feet away.

A waiter with tired eyes came to us, took our orders and drifted away.

"Were you hoping to find old guests from the hotel here?" asked Jim.

"It seemed possible."

"Old men go to bars for company. The hotel guests have all the company they need among themselves."

I was looking for a maverick and there didn't appear to be any, at least not here.

"Maybe he doesn't allow them to move out and mingle with the common folk," I said.

"I can't imagine why."

"Because they might tell secrets. You ever hear of places that take in the elderly and sort of help them out of this world for the benefit of heirs who are willing to hurry the process a little?"

Jim smiled. "That's a rather appalling idea, but it does not seem viable in this case—Camillo's guests are too poor to be valuable, dead or alive."

We had two drinks before I gave up and suggested we go to bed. My companions were agreeable.

I rose at six-thirty in the morning, dressed and went down to the breakfast room. It was not formally open yet, but one of the ancients offered me fresh coffee and I watched as the tables were set by two brisk old men. I tried to engage them in conversation, but they indicated they couldn't understand my Spanish, let alone my English, and kept their distance once my breakfast was delivered.

By eight I was in a car rental office and before eight-thirty I was on my way to the airport. It was, I knew, extremely rude to leave Jim and Juanita with nothing but an enigmatic note telling them I'd be back on Monday, but I was determined that no one should know where I was going.

Connections worked out and by three-thirty I was at the Houston airport.

"I'm sorry this is such short notice," I told Marigold when she answered my call, "but how about we take in dinner and a movie tonight?"

"You promised advance notice."

"Yeah, but I'm getting paranoid—I was afraid the phone at Camillo's might be tapped or the operator'd listen in. This time I wanted to be sure nobody knew where I was."

She was a little grumpy but finally admitted she'd talked with April and the little girl was willing to chance an evening with a stranger. No doubt the promise of seeing a movie had swung the deal.

I picked them up in a cab at six-thirty.

They walked past the doorman who smiled at April when she said "Hi!" to him and grinned broadly when she announced, "*I'm going for a ride in a car-car!*"

April was very thin with a slightly round face, great blue eyes and golden hair cut short. She sneaked a peek at me as she climbed into the back seat and sat down in the near corner, forcing her mother to move past her and sit between us.

Marigold introduced me as "Mr. Champion" and I said, "Hi, Ms. Amsdecker."

"My name is April," she informed me darkly.

"Mine's really Kyle."

She wasn't overly impressed with that and looked away as her mother told our driver the destination.

Marigold was in a dark mood and said nothing while I tried to make small talk. After a few seconds April leaned forward to look around her mother and announced, "I'm three."

"Ah," I said, "you're very blond for your age."

"Uh-huh."

"When was your birthday?"

She looked at her mother who came to life and said it had been two months ago.

"That explains it," I said. "You're already on your way to four."

She looked a little suspicious, but after a moment got up and came around her mother's knees to sit between us. It wasn't hard since we were in a yellow cab and the wide seat provided ample space between everyone.

"That's a very fine dress," I told April.

She looked down approvingly and nodded her gold head.

"Is your mother always in a bad mood when she's hungry?" I asked.

"Uh-huh."

Marigold looked a little more cheerful when we reached her favorite restaurant and inside the maître d' cooed over April, gave us a corner table and left three menus. April picked hers up and examined it with feigned interest for several seconds.

"What's your favorite food?" I asked her.

"Hot dogs and lobster thermidor."

"At the same time?"

"Uh-huh."

"She's never had them at the same time," said Marigold.

"Maybe she's never had the chance."

"Well, she won't get it here."

Marigold's humor improved still more with the arrival of our food and she watched April approvingly as the little girl worked quietly on her lobster thermidor and left the talking to us.

I said again I was sorry about giving such short notice and she waved off the apology, saying she'd intended to break off with the guy she'd been dating anyway.

"Is this the same guy I cut out before?"

She nodded. I tried to feel sorry for him but only managed smug.

We went to see the movie *Annie* which seemed pretty okay to me, but halfway through, April leaned toward her mother and said, "I've seen enough now, let's go home."

"Don't you want to see how it comes out?"

"It'll be all right," she said.

Marigold looked at me and I said let's go.

The apartment was modestly furnished in fine taste and had an impressively large living room. Marigold explained that her mother-in-law had taken advantage of the night off to visit her daughter in a Houston suburb.

As she was led to her bedroom, April turned and said, "G'night, Mr. Champ," and sailed serenely through her door.

When Marigold came back, I said, "That's quite a girl."

"Well, she's not totally spoiled yet, but her grandma's working on it. You want a drink?"

"How about coffee?"

She said fine and I thought I detected a note of relief, which made me feel a little phony since I'd have preferred a good highball.

When she returned, I was standing beside a bookcase that filled a five-foot space between two large windows overlooking the street. The larger bottom shelves held hardbacks, mostly old Randon House Giants like *War and Peace* and *Moby Dick*. Upper shelves held a variety of paperbacks ranging from *In Search of Excellence* to mysteries.

"The ones on the bottom belong to Marcia, my mother-in-law —or should I say 'out-of-law'? Whatever. The paperbacks are mine."

"I wouldn't have expected you'd go for mysteries."

"You figured I was the self-improvement type, right?"

I admitted that was true.

"What's in your library?" she asked.

"Mysteries, some sci-fi, Twain, Hemingway, Keillor, Roth, Fitzgerald, Edmund Wilson, Dillard—sort of a mix."

"A mix is right."

We talked a little more of books before she went back to the kitchen and brought an automatic coffee maker and cups on a tray.

After the pouring she asked what I'd been planning to do when I went to the university.

"It was pretty vague."

"But come on, you must've had *something* in mind—"

"I just wanted to get through okay and wind up rich and famous. Never was fussy how."

"Doing what?"

"Oh, the first year I thought it could come lots of ways. I'd be a star trackman, I'd write great novels, maybe be an actor. The only trouble was there were so many people around who showed up with better equipment. You know, faster, smarter, more talented. So for a while I thought I'd get into journalism. Pursue truth, expose wrongs, learn about everything from the inside. My first instructor in reporting put it in the proper perspective. He was a practicing reporter, taught during afternoons and had an evening beat with the local paper. He said he got into reporting because he was nosy and it was the only job that gave him an excuse to ask people personal questions and get paid for it. He also warned us that most of the time in that business you're asking questions some editor wants answered from people that don't necessarily interest you. And nothing, absolutely nothing in the world, is as simple as a column of newsprint has to describe it. And of course he was right. It's frustrating in the print media, but it's absolutely maddening on TV. All the world in a nutshell and delivered with a plastic smile."

"So you weren't too unhappy about getting out of it?"

"Like hell. It about wiped me out. It made me second-best at best, and a loser at worst. Never liked either role."

"Good," she said, and laughed.

"Yeah, but where am I?"

"As you said when we had the champagne, surviving. You'll do all right."

"What about you, what do you want most?"

She put her empty cup down on the coffee table, sat back and folded her slender hands.

"I'd like to be director of the Foundation."

"Why?"

She raised her shoulders and rested her head against the chair back.

"Lots of reasons. I'd have nice people around me all the time, needing my help and wanting to like and impress me. And other people who have this need to give but want someone to do it for them in satisfying ways. It's the best business in the world."

"With security and power, right?"

"Yes. Is that so contemptible?"

"It's sure as hell good as news or entertainment—probably better than the two combined. How'd you run things different from Fletcher?"

"I'd hire specialists to research problems, examine applicants and their proposals objectively as possible, find ways to make grants that'd show results I could see."

"No more whims, huh?"

"Maybe a few. Small ones. I wouldn't want to be *all* coldly analytical—or predictable."

"Okay, assuming Fletcher's out of the picture, what happens next? You apply for the job?"

"It's up to the board. I will if they'll let me. The Foundation's entirely separate from the estate, so Daphne has no say."

No doubt that was all in Marigold's favor. I asked who the members were and she said Avery, a retired banker, Sutton, Oren's uncle by marriage, and Elvira Mumford, who runs a senior center in Houston.

"Funded by the Foundation?"

She shook her head. "That'd be a conflict of interest."

"Why'd she come on the board if it'd cut off a grant resource?"

"It'd give her access to other grant-makers and I imagine Oren promised to encourage people she knew to help her out."

"The good-old-boy system, as ever."

She didn't deny it. I asked what Elvira was like.

"She's a fine-looking, very intelligent and real sort of person—"

"Sounds good—"

"—she's also opportunistic, manipulative and shrewd. She uses people without making any bones about it and manages to make most of them feel they're important because they're useful and she knows it."

"A born leader."

"Exactly."

I suspected she was also a role model but kept that to myself.

Gradually our conversation became more personal and I was sufficiently bolstered to hold her hand when she offered it as I was leaving and asked if I could do better than a handshake. She said I could try and I did. It was a fine, warm kiss and I left with a mild conviction that better things would follow.

XVII

I located Elvira Mumford the next day in a small office at the end of a long corridor in a decrepit building well removed from fashionable, downtown Houston. A sign on the wall identified the occupant as the Executive Director. The door was wide open and I peered in, meeting a bright green gaze from the woman behind an olive drab desk which dated from World War II. Her sculptured hair was light brown and gray, cut somewhere between a page boy and a Dutch bob. Her tanned face was wide-cheeked, full-lipped and trim along the jaw.

She offered me a slender hand with a firm grip and rose just enough to reach across the desk without standing, and waved me into an uncushioned, olive drab wooden chair.

"It's not comfortable," she assured me. "I don't normally encourage long visits."

I said I'd be brief if she'd be direct.

"Directness," she said with a smile of unthreatening intimacy, "is my specialty. How far has your investigation gone?"

"The only thing sure so far is that somebody doesn't want him found."

"Tell me about it."

I explained while she alternately doodled on a legal pad and examined my face with green eyes that penetrated like a laser beam.

When I ran down, she asked if I thought Oren were dead. I nodded.

For a moment the direct gaze left me while she concentrated on her doodling pad and frowned. When she looked up, the frown was gone. She asked if I had any theories or suspects.

"Nothing worth telling about."

She placed the pencil on her pad, shoved them carefully to her right and rested tanned, rather masculine hands on the desk.

"What do you expect from me?"

"I'd like to learn more about Fletcher. I know he liked playing God and went at it about as arbitrarily as the original at times. I know his general business background and that he kept big chunks of cash handy and there were probably people close who hated or feared him. But none of these people seem like ones that'd try to knock me off using hired hands. Somebody's nervous as hell and that's crazy, because I don't know any reason they should think I'm on to anything."

Her unnaturally green eyes probed again. There were tiny wrinkles at their corners and at the edges of her wide mouth. A high-collared white blouse concealed the lower half of her throat, but what showed was surprisingly smooth for a tanned woman in her fifties. She wore a green eye shadow so subtly applied it seemed a reflection of the bright irises.

"What you really want to know," she said, "is what was going on between Oren and me, right?"

I grinned and said yes.

She nodded, leaned back and rested her elbows on the chair arms.

"All right. I'll tell you about Oren. We grew up as neighbors, went to the same school. He was a year ahead of me, but we knew each other in an easy, comfortable way. I remember him as sober, aloof, even shy; very respectful toward teachers and polite to other students. After his graduation we saw a lot of each other. I think he was rather afraid of young ladies he hadn't known well. At the time I thought he was very romantic; he carried around this air of thoughtful solemnity that at that age made me think he must be suffering some secret sorrow. The fact was, he hadn't a notion as to what he wanted to do with himself. He couldn't imagine any career he'd like. I thought that tragic since *everything* interested me then. I assumed that was because I wasn't as bright as he was. In our world then, women assumed men were wiser and grander than we—especially when they were older. After he went to college, I didn't see him anymore. He went into the family business and that was it."

"How'd you get back together?"

"He heard from mutual friends that my husband had died and came to the funeral. It wasn't exactly like Richard the Third, but he *did* approach me at the funeral and said he wanted us to see more of each other. I was a little put out with myself that I wasn't offended, but the fact is my husband had died after a long illness and his going was more of a relief than a tragedy by then, so it was very nice to have an old friend show up and make it clear he thought I was special."

"Then what?"

"We became good friends again."

"You weren't his mistress?"

"You're a very young man to be using such archaic terms."

"I'm just trying to get to the meat of the issue."

"What an unfortunate choice of words."

I don't blush often, but I felt my face turning warm as the green eyes took me in disapprovingly.

"Did Mrs. Fletcher have grounds for her claim that you were sleeping with her husband?"

"Did you ask *her* if she slept with him?"

"No, but I gather she hadn't been for quite a while."

"Is that terribly pertinent to this case?"

I lifted my hands. "Right now I don't know anything is—or isn't. I'm just trying to find out what the hell relationships were and—"

"And who had a motive for killing him."

"You got it."

"I'd guess Daphne had as strong a motive as anyone."

"That's occurred to me, but if so, why hire me to find him?"

"For legal and insurance reasons, I'd imagine. If she were resourceful enough to eliminate him in Mexico, she'd also manage to hide her connection with the murder, especially working with that lawyer friend of hers."

"You think they're having an affair?"

"Don't you?"

"Yeah."

"Well, thank the Lord. You aren't blind, at least."

"You know a man named Camillo?"

"I know of him. He was a favorite topic of conversation for Oren. I understand he runs something like a port of last resort for aging but agile old men."

"Did you know Oren asked him to submit a grant request, then promptly turned it down?"

"It wasn't quite that way. Camillo asked him for money. Oren said put it in writing, because that's what he always did. Foundations are accountable to government authorities, you know, so they're very legal about giving away money. And he *was* interested in Camillo's ideas, if not the way he ran his hotel. He told me he was thinking of promoting such a program somewhere in Texas or Montana. Texas was handy, but he thought about Montana because up there they have no programs for older people or anyone else for that matter."

"Did you ask him for a grant to help your agency?"

She smiled. "Of course not. He named me to his board of directors. That was his first approach at the funeral. He said he wanted someone with a completely different background than the other directors—someone with agency experience. Of course I was flattered and accepted. I'd already been serving on other volunteer boards, so it didn't seem like a strange suggestion at the time. I thought he was just being considerate, trying to give me additional interests now that I was widowed."

"You didn't think it was part of a hustle?"

She gazed at me for a moment and I assumed she didn't know the slang meaning of hustle, then she said yes, that had occurred to her and her reaction was that that was a ridiculous notion—he had a young wife and liked young women and she was well past that.

"But you found out the interest was more personal?"

"I found out he was not personally interested in his young wife."

"Did he ever mention divorce?"

She shook her head.

"You think he considered it?"

"Not seriously."

"Why not, if he wasn't satisfied?"

"Because she'd demand too much. Oren was willing to give away millions, but he wouldn't let anyone take a nickel from him against his will."

"You know if she ever thought of divorcing him?"

"No. He never told me she had and I certainly never asked."

We talked some more without educating each other much and I asked her to think of people who might have the most to gain by his demise and she said we'd covered all she knew. Of course there was always the possibility of someone a little crazy having been a suppliant who was turned down, but such people were highly unlikely to have engineered the elaborate attempt on my life. I got a vague feeling that she might think there was no connection between that episode and Oren Fletcher—as if she thought I might have enemies of my own.

When I got up to leave, she suggested I be very careful.

I suppose the serious tone of her warning made me feel paranoiac when I saw the cab conveniently moving my way as I stepped out on the sidewalk. Whatever the reason, I turned away and walked south to the next corner, crossed the street and paused for a moment in front of a closed theater.

I saw a cab parked on the street side I'd left but couldn't be sure it was the one I'd spotted first. Two young blacks ambled my way, one carrying a ghetto blaster set at top volume. They walked with elbows back, arms loose, except for the one holding the blaster, like John Wayne walking into a bar with his guns slung low. I began walking slowly their way and we passed each other with covert glances. The one without the radio gave me a dark, antagonistic stare. They both wore cowboy boots and Levi's with blue denim work jackets.

The street was lined with parked cars, but there were few

pedestrians and I studied the nearer ones, looking for men watching me. No one seemed to be paying any attention, but I remembered from all the mysteries and intrigue novels that followers are always casual.

I kept moving west for a block and the neighborhood took on a slightly less forlorn look. Another block on I became convinced that a man in a plaid sport shirt was stalking me. I turned south again, and when I looked back, he was nowhere in sight but another man I'd noticed earlier, wearing blue jeans and a white T-shirt, was strolling along the street across from me. The fact that his T-shirt had no message was enough to make me suspicious when I'd first seen him and now I was sure he was following me. When the guy in the plaid shirt appeared again, I paused at a corner and at the last moment got on a bus. It took me two blocks before I saw a parked cab, left the bus, grabbed the cab and went back to my hotel.

XVIII

I sat in the room awhile, reviewing the past couple of hours, and decided I wasn't satisfied with the Elvira interview and I'd been a ninny about the guys on the street. After a while I got out the telephone book and looked up the number of Elvira's agency.

"I forgot to ask you," I said when she came on the line, "What do you think of Marigold Amsdecker?"

"I think she has the most ridiculous name I ever heard."

"Yeah, but aside from that?"

There was a moment's pause. "She's very efficient."

"You don't think she was hired for her looks?"

"Not entirely."

"Oren did have an eye for the ladies, didn't he? The receptionist isn't exactly a dog either."

"She's utterly charming."

"You think Oren ever fooled around with the help?"

"Oren always meant business."

I wanted her to explain that, but before I could press it, she said she had other things to do and broke off.

I tried to reach Jim at Camillo's hotel and was told that he had checked out the afternoon after I left. He left word that they were returning to Guanajuato. I called him there. He was out and so was Juanita.

It was still early in the afternoon, but I decided to have a beer and went down to the hotel bar. It was nicely deserted, except for an amorous couple at a table in the corner and two characters at the bar. I ordered a Heineken and nibbled on peanuts piled in a wooden bowl. The characters were arguing about the comparative merits of baseball and football. The bigger man was winning. He said if baseball were worth a shit, Texas would have a winning team. What counted was football and Dallas was a winner. What about Houston? asked the smaller man. Don't talk about Houston and football, said the big man.

The little man was facing me, saw my grin and said, "What do you think?"

"I figure if Bum Phillips had stayed, Houston would've had a winner before long."

The big man glanced my way.

"Bum couldn't coach shit."

"I doubt he ever tried."

"He's trying now, at New Orleans."

"You're too much of an authority for me," I said.

After finishing the beer I went to my room and called Marigold. She sounded depressed and I asked what was wrong.

"Mr. Sutton, one of the board members, thinks we should close the office until we know what has happened to Mr. Fletcher."

"Is Sutton the uncle attorney?"

"Yes."

"What'll that do, put you out of a job?"

"It could. I just don't know what'll happen. The board is meeting tonight."

"I thought all boards met for lunch."

"Ours meets at night."

"So you're available after dinner—how about I pick you up when it's over and we'll have a drink. We can celebrate or hold a wake, depending."

She was silent a moment, then, in a voice with some surprise in it, said, "Yes, that'd be nice. You're very thoughtful."

I wondered if it were thoughtfulness, opportunism or overlong abstinence and decided it was some of each.

While I was dining alone in the hotel, I noticed the two sports fans at a table some distance away. The big guy was talking. I tried to imagine what these guys did and how come they would be boozing in the afternoon and eating together at night. They didn't look related; the big one was fair with a moderately red face and hair that covered his ears. He talked while eating and ate a lot. The little guy was dark with unfashionably trim black hair and dark eyebrows that made him look thoughtful, almost brooding, when he didn't smile. He had finished his dinner early and sat smoking a cigarette while watching his partner. Once or twice he glanced around the room but made no eye contact with me. The big guy concentrated on his plate exclusively. His hands made the knife and fork he wielded look like children's utensils.

Probably salespeople, I decided. The monster was an ex-football player brought along to impress the marks and the little guy handled closings.

I was up in my room reading Japrisot's *The Lady in the Car with Glasses and a Gun* when the telephone rang.

"Meeting's over," said Marigold.

"We celebrating or—"

"Temporary victory, I guess."

She sounded tired, and when I commented on that, she said it was just a reaction—she'd be over it by the time I picked her up out front.

"What'd you like to do?" I asked as she popped into my cab and settled back.

"You decide."

I'd been looking through the visitor's guide earlier and directed the driver to a dance place.

It was a little smoky and a lot noisy. Lights came and went, couples gyrated, jumped, jerked and hopped about on the floor and others leaned across small tables and mixed drinks, talking, laughing and occasionally hooting.

I really prefer cuddling dances but get energetic if the music's right and was delighted to find that Marigold had a perfect sense of rhythm and all the right moves. I don't have names for anything I do, I just react to the tune and that can be disastrous with the wrong partner, but we were in sync from the first, and when we sat down to our drinks, we were both sweating and puffing.

She laughed and shook her head after taking a drink of gin and tonic.

"Haven't done anything like this in years—"

"You move like you did it every night."

"Right now I think I'd like to."

I put my hand on the table, conveniently close to hers, but she didn't seem to notice.

We finished a drink, ordered another and got up to dance again. The second set was more sedate and I held her close. She was stiff and withholding at first, then gradually yielded a bit and finally bent her head forward until the pelt-like hair brushed my chin. I turned my head and lowered my cheek for the brushing contact.

When we sat down again, she put her hand on the table and I covered it with mine.

"You are an astonishingly assertive dancer," she said.

"What's that mean?"

"You lead with total authority."

"Is that good or bad?"

"It's good," she said, with a note of surprise. "I enjoy it. Did you dance like that with your married lady?"

"We never danced. Under the circumstances we never had anything like a normal date. Everything was secret—"

Or sneaky, if you got down to cases.

"That sounds awfully sad to me," she said.

"Yeah. Actually, now, it sounds kind of stupid."

"And how long did it last?"

"A couple years—maybe more."

"I wonder if you ever got over it. You still think about her a lot?"

"I don't forget, but no, it's nothing like an obsession. It was part of growing up, and if you don't mind, I'd just as soon drop the subject, okay?"

"Okay. Let's dance some more."

During the first slow number she didn't put her face against my chest as she had before. The second number was fast and near the end of it, as we separated briefly, she broke into a smile that graduated to a laugh, and when the piece ended, she squeezed me hard.

"Aren't we something?" she said.

I ordered a bottle of champagne and we got halfway through it, holding hands and laughing a lot. Suddenly she leaned forward.

"Let's go."

"You want to go home?"

She shook her head. "I want to go with you. Can we do that?"

"Why not?"

She was wildly excited and exciting. I tried desperately to keep from losing control and remembered the college Romeo who'd assured me you can prolong the action by thinking of fishing or baseball during the act, but it didn't work; nothing existed but the woman under, over and beside me.

Later, when I woke her and she responded warmly, I wondered if I'd louse everything up by telling her I wanted this to be permanent. I couldn't believe there'd ever be anything I'd seriously want beyond her.

I woke in the morning as she rose and headed for the bathroom. The naked body, so slender and graceful, disappeared too quickly and I lay back, staring at the ceiling and preparing myself for when she returned. I expected she'd be upset about losing her head and spending the night with me.

Suddenly she peeked around the hall corner.

"I'm going to shower—you want in here first?"

"No—go ahead."

"I won't be long."

I didn't believe that but in almost no time she was out, wrapped in a towel, and I went in to shower and shave. She'd left no mess, just a steamy room and wet towels on hangers. She'd even managed to leave the bath mat almost dry.

When I came out, she was sitting before the bureau mirror, making up her eyes. The short hair was mink-smooth and fluffy. I had a brief, ungenerous thought that hair so styled was very convenient for one-night stands.

"If we do this often," she said, "I'll have to start carrying a larger purse, so I can bring a change of underwear."

"Give me your sizes and I'll buy what you need."

She glanced at me in the mirror.

"Are you big on lingerie?"

"I get big, yeah. Relatively, I mean."

"Relative to what?"

"Relative to when I'm small."

She laughed, put down the eye pencil and turned. The slip was peach-colored with spaghetti straps and a low front. It looked fresh as a summer salad.

"What time do you have to be at work?"

"That's no problem. The board sleeps late."

"How about your—what do I call her—mother-in-law?"

"That's good enough, and don't worry. I called her from the john last night."

"Doesn't she disapprove?"

"I didn't ask—and she's never tried to run my life."

I wanted to ask if she'd done this often before but managed to stifle the impulse. It might have been because I didn't want to know, more likely because I didn't want to make her mad.

Down at breakfast I suggested she return to Mexico with me.

"I need an interpreter, someone I can trust."

She dabbed at her mouth with her napkin and frowned at me.

"You think I can just waltz out on my job?"

"Well, no, but aren't things sort of in suspension right now?"

"This is a very key time," she said with forced patience. "I told you, I want to be the Foundation director and I'm certainly not going to improve my chances by going to Mexico. My work's important, to me and to other people."

I realized she was offended because I wasn't taking her career seriously.

"Well, couldn't you argue that it was important to find out what had happened to Fletcher and you could help me do it?"

"That's ridiculous."

"Okay. Let's look at a few things. Doesn't a foundation director have to know about investing and all that stuff?"

"Those things are the responsibility of the board."

"Okay, how about Elvira—don't you think she might be interested in the job?"

"Yes," she admitted. "I'm sure she is."

"So you've got to work on the lawyer and the banker. Which one do you start with?"

"You make me sound awfully calculating."

"Come on, you've admitted you're ambitious, why be coy about your plans?"

"Okay," she said, turning grim. "Mr. Sutton has always liked me. He flirts in his old-world way, pretending he thinks of me as a daughter. I'm not sure what he thinks of Elvira but suspect he considers her a pushy woman. Sometimes they can be almost chummy, then again things get bristly between them. Her aggressiveness always annoyed him, except when she turned it against Oren. Then it amused him. I think he was always jealous of Oren."

"How about the banker?"

"Avery's suspicious of her but probably wouldn't care what happened as long as he was able to stay in charge of the investments. He keeps insisting bad times are coming and we've got to have an enormous reserve on hand for use when the crash comes."

"Wouldn't a crash make the reserves go blooey?"

"He doesn't think so, not if we're invested strongly in precious metals. He's particularly excited about platinum. He says it's ridiculously underpriced."

"Are you sure Daphne hasn't got any say in any of this?"

"Positive. The Foundation's entirely separate from the estate. Oren was very careful about that."

"Did he tell you as much?"

"Yes, he did."

"Were you two pretty chummy?"

Her eyes narrowed. "We weren't 'chummy' at all. I set employers entirely apart."

"In that case I withdraw the offer for you to be my interpreter."

She smiled, so I knew I'd recovered a little ground, but she didn't laugh, so there was still a ways to go.

"It seems to me," I said, "that there could be an awful lot of legal hassle going on with the Foundation in the near future. Daphne's cozy with a lawyer; I'll bet she goes after the bundle. And there could be big trouble with that cozy little board. You really want to be in the middle of all that?"

"I don't see any choice."

"You've got to have it?"

"I've got to try for it. If I don't make it, I'll survive."

"You're something of a gambler, huh?"

"I'm here with you."

"Being with me's a gamble?"

"Yes. When you called from Mexico, I bought the pills so this time I won't get pregnant. But all things considered, I shouldn't have let myself get involved. You may just be trying to use me— now don't get sore—I don't really know you that well. I don't know what to expect of you. But last night was so much fun I just decided, what the heck, I've been smart and careful so long I'm sick of it, and when we danced, I knew we'd go to bed together. When we did, I figured at first I'd leave as soon as you slept—only it went so beautifully I just had to know what you'd be like in the morning."

"How was I?"

"Lovely. You didn't turn indifferent, or grabby—you stayed interested. Most women don't feel sexy in the morning, you know, they turn practical when it's time to get up."

We drank coffee and talked until we had the coffee shop to ourselves and then the coffee break people drifted in and we became aware of them and a little self-conscious about ourselves and went back to our room.

I found out she could feel sexy in the morning if she'd had breakfast first.

XIX

She went home after lunch and I made an appointment with Sutton, the attorney uncle. I'd expected a doddering old man, but instead he was tall, square-shouldered and domineering. He wore his blue-gray hair stylishly full but trim, his smooth jaw was assertive and his narrow, deep-set eyes darted over my face, clothes and mannerisms so intently I felt like a nude model before a freshman art class.

"So," he said, offering me his crisp, hard hand, "you're the ex-TV man Daphne once romanced."

"Right now I'm the guy she hired to find her husband."

"Whatever," he said, and sat down.

His home was much in the style of Oren Fletcher's but a trifle older and not quite so expansive. A house lady with the looks of a *Playboy* cartoon French maid and the mien of an English butler had greeted me at the door and deferentially led me to the study just off the entry hall. It had no desk, only an ornate table with a gleaming top whose surface held only varnish. One wall was covered with a built-in bookshelf packed with leather-bound works of encyclopedic solemnity. Beside the table stood a magazine rack and I was startled to see the one cover in view was *Penthouse*.

When I looked from that back to the man, his eyes met mine straight on.

"Well?" he challenged.

"I need to ask some impertinent questions."

"Ask."

"What do you think of Daphne's lawyer, Harlan?"

"He's a junior partner in my firm. What would you expect I'd think of him?"

"I'm not thinking of his legal competence. I'm interested in his relationship with Daphne."

"That's none of my business."

"You think he might be planning to marry her?"

He stared at me for a moment and tilted his head back a fraction.

"It's possible."

"You think she's interested?"

"I doubt it."

"Did Harlan have anything to do with preparing Fletcher's will?"

"He drew it up; I approved it."

"Can you tell me who the chief beneficiaries are?"

"The Foundation and his wife."

"No one else?"

"Those are the chief beneficiaries."

"You mind telling me in what proportions?"

"The larger amount goes to the Foundation. He left enough for Daphne to be very comfortable but shorted her enough to let her know he wasn't a fool."

"Who do you think would gain the most from his disappearance?"

"Fletcher."

I watched him for a moment and saw the beginnings of a smile at the corners of his thin mouth.

"What would he gain?" I asked.

"Freedom."

"He couldn't buy that?"

"He didn't have the imagination."

"Would you explain that?"

"No." His grin showed long teeth and receding gums.

"Would you say he had a special interest in young women?"

"Special? No. Marked, perhaps."

"Is that a family trait?"

"Only on the male side so far as I know."

"How did Elvira Mumford fit in with that?"

He frowned. "What kind of a stupid question is that? She didn't 'fit in' to anything with Fletcher."

"Daphne says she was his mistress."

"That's ridiculous—"

He started to say more, then looked past me and closed his mouth. I turned to see the French maid enter with a tray which held a bottle of Courvoisier and two crystal glasses.

She set it on the coffee table between us and automatically poured two generous portions. Her breasts surged forward in the low-cut blouse as she leaned over.

Sutton thanked her. She nodded without glancing at either of us and left.

When he leaned forward, picked up his glass and lifted it in a token salute, I did the same and we both sipped the umber drink.

I asked him to describe the Foundation's procedures for making grants.

"It's quite simple. Ms. Amsdecker screens the mail, picks appeals that either fit our formula or seem interesting enough to intrigue Fletcher and writes briefs on them. These are distributed to board members who supposedly review them prior to the quarterly meetings where we go through the proposals. Since Fletcher had okayed all those included, we could assume they were acceptable to him and the only ones that really came under discussion were those we figured he had no serious stake in."

"Are you saying it was a rubber-stamp board?"

"Mostly. Before Elvira, when the other member was Fletcher's older sister, only I bitched about some of the choices. Then the sister died and with Elvira on my side, we stirred things up now and again."

"Was there a hassle over the Camillo grant?"

"You mean the Mexican deal? Yes. We went into the arena on that one."

"You and Elvira were for it?"

He nodded, grinning.

"Why?"

"Elvira knew quite a bit about the operation—she knows just

about everything there is to know about programs for the elderly. I went along with her."

"How'd Fletcher react?"

"Like his favorite hound had bit his leg."

"But he prevailed."

"Sure. He thanked us for our opinions and had Amsdecker write a denial."

"Was Elvira sore about that?"

He gave me a sour look. "She was annoyed, but I hardly think it made her homicidal."

I grinned, trying to let him know I agreed, but he did not look mollified.

"Ever been to Mexico?" I asked him after we'd both had more of the Courvoisier.

He shook his head. "I'm not interested in primitive societies."

We talked some more, but he was obviously becoming bored, so I finished my drink, thanked him and stood up. The maid appeared magically and escorted me out.

XX

The trouble, I told Marigold, is that when rich men get murdered, you think it had to be for money. You forget they get killed for all the reasons poor people do; jealousy, envy and plain old hate. She said that was very profound. I told her Sutton had said Oren showed a marked interest in young women and thought any notion that he might be involved with Elvira Mumford was ridiculous.

"A lot *he* knows," she said.

"What do you know?"

"*I* believe he was going to marry her."

"Yeah? Why?"

"I knew Oren."

I put down my glass and stared at her. She had a stubborn expression I'd not seen on her before and it stayed as she got up to pour more wine for us. We'd been eating in her kitchen. April and her mother-in-law were off somewhere for an overnight visit with relatives. Marigold had cooked chicken with white wine sauce and pale grapes that left me stuffed as a Christmas goose and almost as lively.

"That was a really great meal," I told her.

"You think I'm wrong."

"No, but how come you didn't mention this before?"

She shrugged. "It's just intuition; I didn't think it was worth bringing up."

"So what's behind it?"

"Oh," she said, waving the bottle in a short arc, "it was the way he looked after he'd been on the phone with her, or an expression he'd get when she spoke up at board meetings. He'd look sort of proud when she agreed with him and a little hurt when she didn't. He never seemed to have any real reaction to opinions of the others—he didn't need their support and he ignored their opposition."

"Sutton said she bucked him on the Camillo decision—and he joined her."

"Yes," she said after taking a drink of wine. "That was one of the times when Oren looked hurt. In fact he was a little angry. That tickled Mr. Sutton."

"Did Sutton and Fletcher disagree often?"

"Not really. But when they did, you could feel Sutton's rancor. I think what bothered him most was that he couldn't annoy Oren. Oren had a way of rising up and flying over opposition, as though he were unaware of it. Mr. Sutton couldn't stand being ignored."

I drank some wine while admiring her golden hair.

"Did you figure Elvira'd be good for Fletcher?"

She laughed. "You think I'm a frustrated matchmaker?"

"I think you're a great cook and a beautiful woman. Can we go to bed now or do we have to do dishes first?"

"People who are married do dishes first."

"But do we want to go to bed thinking after a while we'll have to get up and do them?"

"I doubt I'll think about that a lot."

Tuesday afternoon I had a date to visit Avery Robinson, the retired banker on Fletcher's board. On an impulse I suggested that Marigold come along and break the ice by introducing me as her fiancé. From her expression I knew immediately I'd made a mistake.

"What'd that accomplish?" she asked with a frown.

"It'll impress him, inspire me and maybe commit you."

She stared at me for a moment and the frown became less severe.

"Is this a sneaky proposal?"

"I'd rather call it a bold proposition."

"Marriage is the death of romance."

Dishes, I thought, are the death of romance. I'd got up early and done them.

"Okay," I said. "You want to marry rich."

"You want to start a fight?"

"No. I want you to come along with me."

She suddenly smiled and said okay.

He lived in a condominium, one of those bright, tall, shining memorials to affluence and modernity. From the look of him, as he met us in the living room, he might have been more at home in a primitive cave. His broad head settled into hunched shoulders on a thick body with short legs and long arms that ended in pawlike hands with black hair and yellowed nails. He reminded me of Oscar Homolka, the actor who played the Russian general opposite Michael Caine in *Funeral in Berlin.*

It was disappointing to hear him speak perfectly clear, unaccented English.

"It's a tragedy," he told Marigold as he held her hands after introductions. "Oren was too valuable to lose. Too valuable." He looked accusingly at me. "Something's got to be done. I don't understand those Mexicans—why haven't they done anything?"

I shook my head sympathetically, but he wasn't impressed.

"It's that fellow down there, the one who runs a hotel for old men. He's got Oren somewhere, trying to make him give money to that crazy place. He's mad—he hounded Oren unmercifully—"

"How?" I asked.

"He kept calling him and he tried to work the board. That Mumford woman fell right in with him, so did Sutton. I've never seen Oren more hurt. The whole scheme was right down Mumford's alley, you know—she lives off old people—"

"Come on, Avery," said Marigold, "she works because she loves it. She doesn't need her salary and you know it."

"I know no such thing. You're too trusting, my dear. She'd never work where she does if she didn't have to, no sir! She wouldn't go down to the gutter just to keep from being bored, don't you ever believe it."

"Was this the first grant that those two argued with Fletcher about?" I asked.

"Yup," said Avery, nodding his broad head. "It was a thing to watch, I'll tell you. Sutton, he always resented Oren, you know. He's a fellow used to his own way in the world and here's this whippersnapper nephew who's only related by marriage anyway up there in the driver's seat with all the control. He sees right away where the wind blows. This Mumford woman who's Oren's old sweety that he brought on the board because he's still got eyes for, she turns on him in front of his colleagues. Oh, Sutton loved that. He doesn't give a hoot in hell for anybody that hasn't got a pile, but all of a sudden he's the philanthropist with a bleeding heart for broken-down old men. If I hadn't felt so sorry for Oren, I'd have had to laugh."

I asked him if he always agreed with Fletcher's decisions.

"Always, didn't I, Marigold? His judgment was flawless. He understood these people who run charities, could see right through them, you know? They aren't all saints, not by a jugful. It wasn't the grant requests that shaped his decisions, it was the men and women who made them. He always talked to them himself. He always said, character is everything. Any slick director can hire someone to write a proposal—that's a profession itself; what counted for Oren was the man behind it all because that's who runs the organization that uses your money, not the slick articles that write all the fancy details for hire."

"How'd you feel about his investment judgment?"

His brown eyes darted a glance at me and he scowled.

"It was all right. A little limited."

"Did he depend on you for advice in that direction?"

"Oh yes." He looked at Marigold who gazed back innocently. His eyes returned to me. "He had the good judgment to trust me implicitly and I never gave him cause to regret it. Never."

There was more conversation but not much information, so I suggested we leave, thanked him and drove us back to Marigold's apartment.

"Avery's taken this very hard," she said. "He seems to have aged fifteen years."

I sprawled on her beige couch, clasped my hands behind my head and leaned back.

"The Fletcher Foundation's a trust, isn't it?" I asked.

"Yes, of course."

"Who administers it? Avery Robinson's bank?"

"The bank he used to run, yes. He was chairman of the board until he retired two years ago."

"So he handles investments for the Foundation and makes financial reports at each meeting of the trustees?"

"That's right."

"How're these investments doing?"

"Fine, according to the last report. What're you getting at?"

"I got the notion he was a little defensive about it all. How closely did Fletcher keep tabs on him?"

"Pretty close. He always kept track of everything important to him—he didn't overlook much of anything and don't forget, he was a banker himself."

"Does Avery have connections in Mexico?"

"He knows Juan García, the banker in Guadalajara. He sent a letter of introduction with Oren when he went down there the first time."

I stared at her and she stared back.

"You think there's something strange there?" she asked.

"Yeah. García tried to make me think he hadn't known about Fletcher's account being withdrawn until I showed up. I don't buy that."

She frowned.

"How much do you think he had on deposit there?" I asked.

"Anything from a few thousand to a couple of hundred thousand."

"Would that be Foundation money?"

"Probably. The board authorized foreign accounts for him."

"Why?"

She gave me a rueful grin. "Because it was his, I guess. He

always put money in towns where he spent any time. It was a combination commitment and security blanket, I suppose. It gave him instant access and he knew money made friends, gave him acceptance, you know—"

"Uh-huh. The universal service club of the almighty dollar. Did he have accounts in Guanajuato and Mexico City?"

"I think so. Certainly in Mexico City."

"Can you find out for me?"

"I could ask Avery."

I shook my head. "Don't."

She didn't like that but couldn't think of an argument and just looked worried.

"When's your mother-in-law coming back?"

"Tomorrow."

"Well, let's lie down and think, okay?"

She thought that over, smiled and said okay, let's.

We didn't think a whole lot but we rested well after a while and talked some. She said she didn't believe Avery'd do anything wrong and she positively couldn't imagine that he'd let anything happen to Oren.

"He feels like a father toward him," she assured me.

"Ever hear of infanticide?"

"Oren was no infant."

"I know—but back when I read some history, I found lots of cases where fathers killed sons that threatened them. And I don't figure all the cases got into the history books."

"You're beginning to sound like a cynical reporter."

"How come a woman loved always turns into a critic?"

"Are you generalizing from a very broad experience?"

"Not very, but did you really hear what I said?"

"Sure."

"You maybe heard but you weren't listening. I said a loved woman, not a laid one. A cynical reporter wouldn't have said 'loved.' "

She puckered her lips a touch but didn't seem quite as impressed as I felt she should have been.

"Guys are supposed to be the ones that turn hard when they get soft," I said.

"What kind of a non sequitur is that supposed to be?"

"Ever hear the story of the guy and his girl who passed the jewelry window one night?" She shook her head. "The girl said, 'Hey, look at that beautiful ring—will you buy me that?' And of course he said sure, first thing in the morning. And they went to bed, and when the girl was snuggling up afterward, she asked what time they'd go to the store and he said they wouldn't go and she said you promised and he said yes, he did, but he was always soft when he was hard and hard when he was soft."

She laughed and said girls never got hard, just tender, and she did.

In the morning she was thinking tough and over breakfast told me not to get foolish notions but agreed about Avery and said she'd check out his investments. I said I was proud she took me seriously and she could be damned sure I wasn't going to get foolish notions and I'd check back when I got around to it.

After breakfast, when I was moving toward the door, she asked wasn't I going to kiss her good-bye?

"I was afraid you'd think that was sloppy sentimental."

"That depends on the kiss."

So I came back and our kiss wasn't sentimental. In fact it bordered on the climactic. I went down the stairs wobbly-kneed but with firm resolve.

XXI

"Your girlfriend's teacher was forty-three," Al Lutz told me over the telephone. "Weighed a hundred forty-six, had brown eyes and taught history. He'd been hustling students for over four years when he got involved with the Durado chick and he was so gaga over her everybody on campus knew it."

"How about Jim?"

"From what I hear, it all but got on TV news, so I guess he must've."

"How'd the guy kill himself?"

"Very thorough. He took a short swim through a spillway at a big dam. Below that dam there's a great collection of very big rocks. You get the picture?"

I said I thought so.

"He didn't leave any note or any pile of clothes on a dock. I don't believe any suicide ever did. Why the hell'd they take their clothes off if they wanted to drown, for Christ's sake?"

"Maybe so they wouldn't sink in too shallow water. Did you pick up anything on how Juanita reacted to all this?"

"She went to the funeral and carried a handkerchief. My guy couldn't tell me if she got it wet or not."

"How about Jim, did he go too?"

"Yup."

"Was there any question about this being a suicide?"

"If there was, it was asked too low for my boy to hear about it. What else you need?"

"Got anything on the wife?"

"Not a peep. No leads."

I thanked him, promised a bonus and hung up.

It was late Thursday afternoon when I joined Jim in the bar and
ordered a margarita. He smiled gently and lifted his glass to me.

"Juanita was worried," he said in mild reproof.

"I left a note."

"It was rather enigmatic."

"I'm sorry."

"Tell her."

I assured him I would, and as I drank, marveled at my fickle-
ness. A few days earlier I'd have been tickled foolish to know that
Juanita gave a damn about anything I did. Now, for all the remembered adolescent fascination, I suddenly found her cold,
remote and even a little dull. Was Marigold right, did I only fall in
love with women I'd gone to bed with?

I looked at Jim who gazed back with his sad, benevolent smile.

"Look," I said, "I owe both of you apologies for more than
anything to do with taking off and leaving you a couple days ago."

He lifted his eyebrows.

I drank a little of the margarita and set it aside.

"I haven't been getting anywhere, you know. I've had to start
checking on every conceivable lead, and a few that are just about
inconceivable—"

"So you've made inquiries about Juanita and me?"

"Yeah."

"Have you learned anything disturbing?"

"Uh-huh. Juanita told me her mother died in childbirth. Does
she really believe that?"

"That's what I told her. I hope you haven't told her anything
different."

"Do you know where her mother is?"

"No. If you have found out, I'm not interested."

"I didn't. But I did learn Juanita had a very close friend in
college who committed suicide. An instructor."

"A pitiful episode," he said.

"You know why this guy killed himself?"

"According to gossip, it was unrequited love."

"I hear she loved back pretty good."

He shrugged. "If so, why'd the man kill himself?"

"I wondered about that."

"You have a theory?"

"I'd like to know if you do."

He sighed and leaned forward, resting his elbows on the table.

"I think he wanted her to marry him and she put him off. He was a man with problems. A failed poet, a broken marriage, an unhappy childhood. He had what the young people a few years back called 'bad karma.' A man born to be unhappy."

"It sounds as though you knew him personally."

"Eau Claire is not a big town. It is easy to learn about people there and I made a point of finding out about this man."

"Were you upset by Juanita's involvement with him?"

"Of course, wouldn't you be? Here is a middle-aged failure, a man of experience in a responsible position as an instructor, taking advantage of a naive young girl—"

"Who apparently encouraged but refused to marry him?"

"She had not yet learned how to put off people infatuated with her beauty. She was flattered by his interest and intensity."

"Did you try to make her stop seeing him?"

"My friend," he smiled, "I have never been truly stupid. Foolish on occasion, but never stupid. I never played the stern patriarch. I asked questions now and then, which I hoped would make her think a little. You may suspect that Juanita is not terribly bright because she shows no intellectual interests and has little to say, but she is extremely perceptive. She thinks a great deal and with remarkable clarity."

I had met retarded youngsters like that. They sometimes have very limited range of thought but bring an intensity of focus on areas of personal interest that can give the impression of genius when you see their specialized accomplishments.

"So you figure she turned him down because he was a loser?"

"I think she refused him because she realized that she could not help him."

"How'd she react to his suicide?"

"She was terribly depressed, of course. And angry. I'm convinced she blamed herself as anyone does when a person they have cared about commits suicide. She didn't talk about it much, except to tell me she should have been able to save him. And I said, perhaps foolishly, would it have been worth her life to save his? She thought about that a few days and finally told me I was right, it was better that he died. We never spoke of the man again."

"Did she think people at the school blamed her?"

"I don't know. As I told you, it is a small town and small towns run to gossip, blame and guilt."

I saw Juanita approaching, and before she could sit down, asked if she'd take a walk with me.

"Of course," she said, without looking at Jim.

We walked down the road along the hotel's west wall and I repeated the confession I'd made to Jim about investigating their past. She glanced at me sharply but made no comment.

"Would you mind telling me what you felt when your instructor killed himself?"

She took a deep breath and frowned. "I was angry. He did it to spite me, you know. He said I'd be sorry. That's a mean kind of love, when a person will do something that stupid to punish you. It's all self."

She gave me a direct, accusing look.

"That's the way men are. They think only of themselves."

"Is your father like that?"

She thought for a while as we turned right at the bottom of the drive and stepped up on the walk that ran along the east end of the hotel. The sun made her tanned cheeks glow and her sleek hair shine. She walked with deliberate steps that made her wide skirt swing gently; her toes pointed straight ahead.

"My father," she said at last, "is like other men, only not quite so much."

"I don't think I understand what that means."

She shrugged, letting me know that was my problem.

The walk up the east side of the hotel ascended by widely spaced steps and was separated from the wall by a narrow garden filled with bright flowers unfamiliar to me. Juanita looked only at the steps before her.

"Why didn't you tell us where you were going when you left Camillo's?" she asked.

"I had to be positive no one knew where I was."

She glanced my way.

"It seemed safer."

"You are telling me you were afraid someone would try to kill you again?"

"Yeah."

"Is there a woman where you went?"

I smiled at her. "There are women almost everywhere."

She didn't smile back. "You know what I meant."

"I was after information, not romance."

Her lovely mouth twisted in a brief expression of contempt and she halted to face me.

"When we danced, you weren't thinking of information."

"I sure wasn't."

"This woman, where you went, does she know where you are now?"

"No."

"You don't trust her either?"

"I can't afford to trust anyone right now."

"You don't trust me," she said, "because you think I let Oren make love to me."

"Did he?"

She lifted her chin. "He wanted to. I told him no."

"But you went out with him."

"So?"

"You'd have married him if he got a divorce, wouldn't you?"

She gave me a "who knows?" look and moved up the next step. I walked beside her.

"Did he tell you he was going to get a divorce?"

"We never talked about that."

"What did you talk about?"

"*He* talked."

"What'd he say?"

"He said he liked Mexico."

"That's all?"

"The way he talked, that took a long time to say."

"Did he try to make plans with you?"

"Of course."

"Like what?"

"It is all nothing to do with you."

"It might have everything to do with what I'm trying to find out. Anything that'd give me a clue to his plans would help—"

"His talk had nothing to do with his plans. It was all what you'd call a hustle."

"Did Jim know about this?"

She halted once more and we faced each other. I couldn't tell if there was anger or fear in the dark eyes which flickered over my face. All that was clear was the intensity of concentration.

"Don't ask him about it," she said softly. I felt that she wanted it to sound like a request, but it came out more like a prayer.

"He didn't know?"

She looked away.

"Is he jealous of the men who want you?"

"He's afraid of them." She looked at me again and stepped closer. "He is afraid of being left alone. My mother ran away, deserting him when I was a child. They told me she ran off with a man—"

"Who's 'they'?"

"Kids at school. They knew about it—"

"In grade school?"

She nodded and closed her eyes.

"Back when you were seeing the instructor, did you tell Jim what was going on?"

She shook her head wearily. "He didn't want to know about boys in my life from the time I was very small. He told me they couldn't be trusted, that they'd be cruel, that because I was so pretty, they'd only want to use me and spoil me—as if I were a delicate doll that'd get shabby and dirty with handling—"

"Did you complain to him about that?"

"Yes. When I was in college. And he said, 'Dolls don't get pregnant.' Before that he'd never mentioned anything like the possibility that I could have a baby. I think he refused to face it."

"Did you quarrel?"

"No. Never about serious things. Not ever. We had no confrontations. I never let him know I'd heard about Mother running away, and when I was gone overnight with the man at college, he said nothing to me about it. Just pretended nothing strange had happened. He would just tell me to be happy."

"Were you surprised when your lover committed suicide?"

She stared at a patch of grass beside the walk away from the hotel.

"No. He said he was going to if I said no and I said no so he knew I meant it."

"Wasn't that tough to do?"

"No. I thought it was best for him. He had proved to me that he could not stop drinking and smoking pot and he said I was the most wonderful thing that had ever happened to him and it didn't seem like there was any hope for him, he was bound to kill himself sooner or later and so it might as well be sooner. Killing himself was the only way to save his dignity and make me remember him always."

"I hear your father went to his funeral with you."

She stared at me. "You heard that? Is that the sort of thing a detective can learn just by poking around?"

"He usually needs help."

"You hire people?"

"Yeah."

She continued to stare at me and became very thoughtful.

"So you can pay for information?"

"Yeah, does that interest you personally?"

She was still thinking when Jim appeared at the top of the elongated stairs. I greeted him and Juanita, without turning, said, "Tell him nothing of this." Then, with a smile, she walked up to meet him.

XXII

I went back to my room, pulled off my shoes and stretched out on the firm bed. Through the open window I heard the peacock squawking somewhere near the pool beside the bar. The beams overhead looked black and the arched ceiling glowed as if the great bricks were made of gold.

I tried to think about Juanita and our conversation, but Marigold's face intruded, making me lonely. I dozed and during one in a series of flash dreams saw the green candy mummy which spoke to me and I woke abruptly, thinking it had given me the solution to Oren Fletcher's disappearance. The illusion was so strong I got up, padded over to the bureau and pulled out the figure, hoping it would bring back words in the dream but all it offered was the silent scream.

Where'd be the least likely spot to find a murdered man? How about a cemetery. Maybe the guy who delivered the candy mummy subconsciously gave himself away—the threat to me was based on what had already been done to the original victim.

I sat on the bed with the figure at my side and stared out at the bank of bright blossoms across the sunny courtyard.

Nonsense. Dream-drugged, that's all.

I went down to the lobby, entered the telephone booth and dug out my charge card. Eventually I reached Lieutenant Moreno of the Mexico City police. He not only recognized my name at once, he sounded genuinely pleased to know I was still trying to find Fletcher.

"No," he said, "there have been no new developments here. The car you went over the cliff in was rented under your name with a telephone call. That is, the arrangements were made by that means. No one admits knowing who picked up the car or what they looked like. The signature is an obvious forgery."

He asked what I'd learned and I told him as much as seemed worth mentioning, which didn't include my concerns about Jim and his daughter. Finally I told him about my cemetery theory.

He said that was an interesting idea and sounded as if he meant it. I asked him if such a thing could be arranged.

"Anything can be arranged if one knows the right people and has enough money."

"You think that'd be Camillo?"

"Could be. I will check into it."

"I've got another little problem," I told him. "The police here seem hostile. When I got jumped by a couple local boys outside a nightclub, they acted as if it were my fault and implied I was a lush. I got the impression this all came from ideas they got from the reports of my ride over the cliff near Mexico City. Why'd that be?"

He asked for more details and I went over it all with him. He said he could only assume the local people were unhappy about a foreigner making an investigation in their territory.

"Could you set them straight?"

"To them, a policeman from Mexico City is also an alien. It would not help, believe me."

"I guess what I really want to know is, did you believe me?"

"Mr. Champion, I believed you were sincere when you answered my questions. I believed what you said when I checked the facts."

I told him he was *un caballero* and he solemnly thanked me and concluded, *"Vaya con Dios."*

I walked down the road under the glaring sun and approached the police station gate. The young officer on duty had trouble deciphering my Spanish but eventually dispatched a messenger who returned, nodded and escorted me into Lieutenant Juárez's office. I found him standing behind the table desk, staring at an open file. He looked up as I entered and studied me thoughtfully with his watery eyes.

I greeted him in English, he responded in Spanish.

"Thanks for seeing me—I hope you'll make things easier by speaking English."

"How do you know I speak it?" He had no accent.

"Because of your eyes when I was here with Señor Durado."

He smiled, waved me into the chair before his desk, sat down and said, "When people assume I am ignorant, I try not to embarrass them."

"I only thought you were ignorant when you were offensive—and I thought it then because I was angry."

He nodded and the smile broadened for a moment. Then he became sober and thoughtful.

"So what brings you back to risk further offense?"

"I'm getting nowhere finding Fletcher. All I'm sure of is he didn't go voluntarily. He was an unpredictable man, but not impulsive and certainly not irresponsible. He took great care to establish an aura—"

Lieutenant Juárez's eyebrows lifted. "What is 'ora'?"

"Sorry—it's a style of a man—an impression of something special, like, 'he had a God-like aura.' "

"Ah," he nodded, "of course."

"He liked to keep women confused. I don't think he lied to them much, but he kept secrets and presented different fronts to different women, you know?"

"Yes. That is perfectly clear."

"Okay. So I think he's been killed. I'm positive somebody's trying to keep me from finding out how and where the body is. The last attempt to discourage me was a weird one, but it started me thinking and I need your help to follow up on a theory that's pretty wild but shouldn't be a lot of trouble to settle."

I told him of the green candy mummy. He listened solemnly, stared at me when I became silent and at last, very slowly, nodded his head and leaned forward.

"I will make inquiries."

I thanked him and he escorted me to the gate personally.

"Tell me," I said before going out, "why does this theory seem worth checking?"

"Yesterday afternoon I had a call from Lieutenant Moreno, of the Mexico police. We talked of you and Señor Fletcher. The lieutenant is a thorough, careful man. He had talked with people where you worked on TV. They told him you were a responsible, sober man. I asked why did you leave such employment and he said he had asked that same question and was told it was complicated but had nothing to do with responsibility or character. So."

I thanked him, he said, *"De nada,"* and we parted.

I was still absorbed in the dialogue with Juárez as I walked along the sunny street toward the hotel and was almost upon them when I looked up and saw Rodríguez and his friend with the jackal smile. I glanced around. The street was long and empty with no exits. I could turn and run—the police station was only a couple of blocks away—but the idea was too sensibly ignoble. I kept walking toward them.

They separated just enough to bar the sidewalk and we halted a yard apart.

"Buenas tardes," grinned the jackal.

Rodríguez lunged forward, swinging. I ducked and countered with a solid hook to his gut. He clutched at me as he doubled over and the jackal snuck in two head punches and a kick to my side which was intended for the family jewels. I stumbled while Rodríguez hung on and finally fell into the gutter.

I didn't hear the car pull up and rolled violently into its side trying to avoid more kicks. It gave me a hell of a jolt but didn't break anything and I flattened out to crawl under it as a hand clutched my ankle and someone said, "Whoa, hold on, pardner, you're okay—"

"Rescue," I thought.

I heard a sharp smack and then a few exclamations in Spanish followed by scrambling sounds and then running feet.

I scrambled out from under the car and blinked up at two men standing over me.

"Well, looky here," said an American voice, "it's the guy from Houston."

They helped me up and began brushing me off before I recognized the men I'd seen at the hotel in Houston. They were in great spirits. The smaller one kept chuckling and the big one grinned.

"What was that all about?" asked the lightweight.

"It's a long story—"

"Fine, we got lots of time. Get in the car and we'll take you where you were going."

I thanked them and said that wasn't necessary, but they said don't be silly and the big man bustled me into the car which was large, black and vaguely familiar. I wasn't thinking too well since my head was ringing from the punches I'd taken and my side ached from the kick. Instead of paying attention to what was happening, I kept thinking how much I'd like to catch the jackal alone.

It came to me after a few seconds that my rescuers hadn't asked where I was going, yet the car was moving swiftly and I jerked erect in the seat. The big man's hand, which had been resting on the seat back of me, suddenly gripped my shoulder.

"Relax, pal. Just take it easy."

"Where're we going?"

"Taking you to a doc—you're woozy—oughtta be checked out."

The sense of déjà vu was numbing. Suddenly I was back in Guadalajara, my head muzzy with pain, crowded between big men who told me *"Silencio"* and next I'd be in the gray Volkswagen, plunging over the cliff—

I closed my eyes, relaxed and tried to remember why this car was familiar. Of course, it had passed us the night when Juanita, Jim and I had walked to the restaurant.

I opened my eyes. The street was unfamiliar, narrow and deserted. We pulled up in front of a graying adobe wall with a small dark door and I was helped out firmly. The hand on my arm was big enough to hold a basketball like an orange and strong enough to break me like a dead twig. The small man opened the door and waved us in. The dark room smelled of mold, urine and something worse. We went through another room and stopped in what I assumed was the back of the house. There was a window painted over which admitted only enough light to cause dim shadows. I saw three chairs and a bare table.

"Sit down," said the big man.

I sat.

They took two chairs facing me. The big man wasn't smiling anymore. The little one's teeth gleamed in the shadows.

I wanted to ask, who are you guys, but it seemed foolish, so I just sat with my arms resting on my thighs, my hands crossed between my legs.

"What'd you tell the lieutenant?" asked the little man.

"That I figured Fletcher might be in the Guanajuato cemetery."

"What gave you that idea?"

"The candy mummy."

"Ah."

They didn't look at each other. I wondered, if they did, whether I'd have time to kick the big one and make a break for it. I decided it was very unlikely.

"What'd the lieutenant say to that?"

"He said it was a possibility."

"How much you getting for this job?"

"A hundred thousand."

"American?"

I nodded.

They looked at each other. I came to my feet and swung the chair at the big one. The seat edge caught him in the temple as he was rising. It was a nice solid chair and the contact made a horrible sound. He went down. I kicked the smaller man between his legs as he tried to jerk something from inside his coat and heard the shot but didn't think about it.

The outside sunshine was blinding. I looked both ways. An old man poked his scraggy head out an open door two houses away, jerked it back and slammed the door. I looked in the car, but of course the keys weren't there.

I thought of rolling under the car, hiding in the back, running down the endless, sunbaked street, breaking into one of the closed houses, but none of these ideas seemed safe. I leaned against the wall to the right of the door and listened. There were no sounds of pursuit. A truck appeared to my left and chugged slowly toward me. I bent my head toward the door, trying to listen, but the truck's engine blocked out all other sounds. The truck driver's face was obscured by reflections in the windshield and then the vehicle was moving past the parked Buick and suddenly I was running. I caught the back, threw myself inside and lay panting on the rough truck bed. It smelled of old manure, hay and heat. I looked back toward the driver and was relieved there was no window, only a blank wall. I was in a box open at the back and sat up to stare at the receding street where the black Buick stood, deserted and shrinking in the distance.

Slowly I pulled myself together and sat with my back against the box wall, looking out at the bright pale sky and the brown earth and buildings. I saw a child and then another on the sidewalk, then a shawled woman and a limping old man. Their brown faces were photographed in my mind, the woman with brown fatalistic eyes, a wide, full-lipped mouth clamped shut as if holding in pain; the man wrinkled, with wispy gray hair across his creased forehead, eyes squinting, almost closed. Neither of them glanced at the truck.

I stretched my legs out and felt pain in the right knee. It had been scraped when I jumped into the truck, but I didn't bother examining it or even my torn pants.

What'd the two men planned to do? Why'd they asked about my talk with Juárez and how did they know about it?

The truck made a turn and soon we were in the midst of traffic. I saw drivers behind us who stared at me and realized how strange I must look, a man in a summer suit and sport shirt, obviously a tourist, riding in the box of an ancient, wheezing truck. When it stopped at a red light, I carefully dropped off and limped over to the sidewalk.

There was a pay phone in a small hotel lobby nearby and after some difficulty I reached Lieutenant Juárez. At the end of my brief account he asked me to describe my location, told me not to move and hung up. I was still sitting in the booth when he came after me with two uniformed cops.

We found the Buick still on the street and they went inside while I waited. The old man looked out of the house nearby once more and this time lingered.

Lieutenant Juárez came out.

"You were alone with those two?"

I nodded.

He shook his head and went to the police car. After a few moments on the radio, he returned to my side. One of the escort cops came out, squinted against the bright light and flashed a curious glance my way.

"Both men are unconscious," the lieutenant told me. "One may be dead. I have called for an ambulance."

I remembered the sound of the chair hitting the big man's skull and figured he was the goner. The lieutenant told me to get in his car, and after a few words to the officer in the street, he took the driver's seat and we started back.

"We are going to go over everything you know about this case," he said. "Everything. You understand?"

I agreed.

It took a long time. Two detectives alternated with the lieutenant in asking questions and they spent what seemed to me a ridiculously large part of it reviewing my escape from the empty house.

Late in the afternoon Lieutenant Juárez told me the small man had died. When he tried to draw his gun from his belt, he apparently discharged it. The slug went through his inner thigh, severing the great artery, and he bled to death within minutes. The other man had a severe concussion and hadn't regained consciousness yet. They weren't sure he would.

"It shows," said the lieutenant, "how dangerous a determined man can be."

"Determined hell, I was scared to death."

"With some men, that comes to the same thing."

I tried to take some satisfaction from his obvious respect, but my clearest memory was of fear and the sickening sound of the chair against the big man's skull.

"Who were they?" I asked.

"The large man's name is Duringer. D.B. No idea what the initials stand for. His partner was Clyde Burton. Both from Houston, according to their driver's licenses. We're checking with the Houston police for more."

"Who owns the place where they took me?"

"We'll know soon."

We were in his office. I was sitting, much as I had in the darkened room with the Texans, slouched in a straight chair with my hands between my knees.

"You say you were terrified of these men," said the lieutenant, "yet you've mentioned no threats made or any physical abuse. What brought on the fear?"

"The ride in the car. It was too much like the time in Guadalajara. The deserted street, the empty house, the size of the goon's hand. I remembered going over the cliff and the total helplessness. I knew from the time I recognized them it was no coincidence they were here, and when they asked what I'd told you, it was all damned plain. That's why I didn't play dumb or get cute when they questioned me. There wasn't any point in holding back."

"And it also made them think you were too afraid to try anything, eh?"

"I wasn't planning anything out."

He smiled. "I think, deep in your mind, you were. The mind, she is very complicated. Is there anything else you want to know that we can help you with?"

"Yeah. Could you check out a guy named Camillo? He's a rich retired man, runs a hotel in Guadalajara where he takes care of old men. It's a charity. He knew Fletcher and is a friend of Jim Durado."

"I will make inquiries."

I thanked him, we shook hands and one of the detectives accompanied me to the gate where a car was waiting. The driver was the young cop who'd come around the night I had my run-in with Rodríguez.

He was cordial, as before, but I noticed he was nowhere near as talkative without Juanita's inspiration.

Back at the hotel I slipped into the lobby phone booth and put in a call to Daphne. She was out, not expected back until late.

I called Marigold.

To my intense relief she sounded very pleased and pleasure gave her voice an additionally rich quality. I said I'd been thinking of her. She said that was nice but didn't say she'd been thinking of me. I was suddenly too depressed to speak. After a moment's silence she asked how I was.

"I'd be a hell of a lot better if you were here."

"What's wrong?"

"I killed a guy this afternoon."

She was no more startled by that announcement than I was. I'd had no intention of telling her that when I dialed her number.

"I may have killed two of them. They had me in a room in a deserted house and were asking questions and I hit one with a chair and kicked the other. The guy I kicked shot himself and the other's in the hospital. They don't know if he'll live—"

"My God, are you in jail?"

"No. The police went back to the place with me and they know everything I do. I think they believe me. Maybe it'll turn out okay with them involved. The lieutenant's pretty okay."

"So why're you so down?"

"I panicked in that room. They didn't even threaten me. For all I knew they might've been a couple special investigators or something, but I was scared, and when I saw my chance, I went nuts. The guy I kicked, the one who shot himself, bled to death while I was in front of the house, trying to decide how to get away."

"All right," she said, "try not to think about it. You want me to come down there?"

"Yes."

"Is there an airport there?"

"No. You'll have to land in Guadalajara. I'll rent a car and meet you there. Find out about flight times and I'll call you back in half an hour, okay?"

"Give me an hour."

"Don't change your mind."

"I won't."

I walked to the bar, giddy from the conversation. Calm down, I told myself, you're not a goddamned kid.

"Well," said Jim as I joined him at his table, "you're looking gay."

I thought of telling him that was not a term used loosely in our times but let it go and ordered a beer.

"What happened to your face?" he asked.

"I met Rodríguez and his friend again."

He looked genuinely upset. He asked how I was and what had happened and I told him of the beginning but only said the attackers had been frightened off by people who came to help me. He clucked and said it was terrible, that Juanita really should have identified them as the men who'd jumped me before. My beer was delivered and I sipped at the glass edge while the head settled.

He asked where this happened.

"On my way back from the police station."

His wispy eyebrows lifted.

"I decided to talk with Lieutenant Juárez again. It turns out he speaks English very well."

Jim turned his glass with his slender fingers and shook his head, smiling ruefully.

"So—my role as interpreter was a farce, eh?"

"It wasn't your fault. He apparently enjoyed making us both look foolish."

"He certainly succeeded with me."

We drank and thought our thoughts about Lieutenant Juárez

and each other. I wondered if perhaps I should tell him everything that'd happened, but it seemed wiser to wait until Juanita was present. I wanted to watch them both when I told about the men from Houston.

"How'd you guess the lieutenant spoke English?" he asked.

"I don't know; he just seemed too wise all the time."

"I caught that too," he admitted, "but I assumed he did not speak English well and preferred not to reveal it. What'd you talk to him about?"

"Why I was sure Fletcher'd been murdered and why he shouldn't assume I was an accident-prone boozer."

He smiled and nodded approvingly and his warmth embarrassed me. I was still thinking of him as a suspect while he assumed I was a friend.

Juanita made an entrance.

Her white cotton dress was low at the top and short at the bottom and all it revealed was tan, smooth and glowing. Her black hair flowed over her golden shoulders; the full lips glistened red. She slipped into the chair across from me and frowned as she stared at my face.

"How are you?" she asked.

"Okay."

"I just saw José, the policeman. He says you were attacked and kidnapped."

"Yeah, something like that." I glanced at Jim who stared at me. I gave him a thin smile. "I was waiting for Juanita before telling you the rest of the story. The two guys that ran Rodríguez off took me to a deserted house for questioning. I got away."

"A man was killed," said Juanita. She was looking at me with an expression close to wonder and with something else I couldn't identify. Genuine interest doesn't quite cover it.

"Questioning?" said Jim. "What kind of questions?"

"What'd I told the police, how much was I getting paid for the investigation—"

He insisted on details and I told him. Juanita began to smile. I thought, "If this had happened a few days ago, she'd have come to my bed at Camillo's place. How will she react when Marigold arrives? Is this why men kill men? Because of the effect on women?"

Jim invited me to have dinner with them, but I begged off, saying I had promised to make a telephone call. Juanita said I should join them as soon as I could and I said I'd see how long the call took and left them.

Marigold sounded more efficient than enamored when I got through and said she'd be landing in Guadalajara early the next afternoon. I promised to be waiting and she told me to be extremely careful in a tone that suggested I was an irresponsible child. I convinced myself that she'd simply entered her arranging secretary mode and would warm up again when she saw the hero.

I joined the Durados in the dining room and carried on a distracted dialogue before excusing myself, saying the day had worn me out. They were extremely solicitous, and as I walked through the lobby, Juanita caught up, took hold of my arm and said she had told the cop, José, that if the police wished, she would testify that Rodríguez had attacked me in her presence.

"You didn't have to do that."

"Oh, but I did. It's all too ridiculous."

We went around a little with that and suddenly she gave me a quick, firm kiss and said good night. I headed on toward my room, feeling moderately drunk with power.

Lights hadn't come on yet in the long corridor which led to my room in a series of descending steps. The windows lining the hall faced east and were half dark in the early twilight. The white walls seemed to retain some of the glow from the day's sun and my feet made no sound on the patterned maroon carpet. I passed through the succession of dark, arched doorways to my right, noticed the green plants in huge brown pots on slender wrought-iron stands and glanced up at the beamed ceiling which was reddish brown when the morning sun streamed through the arched windows and now looked black.

I passed through a wide white arch and started down the third series of steps just as the lights came on. Startled, I glanced toward the windows to my left and saw a figure reflected in the glass. It stepped from the small corner to my left and swung a club at me. I ducked, twisted, fell and rolled down the steps. The man stumbled off balance from the miss and tumbled after me, still clinging to his club. I caught him a glancing blow to the temple with my knee, and still rolling, aimed a kick at his jaw. He blocked it with his club, but I drove that back into his face. I heard his teeth click like a closing trap and the next second he was flat on the carpet, bleeding from a deep gash across the right side of his face.

I stood, put my foot on his wrist and jerked the club free. If he'd so much as taken a deep breath, I'd have clobbered him, but he stayed still as a dropped puppet.

I pulled up my pants and went to find help.

XXIII

"He claims," said Lieutenant Juárez with a straight face, "that he was standing in the hall, looking out the window, when you attacked him from behind."

"With a piece of two-by-two I'd brought from the bar?"

"He admits the length of wood was his. He says he found it outside the hotel and picked it up because he likes to carve wood."

"And I suppose he was carrying a Boy Scout knife?"

"No," he grinned suddenly, "it was a switchblade."

"Well," I said, "if I'd known it was Rodríguez's buddy and I'd seen him first, I probably would've jumped him."

Juárez shook his head.

"For a rather harmless-looking young man, you seem to be remarkably formidable. This is the third man you have disabled in less than a week."

"Yeah. He say why he was hanging around my room?"

"Oh yes, of course. He came to apologize for hitting you when he was with his friend. He feels very guilty. Says that Rodríguez is a bad influence."

"That part I can believe."

The lieutenant smiled. "His friends call him Chris, he tells me, but the name is actually Christ. His mother is very religious."

"Well, that explains everything. You think you can learn anything from him?"

"Probably not for a while. When he comes down from his high place, then we see. At first he will not want to talk at all, then he may say much."

"He's an addict?"

He nodded.

I skipped breakfast the next morning and drove straight to Guadalajara. It was a hot, bright day, but off to the west dark clouds edged over the mountain ridges. There was little traffic and I detected no one following me. Every so often, along the roadside, I'd see a ragged peasant wearing *huaraches* and carrying an enormous load of firewood strapped to his bent back. I could only guess he'd been carrying it for miles because I never saw a forest source.

Marigold looked taller and less blond than I remembered, but every bit as lovely. She waved, beaming, as she hurried from customs carrying two Hartmann bags worth more than all my wardrobe. She dropped them, like Liberace discarding his furs onstage, grabbed me and after a hard squeeze pulled back to examine my battered face.

"You look lopsided; is it safe to kiss you?"

I demonstrated.

She responded warmly enough to make my jaw ache, then gathered up her luggage, handed me one piece and we hiked to my rented car.

I asked about the trip and she said she'd tried to watch a movie but the earphones didn't work and she couldn't make much sense of the film.

"Tom Selleck was in it with stubble whiskers and I kept wishing he'd shave but he never did. It was the kind of role where you know the guy'd have horrible breath, ghastly b.o. and whiskers like a wire brush. All that macho crud—"

I felt safe about the whiskers and body odor but wasn't too sure of my breath. As soon as we were in the car, she kissed me again and stayed with it long enough to dispel worries.

"I found out some things about Avery," she said as we drove out of the parking lot.

"Avery who?"

"Robinson. Fletcher Foundation board member, retired banker—remember?"

"Oh yeah—I'm still giddy from your greeting. So what'd you learn?"

"He's been investing Foundation money in precious metals. Silver, gold and platinum. Especially platinum."

"So?"

"They've gone down. Platinum's dropped more than eighty dollars an ounce since he bought."

"Seems to me I've heard they're due to rise any day."

"Sure, but Oren didn't ever want Foundation money concentrated in one area like that and Avery really plunged—I mean, *millions*. At today's prices, the Foundation's lost about twenty percent of its capital."

"Sounds like he'd really be on Fletcher's shit list."

"Oren would call it a feces roster, but yes, Avery'd be in real trouble if Oren were around."

"So what could he have done—kick Avery off the board?"

"It'd be more than that. Avery had a contract for handling investments with a percentage of the earnings. I don't know all the details, but if Avery made a foolish error in judgment, I think Oren would have ruined him."

"I thought your boss was all sweetness and light?"

"You did not."

"Okay, I never have, but you'd pretty well convinced me everyone else did."

"He was fine to all of us when things went his way. But when he was crossed, he was a cool terror. I know he ruined a broker who gave him bad advice back during the silver boom."

The way she said that suggested she thought the broker had it coming. I was tempted to ask if she'd had a yen for Fletcher, but didn't because I thought I knew the answer. She was a practical, planning woman who shared Spock's view that everything should be logical. So why had she suddenly flown into my arms?

I glanced her way and asked if Avery had any Mexican connections.

"Only the banker, García."

"Oh, yeah. The innocent who didn't know his biggest depositor had closed his account six months before I showed up asking questions. Listen, before we go back to Guanajuato, how about we sashay around and visit this bird?"

She agreed and we stopped at the first public phone booth in sight where she promptly got an appointment and within half an hour we arrived at the bank.

García's eyes bugged when he spotted Marigold. I don't think the sight of me pleased him much. He stood up, acknowledged my introduction of Marigold with a bow, and displaying great agility for so rotund a man, darted around the desk and helped her into a chair facing his desk. He let me navigate on my own.

"Well," he beamed once he was enthroned and had his pudgy fingers folded on his desk, "to what do I owe this great honor?"

"When I was here before," I said, "you claimed neither the police nor private investigators had talked to you about Fletcher—"

"Please," he said, raising a fat palm, "I forgot. There was one. Very casual. I thought he was only an acquaintance. Now I realize that like yourself, he was an investigator."

He smiled at Marigold.

I bored on.

"Have the cops talked to you since I was here?"

The smile faded as he regarded me with sad brown eyes.

"Why do you ask about the police? What difference is that?"

"I think they're interested in all that money Fletcher took out of here six months ago."

"So," he shrugged. "Ask them."

We stared at each other. I got the notion that if he played poker he won a lot.

Marigold leaned forward and spoke softly in Spanish. I caught a few of the words, *"importante"* and *"significado,"* and watched while gradually García's antagonism leaked away and his ego reinflated. He responded with lovely, liquid Spanish.

They chatted warmly while I burned. No one apologized for leaving me out or tried to explain a thing. When Marigold was satisfied, she stood up. García leaped to his feet, hurried around his desk to shake her hand and walked us all the way out to the

front door. He even shook hands with me and said adios while
looking me straight in the eye.

"Okay," I said as we walked toward the car, "what the hell did
he say?"

"Oren withdrew his account in cash, packed it in a suitcase and
walked out with two bodyguards."

"His own, or the bank's?"

"They came with him. Both were Mexicans, husky and watch-
ful."

We got into the car and I started the engine.

"García admits he handled this all himself?"

"Yes. He says he was evasive with you because he didn't know
you represented Mrs. Fletcher. He was quite apologetic about
that."

"You must've soft-soaped the bejesus out of him. Didn't he
think there was something fishy about the cash withdrawal?"

"He said a man of his experience doesn't ask a man like
Fletcher any questions about handling his own money. He says
they were able to come up with the cash because by coincidence
they had received a large cash deposit that morning."

"You buy that?"

She shook her head. "I got the feeling he was overacting all the
time. I think he's afraid."

"Of what?"

"Not us."

We drove in silence for a while and then I said, "I think Camillo's behind all of this. He's got the connections, like this Morales
guy, and he's just flaky enough to pull it off. I figure García'd go
along with anything that'd make him a buck or keep him in good
with people he'd be doing business with."

"Maybe. But I don't think he'd take any chances. He doesn't
strike me as a man with that kind of nerve."

Our conversation got suspended as we passed through a series
of small towns where I had to concentrate on not getting lost.
Back on the open road I asked what had made her suddenly
decide to come and join me.

"Oh, a lot of things. There's nothing really going on at the Foundation so I was feeling kind of useless, and listening to you, I just decided I wanted to get involved in all this."

"Were you worried about me?"

I glanced her way and she looked back. "I didn't think you needed mothering."

That wasn't what I meant and she knew it. What I wanted was for her to admit a personal interest, but I had strong doubts that it was anything more than she'd stated.

So why in hell had she been so lovey when she got off the plane?

"I've reserved a room of my own at your hotel," she said very casually. "I thought it might be wiser to keep up appearances."

I turned to glare at her.

"Don't get peevish, I'll let you into my room, okay?"

"Who are we trying to impress with our propriety?" I asked.

"I'm not trying to impress anyone. I'd just rather avoid making things complicated, and you'd do well to remember you've got to please your boss, Daphne."

"All she cares about is finding her hubby's corpse so she can collect her inheritance."

"And she'll be expecting you to spend full time at it."

"I don't like it," I said. "It could be dangerous for you to be alone."

"Come on, you're the lightning rod in this case, lover-boy. Being in your bed isn't the safest place in Mexico these days."

"Maybe you shouldn't have come."

"You want me to go back?"

"You want to?"

"Come on, Kyle, quit playing games. I came because I thought maybe I could help you and you needed me. Okay?"

"Yeah," I said, but I'd have felt better about her admission if she hadn't put it so belligerently.

She suddenly reached over and touched my right hand which rested on the steering wheel.

"Don't try to press me," she said. "I have to go along at my own pace in my own way, okay?"

"Sure."

Our dialogue died after that and it wasn't until we were entering Guanajuato that I made myself warn her of what to expect.

"It could be," I said, "that by now Lieutenant Juárez has found Fletcher's body."

I felt her staring at me.

"I thought I should warn you."

"Thanks." Her voice had a great distance in it. "I didn't think you said that because you were sore at me."

XXIV

The desk clerk greeted us at the counter and handed me two call slips, one from Daphne, the other from Lieutenant Juárez.

I went to the telephone booth while Marigold checked in.

"Where have you been?" demanded the lieutenant.

I told him. There was a long, frosty silence. I apologized for not having notified him of my intentions. The silence went on.

"Have you found Fletcher?" I asked.

"We have found out who owned the house where you were questioned."

"Great."

"The owner is a man named Manuel López. He deals in real estate. He is also a director of funerals."

"Aha!"

"*Sí.*" His voice began to defrost. "We have also found that this director had two funerals in the week Señor Fletcher disappeared. Both bodies were interred at the Panteón."

"So what happens next?"

"We have made arrangements to open these two crypts and make certain who occupies them. I thought you might like to join me."

"Hell yes—when?"

"Very well, if you are truly interested, I will pick you up in front of your hotel. It will be about fifteen minutes or so."

I charged from the booth, stopped to get Marigold's room number from the desk clerk and rushed off to report. Fortunately it occurred to me before I was halfway there that my news was not exactly going to thrill her as it did me and I slowed down while trying to think how I'd fill her in in the least painful way.

She answered my knock at once and stepped back, looking at me apprehensively.

"What'd the lieutenant want?"

"To chew me out for leaving town without his okay."

"That wasn't all," she said, studying my face.

I took her arm and moved her to the bed where we sat side by side while I told her what I'd learned.

"Oh God!" she said.

"It's still not certain—"

She shook her head.

"It's him. I can feel it." Suddenly she looked up. "I won't have to identify him—?"

"No, of course not—"

She looked away. "That's right, after six months it isn't likely anyone would know him."

"Look, don't make it any tougher than you have to till we know for sure, okay?"

She nodded, took a deep breath and straightened up.

"You'd better get out in front. You don't want to make the lieutenant mad again."

"Right, I'll be back as soon as I can—"

I leaned her way for a kiss but she turned her head, so I patted her shoulder awkwardly and took off.

There were two cops in the front seat. Lieutenant Juárez waved me into the back beside him and the car pulled away swiftly.

There was no conversation as we drove up the long, wide street to the Panteón. We pulled into a reserved spot beside the wrought-iron gates, an officer opened the car door and we marched quickly past the young street vendors and staring tourists until we reached the high-walled area of the aboveground crypts.

"This," Lieutenant Juárez told me, "is the poor people's side. Those with money are interred over that way." He waved toward the opposite side of the hall of the mummies.

I could see the wealthy side was closed to tourists and there were trees in the courtyard. The poor area had a pile of dirt near its center and a few bushes along one side. The stacked crypts, six high and forever wide, stood enclosing the square like massive walls.

We went through the entrance, turned right and approached a spot where several men were clustered around a recently unsealed unit. Each of the crypts was fronted by an engraved stone, a few simply with bricks. I saw no vacancies.

Four men were struggling to pull a casket from a slot on the second level. For a time it resisted, then suddenly it gave and they hauled it out and carefully set it on the earth. It took a few moments for one of the men to unseal the lid and we stood watching and sweating in the fierce sun. I glanced at Lieutenant Juárez. He was scowling darkly.

The lid was opened and we all stepped close. I expected a stench and was breathing through my mouth as I stared down at the shriveled body and the contorted mouth frozen in mid scream. The skin was like parchment.

"It looks like Fletcher's hair," I told the lieutenant. "I've seen his picture. Are we going to check the other body?"

"That's already been examined. It's a woman. I believe our missing millionaire is before us."

He leaned closer and pointed at the left hand of the corpse.

"Observe. Each finger has been broken. Very interesting."

As we moved away, I asked how long identification would take and he said probably not long, it appeared there would be no problem about getting fingerprints.

I went directly to Marigold's room after he dropped me off at the hotel. It took a few moments before she answered my knock, and when she let me in, her face was flushed and her eyes puffy.

"You okay?" I asked.

"I slept," she said. "Can you imagine? That's what I do when I can't face things."

I sat beside her on the bed, holding her left hand. She leaned against me and put her head on my shoulder. After a while I told her what we'd found at the cemetery. I skipped the broken hand.

"Poor Oren," she said.

"There's still not a positive I.D."

She lifted her head, nodded and blinked. A tear ran down her smooth cheek.

I suggested we go to the bar for a drink.

She stiffened. "Thanks, but I don't feel a whole lot like celebrating."

"That's not what I had in mind."

"No, I suppose not."

She slipped her shoes off and laid back on the bed. Tears kept leaking down her cheeks and she brushed them away with one hand, then the other. When I started to bend over her, she rolled away and curled up on her side, facing the wall.

"I'm sorry," I said.

She acknowledged that with a nod and said shouldn't I be making a call to Daphne?

I suddenly remembered the call slip the clerk had given me and said yes, I'd have to do that. I went, disgusted with myself for thinking that Marigold would want my comforting presence when I knew what she really wanted was to be alone with her thoughts of Saint Fletcher. Instead of feeling sorry for the guy, I was just jealous. The smallness of that was shriveling.

The line was busy when I placed my call and I stewed around in the lobby for a while, then tried again. Daphne's stiff-necked servant answered on the first ring and went to fetch his lady. After several seconds she said, "Hello?"

"I tried earlier but your line was busy—"

"Yes. I was talking with your policeman."

"Lieutenant Juárez?"

"I guess so."

"What'd he tell you?"

"They found Oren."

So, it had been confirmed already.

"Did he tell you how they happened to be checking out the cemetery?"

"What? What do you mean?"

"It was my idea. I figured out he was there."

"Oh?" She didn't sound that interested. "No, nothing was said about you."

She spoke slowly, as though half asleep. I wondered if she were drugged.

"What's the matter—you on tranquilizers or something?"

"What?"

"Are you doped up?"

"Of course not," she said with sudden petulance. "I'm grieving, for Christ's sake."

"What?"

That popped out with more incredulity than was tasteful under the circumstances, but the notion that she was really moved by Fletcher's death was more than I could cope with at the moment.

"Don't speak to me like that," she said softly. That was so out of character I began to feel like a real bastard.

"Hey, I'm sorry—are you okay?"

"I accept your apology. And I believe you are responsible for finding Oren and you'll get your money, all right?"

"Well sure, fine—"

"I'll be coming there as soon as I can arrange things. Stay till I come. I'll be in touch."

I hung up more than half convinced she actually was grieving. Every woman I knew was grieving for that eleemosynary bastard. Even dead he had them all mesmerized.

As I emerged from the booth, I almost bumped into Juanita.

"You look upset," she said with a radiant smile. "Is anything wrong?"

I said no, thinking how nice it was to find a woman not devastated by the news of Fletcher, then realized she hadn't heard yet.

"We wondered what had happened to you," she said. "You've been missing all day."

"Had to make a little trip."

"Because of last night's attack?"

"Huh?"

"Right after we parted last night. We heard about the man who attacked you in the hall—that's horrible!"

"Practically routine," I assured her with a casual wave.

"Will you have dinner with us?"

"Well, uh, if you don't mind my bringing a friend—"

She said of course not and we parted. It bothered me that I'd turned chicken and hadn't told her the friend was a woman. That sure wouldn't smooth things over when they met.

I found Marigold standing in her room by the tall windows, gazing into the flower-fringed courtyard. When she turned, the outside light haloed her fine hair, shading half her face and turning the other half to gold. Her smile was melancholy as I approached.

"How is Daphne taking it?" she asked as I halted, almost touching her.

"She said she was grieving, but she sounded stoned."

"Well, these days one often follows the other."

"When I said I was sorry, I meant it. I was sorry that you felt so bad; I wasn't pretending anything about Fletcher—"

She put her hands on my shoulders. "Don't worry about it; everything will pass. Just be patient."

"Sure," I said, putting my hands on her slim waist. She pushed off gently and looked out the window again.

"Why'd you really come here?" I asked.

She gave me a cold glance. "I thought we'd already gone over that."

"No, we just waltzed around it. Why do you always blow hot and cold?"

"That's the way I am. I don't put on any act, anytime."

"Did you come because of him, or because of me?"

She tipped her head back. "I offered to come because you sounded so down and I thought I could lift you up. By the time I got to the airplane, I was coming for other reasons not so clear or simple. I have instant emotional reactions usually followed by common sense. That's the way I am and there's nothing you or I can do about it."

Then she took my face in her hands and kissed me while pressing her body close. A few seconds later we were on the bed.

It took a while before her practical sense took over and she said we'd better get down to the dining room before it closed. To my surprise I realized I was ravenous and I didn't even think of the impending confrontation with Juanita until we were approaching the dining room door.

To my relief there was no sign of the Durados and we got a table behind a pillar and sat looking past a candle at each other.

"We're very good, aren't we?" she said.

"Earth-moving."

"I think you have to do it in a sleeping bag on the ground for that to happen."

"I figure if you can tell it moved, you haven't been paying attention to business."

"Very profound. You ought to be a writer."

"I'm better at that than detecting."

"You're best of all at making love."

"You really know all my weaknesses, don't you?"

"That's no weakness—"

"I meant I'm a sucker for flattery. It's you that makes it work. I remember a great cartoon—this guy's sitting on the edge of the bed and his girl is still on her back and he says, 'The part I liked best was when you moved.' What I like about you is, you never stopped moving."

"Oh, I stopped all right. At the end, I absolutely died."

"By then, if you hadn't, I would've."

We were trying to decide on an after-dinner drink when I became aware of the waiter at my side. As I looked up, he handed me a note.

"Come to room 207. Juanita," it said.

Marigold stared at me and asked what was wrong.

I told her.

"What do you think she wants?"

"To sell some information, I'd guess."

"Well, hadn't you better go buy?"

"My job's finished. All I was supposed to do was find the man, not his killer."

"You don't care who killed him?"

"If you want me to, yeah."

"Care, or find out?"

"Either."

"Go."

I went.

XXV

Juanita opened the door at my first tap. Her face was stiff, her eyes puffy and lines showed at the corners of her wide mouth.

"You knew when we met in the hall," she said bitterly.

"It hadn't been confirmed yet."

"You knew. You let me prattle on like a fool—"

"I didn't want to upset you when it wasn't for sure. How'd you find out?"

"José," she said. Then she drew back and gestured me into the dimly lit room. I sat in a chair beside curtained windows; she perched on the bed's edge and crossed her ankles.

"There are a lot of things you don't know," she said.

"That I know."

"Like, do you know Elvira speaks Spanish and her husband used to spend half his time traveling in Mexico and she traveled with him?"

I shook my head.

"Well," she said with satisfaction, "she did. She also knows Morales, the man who owns the nightclub, García, the banker, and she met Camillo and visited his hotel of the ancients."

I said that was very interesting.

"Oren told her about the hotel and she wanted to see it and went there with him. She thought she would be staying with Oren, and when he got separate rooms wherever they went, she learned better. That's when she began to hate him. And that's why she had him murdered."

"She traveled with Fletcher after she became a board member?"

"Yes."

"It seems to me Fletcher made Camillo sore at him too, is that right?"

"Oh yes. He suggested, in front of Camillo's friends, that he write some kind of a letter asking for money—"

"A grant proposal."

"Whatever. Camillo was insulted. He said he'd run his hotel for ten years by explaining to gentlemen what he was doing and making them understand the need, and like gentlemen, they gave it to him. Oren laughed and said he'd like it that way too, but in the United States foundations could not do things that simply."

"So Camillo sent a request and got turned down?"

"That's right. With a snotty little note written by that icy blonde in the Foundation office. Not a visit or a personal telephone call, but a letter from a secretary."

I could believe that'd gall him.

"And while she was down here, Elvira found out about me and Oren and then she knew that he'd never settle with a woman as old as she is, so she worked to have him killed."

"How?"

"You're the detective," she flared, "must I do it all for you?"

"I need all the help I can get."

"I've given you all the help you should need. You can catch her, I know you can."

I told her I was grateful and stood up.

"You will get her, won't you?" The prospect almost erased the recent signs of grief.

"If I can find proof or convince the police. I take it you'll be willing to talk with Lieutenant Juárez?"

"To anybody, anywhere, anytime."

"Without pay?"

She drew herself up. "Absolutely. When we spoke before, I didn't know he had been murdered."

"Okay, I'll get on it."

She slipped from the bed and grasped my hands.

"I'll be very grateful—you'll see."

"Well," said Marigold as she let me into her room, "that didn't take long."

"You figure I'd stay all night?"

"It wouldn't have surprised me—I've seen your recuperative powers. What'd you find out?"

"Quite a bit. She says you wrote the rejection letter to Camillo. Was that the usual procedure?"

"Yes. Oren only signed good-news letters."

"That was shitty."

She frowned. "Why?"

"He made you the heavy."

"Not really. Everybody knew who made the decisions."

"Don't kid yourself. People who're badly disappointed don't always think logically."

She dismissed that and asked what else Juanita had told me.

I laid it all out. She listened with growing annoyance, and when I ran down, shook her head violently.

"I don't believe it."

"Which part?"

"The claim that Elvira planned to sleep with Oren when they traveled together. How in the world would she know that, even if it were true, and I don't believe it was."

"Juanita says he told her himself."

"Juanita's a liar."

I agreed that was possible but suggested, just for the exercise, that we figure out what might have happened if it were true. Certainly that would've made Elvira the scorned woman and we both knew she was enough of a manipulator to use Camillo and Morales to get the job done.

"How?"

"She knew Fletcher had money in Mexico. She could tip off Camillo that with a little imagination he could not only square accounts with Fletcher for the humiliation, but he might get some money for his hotel in the bargain. So Morales provides the muscle, they persuade Fletcher to withdraw his bundle from the bank, then they dispose of Fletcher and with the help of a funeral director friend, stick him in a crypt at the Panteón."

She frowned at me and finally said, "Would it hurt you to call him Oren?"

"No, but—"

"It would make me feel better about you."

"Okay. Sure."

We were silent for a moment while she sat on the bed and stared at the floor. Finally she took a deep breath and looked up.

"The trouble with that theory is it sounds to me as if there wouldn't be anything in it for the banker—García. Why would he go along?"

"He might not have known what was going on. Or maybe Camillo and Morales have money in his bank, or some control of it. He might simply be afraid of Morales's gorillas. And if he had a genuine signature from—uh—Oren, who'd fault him for giving the man his money?"

"The police might, knowing he was familiar with Morales."

"Not likely. And anyway, the beauty of the crypt business was, it looked foolproof. Without a body there's no serious investigation and every day that passes makes a hell of a difference in a murder case. They gained half a year. They probably thought they had forever."

We talked it over some more without making any progress and finally went to bed and, at least to my surprise, just slept.

XXVI

Lieutenant Juárez was standing in the hotel lobby when Marigold and I returned from breakfast a little after 9 A.M. His uniform was sharp as a display case filet knife and I half expected a snappy salute, but he only nodded gravely in response to my greeting.

"I've been talking with Mrs. Fletcher," he said. "She plans a memorial service here in Guanajuato and is bringing some people to attend with her."

I glanced at Marigold who kept her innocent blue eyes on the lieutenant. From the composure of her smooth face I guessed that she had finished with grief.

"When'll it be?" I asked.

"Tomorrow. Mrs. Fletcher plans to arrive around noon at Guadalajara in a chartered plane. She wants you to invite the Durados, the man Camillo, Mr. Morales and Mr. García as well as any others you know in Mexico who were close friends."

"Sounds like quite a party. Was all this your idea?"

He shrugged. "If you can't persuade any of the local men to come, give me their names. I will talk to them."

I agreed, he nodded solemnly and left.

"You want me to make the calls?" asked Marigold.

"I'll handle the Durados if you'll take the others."

"Okay. Let's do it now."

She reached Camillo first. He was, he assured her, devastated by the news of the tragedy and would absolutely come to the service. Then he asked her to repeat her name.

"Ah yes, you are the Foundation assistant who sends the letters, right?"

"Yes."

"It must be difficult for you, always to send the bad news, right?"

She agreed politely.

"I understand that you are a lovely blond young lady, without a husband?"

"I am not married."

"I look forward to seeing you," he said, and hung up.

I asked, after she related this to me, if his last comment sounded like a threat.

"It sounded more lecherous than threatening."

As she was dialing García, I decided it was nice she did not consider lechery threatening.

García also agreed to attend and expressed his eagerness to see Marigold again.

She couldn't reach Morales. His man told her he was unavailable, and when she tried to leave a message, he hung up.

I reported this to Lieutenant Juárez.

"Thank you, we will take care of that."

We went into the dining room. I spotted the Durados right away but got Marigold seated before I went over to see them. I told them about the memorial services and they agreed to come. Juanita did not invite me to join them and did not look over toward the table where Marigold sat. Jim looked unhappy.

Daphne arrived in midafternoon wearing a splendid black dress and an expression more brooding than mournful. Harlan stayed at her side, movie-star handsome in a charcoal-gray summer suit with a plain black knit tie and a silver tie tack. He was working on a thoughtful expression which got lost every time he glanced Daphne's way and broke into a flashing smile.

Elvira was a surprise in a very becoming dark dress and black nylons. She looked trim and youthful despite her gray hair which was trimmed short and styled close to her handsome head. She took in the hotel courtyard, Marigold and me with equal attention and bright interest. Sutton gave me a sharp glance and a curt nod, grinned at Marigold and ignored Lieutenant Juárez.

Avery Robinson blinked like an owl in the sunlight, avoided my eyes and acknowledged Marigold almost brusquely. Behind him was Daphne's long-necked servant, looking more than ever like an old-fashioned undertaker.

Daphne insisted on examining her rooms before moving in, found them satisfactory and announced that we would all assemble in the dining room. All her group had taken lunch on the plane, so everyone settled for coffee or drinks. The hotel staff gave no hint that they were not delighted to serve this self-centered pack of foreigners.

I grabbed a chair next to Elvira.

"So," she said, giving me an arch look, "you've accomplished your job. Does this mean you'll become a full-time private detective?"

"That'll depend on how my new assignment goes."

"And what's that?"

I smiled at her. "Finding out who killed him."

Her eyebrows rose as she glanced toward Daphne. The fresh widow was talking to Marigold who'd managed to slip in between her and Harlan, much to the latter's annoyance.

"That's very interesting," said Elvira, turning back to me. "Daphne didn't mention this during our flight."

"She probably didn't figure it was important to any of you."

She laughed easily and tilted her head.

"You're saying she doesn't think any of us are suspect, but since you've made a point of moving in on me, apparently you have your own ideas. Why pick on me?"

"The last time we talked, two guys got on my tail the minute I hit the street. It made me wonder."

"I see. But isn't it possible they had simply followed you to my office?"

"Yeah, it's possible, but I didn't notice them before."

"Oh my." She pretended to be worried but looked only mocking.

A trio of musicians strolled in, approached Daphne's end of the table and started a Mexican ballad. The tall, slender lead guitarist sang in a strained tenor. His expression suggested the effort was painful.

I leaned closer to Elvira.

"Did Fletcher ask you to marry him?"

She drew back. "Whatever gave you that idea?"

"What's the difference? Did he?"

"No. Oh, he talked around it, but usually he seemed to be saying it would have been an ideal relationship if we'd done it when we were young."

"I thought tycoons always knew what they wanted and went after it."

She laughed. "He knew what he wanted all right. But he enjoyed being sentimental now and then. What I'd once been was something he'd left behind—he was sorry to have missed it, but he wasn't foolish enough to think he could pick it all up at this late date."

"He had to have the young ones, right?"

"Yes."

"Like Juanita?"

"And your blond friend, yes."

"Are you pretending that didn't bother you?"

"I'm pretending nothing. I was a little disappointed—it would have been much nicer if he'd grown up to be what I thought he was when we were children—when he seemed so mature to me. But he never truly grew up, which is probably just as well, he might have lost all his charm and that would've left nothing at all."

I thought I picked up more bitterness from that than she intended, but it hardly seemed sufficient to hang a murder motive on.

"He'd still have his money," I said.

"A consideration never to be overlooked by a practical woman."

"I hear you speak Spanish and spent a lot of time in Mexico with your husband."

"Where'd you pick that up—from Marigold?"

I said no and she called me a liar with her green eyes.

"Did she tell you how much time *she* spent in Mexico and that
Oren picked her up down here?"

"She told me they met here, yeah."

"That's right, they most certainly did."

"You don't like her much, do you?"

"I have the greatest admiration for the dear girl. She'll go far.
You might say, to any lengths."

"You think she'll be the next Foundation exec?"

She smiled gently. "Is that what she's after?"

"She thinks her chances are good if you don't get the job."

"I guess that means I should be very careful," she said, and
with that, turned to Sutton, abandoning me.

I looked at Avery who sat on my left. He was holding a cup of
coffee cradled in both hands and stared at the musicians with the
expression of a man watching a pup wet his Persian carpet.

"I understand you know a Mexican banker named García," I
said.

He blinked, sipped his coffee and placed the cup on the table.

"Slightly, yes. He keeps me posted on Mexican oil interests and
silver."

"How is silver these days?"

"Stable."

"You consider it a good investment?"

He gave me an aggressive stare. "Not good. Excellent. Better
than gold or just about anything else you could imagine. A sterling investment, you might say. Long range, of course."

"I hear Fletcher didn't care for long-term investments."

"Oren Fletcher," he said with some heat, "was a babe in the
woods when it came to investments if you really want to know the
truth. The best thing that ever happened to him was that stroke
he had. Made him get out of investing and into giveaways. The
minute he got out of banking, turned over investment matters to
experts, his value soared. Absolutely soared."

"And you were his expert?"

He spread his hands generously. "The principal one, yes. And
let me tell you, he respected my judgment completely. Some

people will try to tell you he wouldn't approve of my putting
Foundation money into precious metals but that's hogwash. He
trusted my judgment and would have backed me to the hilt."

"But he didn't know you'd done it, right?"

"The subject never came up. He was preoccupied with other
matters and then he was gone—"

"Preoccupied by what matters?"

He gave me a sly look. "Foundation grants, what else?"

I glanced over my shoulder at Elvira, then looked back at
Avery.

"How about women?"

He drew back slightly and allowed himself a condescending
smile.

"Oren had less acumen about women than about investments." The smile was replaced by a frown of concern. "I hate to
speak ill of the dead, but that's simply a fact."

The statement depressed him into silence. I kept watching him
while listening to the conversation behind me. It took several
seconds before I realized they were speaking Spanish. When I
turned to stare at them, Sutton grinned at me.

I turned back to Avery.

"I notice Daphne brought her servant along. Does she always
take him on her travels?"

"I guess so."

"How long's he been with her?"

"About as long as Harlan."

I stared at him and his grin became foxy.

"Before that," he said, "Warden worked for Sutton. His full
name is Theodore Warden. A convicted forger. Harlan was his
lawyer. Helped him get parole by guaranteeing him a job. Harlan
talked Sutton into hiring him and he worked for a couple years
and then went over to work for Fletcher. Sutton was glad to let
him go—he wanted to hire the maid he's got now. She's something."

"Is she another convicted felon?"

He chuckled and nodded. "Contrary to what you might guess, she was a forger too."

"They have anything else in common?"

"Yes. They both have a need to be dominated."

"I guess they found the perfect employers."

"Yes, it's worked out very well for everyone."

Daphne stood up, dismissed the musicians, asked for our attention and announced that arrangements were under way for memorial services to be held the following afternoon at one-thirty.

"I'll host a private dinner this evening at eight-thirty in one of the hotel's meeting rooms. Ask for directions at the registration counter. Memorial services will be in the same room tomorrow."

She dismissed the court and we filed out through the dining room's front door where I joined Marigold.

"How'd you get along with the empress?" I asked.

"Fine. She's asked me to make arrangements and I agreed."

"Well, considering who asked, you hardly had a choice, did you?"

"She was very gracious, actually. I think she's moving into sort of a Jackie mode."

"Looking for an Onassis?"

"Probably. See if she's got eyes for Sutton."

"I think that old bird's got eyes for Elvira."

"Isn't she a bit mature for his tastes?"

"I'd have thought so until I heard them chattering in Spanish. That's a Romance language, you know. They talk it too fast for me to follow."

"She didn't speak Spanish when she was talking to you—"

"No. She started in English and wound up in vitriol. I don't think she's nuts about you."

"Really?"

"She hinted that you are ambitious and ruthless."

"Did you leap to my defense?"

"Not me. Us private eyes only defend ourselves. When I told

her you wanted the exec job, she told me she guessed she'd better be careful. Are you ruthless enough to deserve that crack?"

"I wish I were. Now excuse me, I've got to go and arrange things."

"For Elvira?"

"That's not funny."

I wondered if I'd meant it to be, but managed to grin and wave as she headed for the hotel office.

XXVII

I drifted toward the bar well behind Sutton and Elvira and caught up with Daphne and Harlan by the pool.

"Has everyone been invited?" she asked, squinting against the sun.

"All but Morales. Lieutenant Juárez will get him."

"I want everybody there."

Harlan watched me with a small smile. He looked like an Italian movie star behind his silver-framed glasses.

"How do you like Mexico?" I asked him.

"Fascinating. It's sort of a shabby Disneyland, right?"

"Exactly. You've capsulized the entire country in one neat phrase after one glance."

He grinned with self-satisfaction but sobered quickly when Daphne gave him a sharp, warning look. I smiled sweetly and moved on.

Jim was at his usual station in the bar, invited me to sit down and asked who else would be at the memorial services. I rattled off the list and he smiled.

"Shades of Agatha Christie and Rex Stout."

"Yeah, but without a genius detective or a prepared script. Listen, I've really got to get some things straight. I hope you won't be offended—"

He took a slow drink and watched me thoughtfully.

"I hear you made a lot of money in Wisconsin. That you were a behind-the-scenes power in local politics, big in real estate. Is that right?"

He nodded. "I did fairly well, yes."

"You had clout, that's what it came down to. So tell me, what would you have done if you thought Fletcher was fooling around with Juanita and didn't plan to do right by her?"

He lifted his head, leaned back and didn't quite laugh.

"I'll tell you one thing for sure, I wouldn't have tried to use my Wisconsin clout in Guanajuato, Mexico."

"Yeah, I know that, but you've still got money, you know how to make friends and influence people. That's my point."

"That is true," he conceded and turned his sweating glass on the moist paper napkin as he frowned. Then he glanced up at me very soberly. "So, I *was* concerned. But there was nothing I could do. She is a grown woman. I accept that. Being successful in business never made me think I could arrange the world to suit me."

"Things would take care of themselves, like in college?"

"I hardly expected Oren would kill himself." He leaned forward and rested his elbows on the table.

"What you must do," he told me, "is consider what I'd have to gain if I became vindictive toward Oren and his exploitation of Juanita. As you have no doubt noticed, I am dependent on her. Emotionally, sentimentally and almost any other way you care to think about. But if Oren betrayed her, she would not turn away from me. If anything, that would bind us together more tightly than ever. If she married him, obviously our relationship would change, but it wouldn't end. Becoming the wife of a rich and important man wouldn't turn her from me. And Oren liked me. We were genuinely friends."

"It didn't bug you that he made her his mistress?"

He smiled gently. "You want me to play the Victorian father, enraged by the seducer who trifled with his virgin daughter? Can you actually see me in that role?"

"I don't know you that well."

"You are perceptive, you should know I'm not a man to live outmoded poses. And take a look at Juanita, she's no innocent."

"She cried over Fletcher's death."

"Of course. But she wouldn't be ruined by disappointment and she's too clever to be disillusioned. Oren was a goal, not a god. She will look for a replacement and dismiss the past."

"You're very pragmatic."

"And realistic." He pulled back, drawing his glass with him. "What do you think of Elvira?"

He shrugged. "Juanita says she wanted to marry Oren but he never considered it. I've no way of assessing that."

"Did Fletcher confide in Juanita?"

"From what she's told me, I believe so. He was surprisingly frank with her, as though he felt there was no need to kid her about anything. He at least pretended a relationship that was absolutely open and honest. He wasn't afraid to show her his mean side. He talked freely about the people he dealt with and despised in so many ways. She let him know early on that she was deeply interested in money and its power and it gave him a freedom he found stimulating."

A shadow fell across the floor to my right and I looked up to see Lieutenant Juárez entering the bar from the pool side. He greeted us, sat down, ordered a *cerveza muy fría* and glanced around the room. He looked gloomy.

"Qué pasa?" I asked.

"Christ is dead."

Jim looked shocked; I probably looked jolted myself.

"The young man we were questioning," said Lieutenant Juárez. "He hanged himself in his cell."

I started to ask how, but he glared at me and I shut my mouth.

"We are investigating. I will not accept that this is a piece of carelessness by the guards. And no, he was not beaten to death. We had no need to touch him, only refuse him drugs. He was ready to break."

The waiter brought him his beer and he drank deeply.

"We had to issue a pickup order on Morales. He's not at La Reata or his home."

I waited awhile and finally said, "Whoever's running this operation has got to have a police connection. The Houston hoods didn't know I'd been talking with you personally through clairvoyance. Someone told them."

He sighed, took another drink and leaned forward on his elbows.

"How about Juanita's friend, José?"

"He is being watched. I know already that a fellow he knew in school, a neighbor, works for Morales."

"Have you questioned Rodríguez?"

"There is nothing there. Only a vicious drunk. Tomorrow we will talk to the ones from Guadalajara—if they come."

As I passed through the lobby heading for my room, I saw Sutton and Elvira parting. He walked over to the cigarette machine when she was gone and I drifted over to his side.

"You're full of surprises," I said.

He put coins in the machine, poked the button for Salems and picked up the package before turning to me.

"So?"

"You said you weren't interested in primitive societies, yet here you are, and speaking like a native."

"Spanish is not primitive; Mexico is. And I'm here for obvious reasons."

"Elvira?"

"I don't have to visit Mexico to see her."

"You came to honor your old friend and nephew, right?"

He opened the package with precise fingers, inserted the tip end of a cigarette in his mouth and pulled a slim gold lighter from his pocket.

"How was Oren's Spanish?" I asked.

"He spoke it like a French cow."

"I heard he spoke it well."

"Who told you that?"

"A Mexican guide."

"So," he grinned, "consider the source."

"I also heard Fletcher planned to marry Elvira."

"The same source?"

"I've used lots of sources."

"So why ask me?"

"I'd like to get things straight."

"You'll never make it."

"Probably not. Has Elvira ever visited your house?"

"Why do you ask?"

"I just wondered if she'd ever seen your maid."

His voice turned sharp. "What kind of a TV show'd you have, morning interviews with gossip columnists?"

"Actually I specialized in fraud and crime. What kind of law are you in?"

"Corporate."

"That figures. What's going to happen with the Foundation?"

"It'll survive the loss of Fletcher. Surviving Avery might be another matter."

"You're not impressed by his investments?"

I was beginning to bore him. He looked past me and didn't bother to comment.

"Who'll be the next exec, Elvira or Marigold?"

His attention returned to me and he frowned.

"It's a little early to worry about that, don't you think?"

"Is that what you two were talking about in Spanish?"

He grinned. "I don't talk business in a social setting."

He lifted his head and looked past me once more. I turned to see Elvira walking toward us. She had changed from high- to low-heeled shoes and smiled at Sutton.

"Ready?" she said.

He nodded, took her arm, tilted his head my way and they walked off.

XXVIII

Theodore Warden, Daphne's servant, showed no surprise when I appeared at his door and agreed to let me in when I said I'd like to ask him some questions.

I'd expected an immaculate room, but obviously he enjoyed clutter in privacy. Shaving equipment, toilet articles, change, keys, brochures and a pair of discarded socks were spread over the combination bureau and desktop. His suit coat was draped over the desk chair and his tie had fallen to the floor nearby. The rumpled spread showed where he'd been stretched out watching the TV. The sound was off, but I could see a commercial going on for Rolaids.

I sat down in an armchair. He stood near the bed, watching me with enigmatic brown eyes.

"Who takes care of the mansion while you're away?" I asked.

"Raquel."

"Is she a maid?"

"If you mean a virgin, I doubt it. If you mean a woman who serves, no. She's the cook."

"And you're the house pedant, huh? How'd you like Fletcher as a boss?"

"He was ideal."

"In what way?"

"He was seldom home."

My grin brought no response.

"How about Mrs. Fletcher?"

"She's not home much either."

"Sounds like you've got an ideal job."

No comment.

"You see a lot of the lawyer, Harlan?"

"Some."

"Does he stay overnight?"

"I couldn't say. I've never been asked to serve breakfast in bed to the two of them."

"But you'd notice if his car stayed out in front overnight, wouldn't you?"

"Probably."

"Did it?"

"I don't recall."

"You've been convicted of a felony, haven't you?"

He had been standing about four feet away up to this point in a pose that suggested he was waiting for me to order tea and crumpets. Now he looked bored, moved over to the bed and sat down.

"I take it this is going to be a long session?" he said.

"It could be. What about the question?"

"Yes. Forgery."

"And Harlan was your lawyer. How'd you happen to get him?"

"I was a waiter in his club. He always sat at one of my tables when there was room."

"So when he couldn't keep you from going to prison, he helped you get parole, right?"

He nodded.

"How long ago was that?"

"I got out four years ago. For two years I worked for Mr. Sutton. Then I went to the Fletchers'."

"And Harlan arranged that?"

"Yes."

"You ever talk with Sutton after you left him?"

"Of course. When he came to the Fletchers', he'd say, 'How are you doing?' and I'd say, 'Fine, sir.' He'd say, 'I'll have another Scotch' and I'd say, 'Right away, sir.' We were very close."

"Was it the same with Harlan?"

"No. He orders white wine."

I stared at him for a few seconds and he stared back calmly.

"Did Harlan suggest to Mrs. Fletcher that she hire me?"

"No. That was her idea. Mr. Beck was surprised when she told him."

"Beck is Harlan's last name?"

He nodded.

"Was he against the idea?"

"No. He thought it was fine."

I asked how his employers got along together and he said fine. No, he never heard them argue. They were rather formal with each other, but of course they were often separated since he traveled so much.

"How was her relationship with Harlan?"

It was less formal, he admitted.

"Did Mr. Fletcher sleep with Mrs. Fletcher?"

"I wouldn't know. They have their own bedrooms and both beds are used."

"Does she stay away from the house overnight when her husband is out of town?"

"Occasionally."

"How about when he's in town?"

"Never."

"Does she drive herself when she goes away for an evening?"

"Sometimes. Other times she is picked up."

"By who?"

"Mr. Beck."

I stared at him for a moment, trying to figure out why he answered that question directly.

"Did Mrs. Fletcher tell you to be honest with me?" I asked.

"Yes."

"No reservations or qualifications?"

"I am to give no opinions. Just facts asked for."

"She's a shrewd woman, don't you think?"

"I have no opinions."

"Do you respect her?"

"Yes."

He said that as a fact and I believed him. Of course I didn't have any way of knowing what qualities earned his respect.

"What was the relationship between Fletcher and Harlan?"

"Mr. Fletcher treated him with elaborate politeness."

"Maybe a little condescension?"

He thought about that, trying to decide if it called for an opinion.

"I would say yes. Perhaps more than a little."

"Did you detect any resentment in Harlan?"

"No. Mr. Beck is not a sensitive man."

Fact.

"Is he ambitious?"

"He's an attorney."

I might as well have ended the session there, but I went on to ask if he'd been in regular touch with Harlan, keeping him posted on what went on in the house, and he denied any such arrangement. His responsibilities were to the lady and he was not indebted in any way to Mr. Beck.

As I got up to leave, I sensed that he was quite satisfied with the way he had handled himself and I couldn't resist leaving him with something to think about.

"Tomorrow," I said at the door, "Lieutenant Juárez will be questioning you. I don't think he's going to swallow your claim of total loyalty to Mrs. Fletcher."

"He can't prove anything else," he said.

"I wonder."

I thought that reached him even though his face gave nothing away. He made no response when I wished him good night.

XXIX

I stopped by the desk before going to Marigold's room and found a message asking me to call Lieutenant Juárez. He came on the line at once.

"The Guadalajara police have been questioning García and other people at the bank. García sticks to his story that all was proper and cannot describe the bodyguards. But the chief clerk at the bank says that Fletcher entered looking dazed, kept his left hand in his pocket and seemed to need help from the two escorts as he walked to García's office. When they left, one of the guards was carrying the suitcase.

"García claimed he'd never been in Morales's bar, but they have found people who remember seeing him there several times. He's under surveillance and they're letting him know it. He is very frightened. I think we will be able to do business with Mr. García before long."

"So what do you think happened?"

"Fletcher was probably tortured into making the withdrawal. They worked on his left hand so he could still use his right to sign papers, and after leaving the bank, they killed him."

"Have they located Morales yet?"

"No. He may very well have skipped Mexico entirely."

"Maybe he's here in Guanajuato."

"That seems unlikely, but we won't overlook the possibility. Do you have anything new for me?"

I told him of my interview with Theodore Warden and he was not much impressed. He did say that he would talk with him in the morning.

Marigold was more encouraging. She thought I'd handled the servant very well and liked my idea that Harlan was behind everything.

"Oren called him Daphne's pet poodle, and he knew it. He pretended it didn't mean a thing, but I suspect it made him boil."

We talked awhile before getting personal and finally passionate. She wanted to talk more about the case afterward, and when I got too sleepy, she said I should go back to my room. That made me sore, but I finally dressed and headed down the softly lit corridor toward my room. The windows were black and ominous on my left and I watched the corners for lurking killers, but there were none around and my footsteps on the carpet made no sound.

I reached my door, unlocked it, stepped inside and turned on the light.

"Hi," said Harlan.

He was stretched out on my bed with his dark head propped up by the pillows stacked against the heavy headboard. His eyes blinked against the soft light from the wrought-iron wall fixture. I glanced at his empty hands, looked around the room and settled into the armchair by the window.

"How'd you get in?"

"Bribery. Not expensive or complicated." He clasped his hands behind his head and grinned at me. "I thought we'd ought to talk. You're a very resourceful guy and I figure we can do each other some good."

"Like how?"

He brought his arms down and sat up straight.

"It's like this: Daphne really wants to know who killed Oren. It's become an obsession. And since she's my obsession, I plan to get whatever she wants. Now, I've got my ideas about what happened and I thought if we got together, exchanged information and brainstormed this thing, we might get it solved. Fair enough?"

"What are your ideas?"

"The way I see it, Marigold has conspired with this Morales character to have Oren put away and put her in line as the exec of the Fletcher Foundation. She has multiple motives." He raised one finger. "First, she was jealous because he fell for the Spanish girl, Juanita, and besides that, he was messing around with Elvira and evidently intended to make her the next exec. Now, our Marigold is the greediest little blonde on two feet. She wants that Foundation job and all the perks that go with it. She knows Mexico and all the people involved with Oren here, she speaks the language like a native and she's the greatest little organizer since Napoleon. She also knows exactly which buttons to poke. Including yours. How do you like it?"

I crossed my legs.

"It has some good angles. You figured out how you're going to prove any of it?"

"The weak link is the banker. García. He'll fold like a paper napkin once the police go to work on him. When they do, they'll find Marigold was the connection, the setup artist. She was the one who wrote the rejection letter to Camillo, so she knew *he* was sore, she knew he had connections with Morales who'd knock off his own mother if the price was right and he had the army to handle the job."

"Sounds simple. So what do you need from me?"

"Well, things are rarely as simple as they seem. I'd feel better about my theories if I knew what you'd found out. After all, you've been working on this quite a while, you must know things I don't."

"That doesn't seem too likely."

He grinned again, sat up and put his feet on the floor.

"You're turning sarcastic. You're sore because I've just told you that Marigold's been playing you for a sucker. But think about it. How much do you know about her? Who's a more likely suspect?"

"I kind of like you for it."

"Really?" He laughed. It didn't sound phony at all. "What's your theory? That I wanted Daphne widowed so I could marry rich?"

"I think you'd settle just for her, but the money wouldn't exactly be a deterrent."

"Oh, hell no. Money's always nice and all the better when it comes with a great woman. You know all about that, don't you? I don't have to tell you a thing when it comes to Daphne."

He said that lightly, but I suddenly felt sure he hated the idea that I'd been ahead of him there.

"I guess she's okay, if you like the bossy type."

"That's just a front," he said, waving casually. "If you'd really got to know her and had been able to handle her, you'd have realized all she wanted was a strong man. That's why she married Fletcher. She thought he had real power. She found out in a hurry that in fact he was just a rich juvenile who had the hots for any young girl he saw."

"Which seems to suggest that she had the strongest motive of anybody for wanting him dead."

"Huh-uh," he said, getting up and moving to the window near me. "Give credit where it's due, friend. The wife is always the first suspect in a case like this and she'd be the first to know it. Daphne's not foolish or reckless, believe me. That's why she was so careful in our relationship. She never made the man look foolish. From the very start she knew he wasn't jealous of me. Hell," he laughed, "he couldn't take me seriously if you want to know the truth. That's embarrassing, but it's a fact and I'm big enough to admit it freely. He was perfectly willing to let her have some fun as long as she didn't make him look bad. I'll even admit she got involved with me in the beginning purely on a spite level —you know—getting even. I'm younger than she is, you know. Not much, but enough for the token effect. If he was going to fool around with younger ones, so could she."

He looked down at me.

"Remember, she hired you to find Oren. If she'd arranged the death, she wouldn't have needed you to find the body, would she?"

I looked up at him and he turned to gaze out the window. There were lights in the courtyard by the hotel entrance but they weren't strong enough to wipe out the reflection of his figure in the mirroring window.

"Did you hire the private detectives that began the investigation?" I asked.

"Did Daphne tell you that?" he asked easily.

"She didn't tell me a thing about private detectives. You did."

He shrugged. "I'd forgotten. Yes, I handled that. It was automatic."

"Who suggested hiring me?"

He gave me his ingratiating grin. "Well, *I* certainly didn't. I'd never heard of you till she came up with the idea when she heard at a party that you'd been canned by the TV station. She suggested the idea when we were leaving in my car. I'll have to say, she made you sound like something between Mike Wallace and Dan Rather."

"I'll bet. What'd you say the name of the outfit you hired was?"

"Don't kid me," he said, still grinning. "You don't forget a thing."

"I just wondered if you did."

"Every now and then. But not in this case. It was Gavillan's."

"Who'd you talk to there?"

"Now that, I don't remember. A fellow named Sullivan, I think, but I wouldn't swear to that in court."

"And the second guy, he was from the same firm?"

"That's right. If you mean the second investigator."

"I guess you won't be offended if I confirm this business?"

"Not in the least. I'm just sorry I can't give you the number. My secretary looked it up at the time and I don't have it in my book."

"What's your secretary's home number?"

He laughed. It didn't sound quite so genuine this time.

"You *are* a tiger, aren't you? Why'd I have her home number?"

"It just seemed likely."

"Well, I don't." For the first time I saw his frown. I guessed it had chilled many a witness.

"How about her address? I'd like to call her now. Might as well clear this up right away."

"I don't know her address. As a matter of fact, she left our office to get married. I don't even know her new name."

"Maybe she kept the old one, lots of women do that now. What was her maiden name?"

He shook his head and managed a new grin.

"You really are something. Okay, it's Alice. Alice Ann Smith, so help me God. And now that you ask, I do remember the new name, it's LeTourneau."

"Great, I'll go down to the lobby and use the phone, there isn't one in here."

"The joys of a Mexican hotel," he said cheerfully. "No telephone, TV or radio. But listen, I really wanted to talk with you some more—"

"Fine. Relax on my bed again. If I can confirm your claims, we'll have a lot to talk about. If I can't, we could really have a long session. It's a no-lose situation, right?"

The first number I called was Lieutenant Juárez's. He wasn't in, but finally I got hold of a sergeant with good English who listened to my story and gave me the lieutenant's home number. He answered on the first ring and we talked briefly.

Then I called information in Houston. I told the operator it was imperative that I reach an Alice Ann LeTourneau, since her mother had been seriously injured in a vacation accident and wanted to contact her but couldn't give her number or address. I gave her my charge number and asked her to go to any expense to make the connection. She assured me she'd do all that was possible and began calling.

I went to the checkout desk, told the clerk I'd be in the bar if a call came for me and a moment later found Daphne sitting with Jim and Juanita. She waved me over to their table.

"Where's Harlan?" I asked.

Daphne said he was having stomach problems and had gone to bed early.

"I understand you know these people quite well," she said, nodding at the Durados. "Jim tells me you consider him a fine suspect."

"I've considered everyone," I assured her, "even you."

That didn't amuse her. She scowled, drank off her margarita and looked for the waiter.

"You've fallen off the wagon," I said.

"I'm not married anymore."

"Well, I suppose that makes some kind of sense. What was the name of the firm you hired first to find Oren?"

"I haven't the slightest idea. Something Irish, I think."

"Who handled it?"

"Harlan."

"You sure he hired anybody?"

She stared at me as the waiter arrived, looked up, impatiently waved her glass for a refill and looked back at me.

"What do you mean? Are you telling me Harlan lied?"

"It'd be interesting if he did. You remember signing any checks to this investigative outfit?"

Her scowl faded into a thoughtful frown.

"No," she said at last. "But that doesn't mean much, I sign a lot of checks . . ."

She turned her glass on the table and stared at me once more.

"Do you actually think he's behind all this?"

"I'm considering everybody, like I told you."

"How about Elvira?"

"Her too."

Juanita's eyes flashed from Daphne to me and back, over and over. Her mouth was open slightly, as if she were about to smile. Jim sat, completely relaxed, while his brown eyes calmly regarded me.

"What you're saying," said Daphne with growing anger, "is that you still don't know a damned thing. It could be just anyone at all, right?"

"I think it narrows down to a chosen few."

The desk clerk approached, leaned over and told me there was a call for me in the lobby. I thanked him, excused myself and headed back.

The blow struck me just above the right kidney, tearing out a sound somewhere between a grunt and a scream that was cut off by a hand slapped over my mouth. My knees buckled, strong hands gripped my elbows and the next moment I was stumbling between two men through the lobby door and into the courtyard. My head was shoved down, I was slammed into a waiting car which immediately purred to life and moved off.

"What made you wise?" asked Harlan. "It wasn't just the investigator business, was it?"

I managed to lift my head and saw him looking back from the front seat. I turned to my right and saw Rodríguez, grinning at me. José, the cop, sat on my left.

I swallowed and drew a shallow breath.

"You just seemed most likely," I said. I was surprised that speaking didn't hurt more.

"Why?"

"You're young, impatient, ambitious, in a hurry. Nobody else seemed really right for it. All too old or too conservative or both."

He shook his head and smiled. He was feeling very good.

"I'll tell you the real reason," he said. "It was because I got the woman you wanted. She'd dumped you and you knew I was sleeping with her and that galled you. That's all there was to it. You're no Mr. Bright Boy; you're just a jealous reporter making up his story to suit himself."

"Could be," I admitted. "Where are we going?"

"You don't really want to know."

"I suppose not."

"I'll tell you anyway. I'd like to stick you in the crypt we used for Oren so you could wind up on mummy row, but you've bitched up that routine, so we'll try something else. We'll dump you in the tailings pond up above town. With a few weights. You'll be like silver-plated, isn't that nice?"

I couldn't think of a good response to that.

"Why'd you put Oren in the crypt?" I asked.

"Because I heard the mummies terrified him. It seemed a fitting windup for the smug, condescending son-of-a-bitch."

"You hated him that much?"

"You bet your ass. If you'd known him, you'd understand, believe me. He absolutely *believed* he was God Almighty. He wouldn't give Daphne a divorce and all the time he had those goddamned girls fawning on him, like a bunch of groupies around a rock star. It nauseated me."

Theodore Warden had been wrong. Harlan was sensitive.

I wondered what Harlan would've planned for me if I'd been more deferential.

"How'd you get Morales involved?" I asked.

"Simple. I offered him the money Oren had in García's bank. García cooperated because he's scared to death of Morales and on top of that, Morales offered him ten thousand dollars for simply closing his eyes to what was really happening."

"So how'd they force Oren to withdraw cash from the bank?"

"They broke fingers on his left hand until he turned cooperative. He was surprisingly tough. Didn't give in until they got to his thumb."

The pain was beginning to recede in my back and I decided at least that wasn't going to be fatal. That didn't offer me a great deal of comfort when José removed my belt and strapped my ankles together. Then he removed my shoelaces, linked them with a square knot and tied my wrists together. They were fine new laces; I didn't think I could break them.

I looked up at Harlan when José let me sit back once more. He was resting his cheek on his left arm across the seat behind him. A light flashed through the rear window briefly, turning his face ghostly white.

"Hey," he said, lifting his head and looking at the driver, "someone's following us."

The driver answered in Spanish. I recognized the voice from my first night in Guadalajara. It was the round-faced, balloon-handed guide who'd taken me into the church where I was sapped.

"Turn left at the next crossing," ordered Harlan.

The car turned and moved cautiously over the narrow, rough

street and slowed at the corner. Lights approached from our right. There was no opening ahead.

"Gun it!" yelled Harlan. Carlos obeyed, the big car slewed around the corner and plunged up the hill. A siren wailed behind us.

"Untie him," Harlan told José. "Hurry!"

Rodríguez bent over to remove the belt from my ankles while José struggled with the laces on my wrists. He was still at it when Carlos hit the brakes and brought us to a shuddering stop just short of the police car blocking the crossing.

"Everybody relax," said Harlan. "Leave the talking to me, understand?"

José succeeded in freeing my wrists and my hands felt the needles of returning circulation as I pulled them around into my lap. I saw large figures approaching the car on each side. Lights from the second car shone through the back window.

Harlan leaned casually to his right and stuck his head out the window.

"Qué es el problema?"

The nearest officer told him to open the door slowly and get out with his hands up. I could see the pistol in his hand. I looked at José. His smile was a tortured grimace as he reached to open the door, turned, lowered his head and started out. Rodríguez suddenly lunged across me, snatched the pistol from José's holster and threw himself back at the right door which was being opened by an officer.

I rammed my right elbow into Rodríguez's back and hooked his left elbow with my left hand. He grunted as I yelled, "He's got a gun!"

The officer jerked back and fired. I felt the impact on Rodríguez's body and snatched back my hand. Rodríguez slowly tumbled out of the car and into the street, headfirst.

I was dragged out of the car and braced against the rear fender before Lieutenant Juárez reached my side and roughly told the cops to let me go.

"You okay?" he asked.

"Beautiful, absolutely beautiful."

I had lost a shoe when the cops jerked me from the car and Juárez had one of his men retrieve it and hand it over. I asked for my laces and belt, put them in their proper places and described what had happened before we reached the police station.

"You'll be happy to know," said Lieutenant Juárez, "that we caught Morales's number-one man in the midst of an attempt to assassinate García. Even better, Morales was driving the assassin's car personally. I think we will be able to wrap up this case very neatly."

"Maybe—but don't forget—Harlan's a lawyer."

"I won't. Just you remember, he will be tried in a Mexican court."

The memorial service was mercifully brief. Daphne and Juanita wept, Marigold did not. Mourning became Elvira. Her face radiated the serenity of a mature woman who had accepted tragedy and transcended it. I've never witnessed a nobler performance.

The farewell luncheon was a relaxed affair, free of the fear and suspicion that had been with the participants ever since Oren's disappearance. No one congratulated me during the civilities or even expressed concern over my close call, but I felt there was a touch of deference in the way they looked at and spoke to me when they were near. All but Sutton.

I made the mistake of asking if he'd be defending Harlan. He told me that was an idiotic notion.

"You don't assume he's guilty?"

"Of course not, but I'm not a court lawyer and I don't know Mexican law. We'll get him counsel from Mexico City."

"We? Does that mean your law firm or the Foundation?"

"The law firm, of course."

"You think you can get him off?"

"I'm a lawyer, not a prophet. We'll do our best."

I cornered Daphne and asked how she was handling the discovery that Harlan had managed her husband's death. She held her margarita in both hands and stared through me for a moment.

Finally she shook her head and frowned. "I still haven't really accepted it. He was always so respectful toward Oren—" Suddenly she smiled. "You know, there were times when Harlan actually defended Oren. Times when I was mad for one reason or another and said critical things. I honestly believe that Harlan was sincere when he did it. I suppose it was one of those love-hate relationships. I mean, he admired Oren, but he was in love with me and it got him all mixed up. You know what I mean?"

"You figure he can cop an insanity plea?"

She glared for an instant, then softened and gave me a tolerant nod.

"It's natural that you'd be vindictive, considering your experiences—"

"Yeah. So who'll be your lawyer now?"

"Oh, that's no problem. Uncle Milt will take care of me."

"Uncle Milt?"

"Milton Sutton, *you* know."

"Oh, of course, Uncle Milt. What could be sweeter? The guy whose firm is going to defend your husband's murderer."

She waved that off impatiently.

"At least I was right about you, wasn't I? You found Oren despite all sorts of perils, from the glacial blonde to the exotic brunette."

"Too bad I loused up your romance."

"Don't take too much satisfaction from that—it wasn't going anywhere. But speaking of romance, which of the ladies will you settle on?"

"I'm partial to the blonde," I admitted.

"Men usually are. Unfortunately this one's all set on her career. I'm afraid you're out of luck. It's not likely she's going to have much time for an unemployed TV announcer."

I thanked her for such heartwarming encouragement and moved off to find the lady.

We had spent the previous night in my room. It had been perfect; Marigold kept telling me how brilliant I'd been and what a great lover I was, and the way things went, I had to agree she was absolutely right. Except in the morning it was discouragingly easy to remember how feeble my prospects were.

She was floating away from Elvira, Sutton and Avery when I spotted her, and at first glance I knew Daphne had been right. Marigold had the executive director's job.

"Don't tell me," I said as she grabbed my hands, "let me guess—"

"I've got it, Kyle. I've got it!"

"Hell, as far as I'm concerned, you've always had it."

She laughed and hugged me, and as I squeezed back, I looked over her shoulder and caught Sutton's eye. He grinned maliciously. I wished just then that the killer hadn't been Harlan, but knew that if it had been Sutton, I'd never have been able to trap him.

"Okay," I said, "let's go upstairs and pack."

She said that was a wonderful idea and up we went, but we didn't get around to any suitcases for quite a while. This time she didn't tell me how great I was; she talked about how wonderful everything was going to be. Her happiness was so pure I didn't worry about the implications and just shared in her triumph.

We returned to Houston in Daphne's plane, and before long I was wishing we'd taken a commercial flight. The private jet was like a lounge and Marigold spent the trip in conference with the Foundation crowd talking about grants, investments and personalities in the social service world.

I talked some with Daphne who was happy to explain why Elvira didn't get the Foundation job.

"I told Milt straight," she said, "that if that woman was made the executive director I'd sue for control. He tried to give me some guff about the will leaving me out of that picture, but I let him know I could prove that senior-citizen siren had been working on Oren and he folded in a hurry. Not that he was all excited about her getting the job anyway. The old lecher's got his own plans for her."

Things didn't improve any in Houston. Marigold's apartment had no room for me, so I stayed in a nearby hotel and we grabbed a couple of meals together and quickies in my room, but mostly she was buried by her job.

I spent a lot of time on long-distance calls and took off one afternoon to borrow April from the mother-in-law who gave me the feeling she didn't trust me.

April did. We went to a park near her apartment and got along great with the help of swings, a slide and a Dairy Queen with chocolate which only slightly stained my new sport shirt. When we parted, she gave me a hell of a squeeze and a solid kiss, which convinced me I had a strong booster in the family—for whatever that was worth.

That night I got a call from Al Lutz in Milwaukee. He said their top investigative reporter had been shot and they needed a good man to finish his assignment.

"That is," he said, "if you could condescend to work for the print media after being a TV star."

"I'll take anything but obits. How bad was this guy shot?"

"Bad enough to get an obit."

I thought about that.

"Was the shooter somebody he was investigating?"

"That's one of the things you'd be expected to find out."

"It sounds like you want an expendable man."

"We got to consider staff morale, sure. Come on, you want the job or not? This call's costing—"

I told him I'd think it over and he said fine, he'd already found out there was a plane I could catch at 7:10 A.M.

Actually it didn't take off until 7:25 A.M.